Leave Everything You Know Behind

Ginny Fite

MILFORD
HOUSE

an imprint of Sunbury Press, Inc.
Mechanicsburg, PA USA

MILFORD HOUSE

an imprint of Sunbury Press, Inc.
Mechanicsburg, PA USA

For information about special discounts for bulk purchases, please contact Sunbury Press Orders Dept. at (855) 338-8359 or orders@sunburypress.com.

To request one of our authors for speaking engagements or book signings, please contact Sunbury Press Publicity Dept. at publicity@sunburypress.com.

FIRST MILFORD HOUSE PRESS EDITION: December 2023

Set in Adobe Garamond Pro | Interior design by Crystal Devine | Cover by Nataysia Akmatova | Edited by Gabrielle Kirk.

Publisher's Cataloging-in-Publication Data
Names: Fite, Ginny, author.
Title: Leave everything you know behind / Ginny Fite.
Description: First trade paperback edition. | Mechanicsburg, PA : Milford House Press, 2023.
Summary: Anne Canfield doesn't know she only has months to live, but even death won't stop her from saving a stranger or protecting her son. An unexpected friendship changes everything for two women facing the hardest challenges life can dish up.
Identifiers: ISBN : 979-8-88819-170-5 (paperback).
Subjects: FICTION / Women | FICTION / Family Life / General | FICTION / Psychological.

0 1 1 2 3 5 8 13 21 34 55

For the Love of Books!

To Ann and Eileen

"For whatever things a man thinks of at the final moment when he leaves the body - that alone does he attain"

—THE BHAGAVAD GITA

Also by Ginny Fite

Chapter 1

Anne inhaled tart winter air deep into her lungs, savored the sensation, and leaned on her walking sticks. Everything at the cove was just as she would have arranged it if she had been in charge of the world.

Old white pines, bare red oaks, and leafless ash trees lent the hilly lakeside that primeval look she loved. A ribbon of rosewood-colored mountains skirted the distant western shore. Across the water, a gray loon leaned into the breeze and called for its mate. Snow spiraled onto the lake's frozen surface, mirroring the cobalt sky.

Contemplating whether she had the nerve to walk out on the ice, Anne spotted a dark shape hovering at the water's edge. "Is that a bear?" The tremble in her voice embarrassed her as she slipped behind a winterberry bush. "Better safe . . ."

It's a figment of your imagination.

Anne ignored her dead husband's remark and peered at the shape again to assess her situation. Whatever it was, it didn't know she was there. She could still enjoy her moment, although now she'd been cheated of the tranquility the two-mile tramp to the beach at dawn usually provided.

Watching the sunrise always put the hurly-burly of her life into perspective. Some days the sun's steady ascent above the mountain was the only thing she could count on. On the worst days, she couldn't acknowledge the morning light and instead burrowed into the cave of blankets on her bed. She hoped today wouldn't deliver more trouble than she could handle.

Images of a bear lumbering toward her raced through her mind. She would freeze in her tracks and pee her pants in fear. She couldn't decide which was more awful, being mauled to death or having to walk all the way home in cold, wet pants.

"I'll stay right here. Far enough away from whatever it is, just in case."

As usual, you're creating drama out of thin air.

"Poor Howard," Anne retorted. "Dead five years and you still get everything wrong." This is what she got for being married for fifty years—a never-ending conversation with a man she despaired of ever silencing. Pushing back the hood of her parka, she straightened her back and sidled closer to get a better look at what the interloper was up to.

Usually, the solitude in the cove fortified her for the chaos of the newspaper office. There, tapping keys, the nearly constant drone of simultaneous telephone interviews, intermittent squawks from the police scanner, and endless consultations or demands from reporters drowned out her thoughts.

At home, the five sons and one husband who'd once lived with her had left an everlasting hum, like contrails hanging in the sky long after the jet has passed. And now, out of the blue, the serenity she'd hoped for was shattered by an intruder standing in her exact spot and waiting for God knows what.

"Not promising at all," Anne muttered.

The sky lightened, the snow picked up, and the shape stepped onto the ice. *That's a woman! What on earth is she doing? She must be a tourist.*

"Hey, wait." Anne's voice caught in her throat. Her mind whirled like the snow swirling around her, unsure whether to tell the woman the ice was dangerous this time of year or ignore what was happening right in front of her. She had never been one to shirk the obligations of good citizenship, even if that meant other people thought of her as a busybody.

Whatever she's doing, it's none of your business, Howard said.

Anne shuffled closer to the shore. *I should be careful.* After all, what kind of person would be here at this hour of the day?

You. A person like you.

"Be quiet, Howard. I'm thinking."

She flinched as snow crunched under her boots. A branch snapped. The woman, completely unaware of her, took another step as if testing the solidity of the ice. Anne felt some relief at the stranger's caution. At least she wasn't running willy-nilly out into the center of the cove.

"What if she's dangerous?"

A quick retreat was impossible. It was two miles to Anne's house, she was alone, and she had no way to defend herself except her walking sticks. She'd have to confront whoever this was on her own. And yet, instead of sneaking quietly away as any prudent person might, she was anchored to the spot by curiosity.

The last thing she wanted this morning was to waste time chatting with a stranger. Yet, something was happening here that she needed to pay attention to, even if she didn't want to. Anne leaned over to fend off a sudden bout of dizziness.

The woman slid farther out on the ice. "What's she doing? Doesn't she know the ice won't hold?" Everyone in Queenscove knew that Lake Champlain's southernmost shore froze in December, particularly in the coves. This early in the winter what looked like solid ice could fracture beneath a person's weight and plunge a body into frigid water. The sign on the beach proclaimed the risk.

An image of her son, Luke, barricading himself in a distant motel blew through Anne's mind—the pitted grout around the tub, the peeling linoleum, the moldy shower curtain wrapped around his body. She'd studied pilfered crime scene photos for clues of what had gone wrong, desperate to understand what she could have done or said before it was too late.

Anne closed her eyes and shook her head to clear it. When she opened them, the stranger had flung out her arms and lifted her face to catch the light spilling over the horizon. Bare tree branches transformed from black to gold as light slid across the lake and illuminated the woman.

Luxurious sable-colored hair draped her shoulders; a teal scarf flapped steadily in the breeze; the pockets of her slim coat bulged. The woman edged closer to the point where the lake abruptly deepened.

Anne squinted to improve her vision. "Do you see that, Howard? She has rocks in her pockets."

You're jumping to conclusions for which there's no evidence.

"You're right. Those bulges in her pockets could be anything—a wallet and phone, a jumble of keys, a leftover bagel wrapped in a napkin."

You're overreacting, as usual.

Anne waved Howard off, but he was right. This time. She didn't know anything about what was happening. The woman should be left to her ritual. Maybe this was her one moment of awe in a long boring year. She had expected to be alone here at sunrise. No one was supposed to be her witness.

But the ice might break, and apparently, she didn't know that. "Or does she? Should I warn her?"

You should mind your own business.

The woman took a step closer to peril. Anne imagined her crashing through the ice, submerged and flailing beneath the surface—hair floating, eyes wide, mouth open in regret—ice reforming above her head as she drowned.

"Oh, for God's sake, if I were young, I'd race across the lake to stop her. She'd thank me for the warning. We'd laugh at my officiousness."

Assessing the distance between them, Anne knew she wouldn't make it to the woman in time. At seventy-five, she didn't have the strength to run across the frozen lake to pull anyone from a break in the ice. They would both fall in. The metallic taste of fear thickened her tongue.

Drowning was not on her agenda today, but she couldn't leave the woman to die, and if she didn't stop her now, it would be too late. After all, she wouldn't just drive around a woman lying in the street. On the other hand, the woman's choices were none of her concern.

After fifty years of making dozens of decisions a day, this question was impossible to resolve. Her mind couldn't hear itself think, and her indecision was exhausting. "What if she were my child?" Anne turned the question around the way her philosopher husband taught her. "She's someone's child."

Veering off the path, Anne scurried as fast as her walking sticks could pull her across the narrow wooden footbridge onto the snow-covered beach, closing the distance between her and the woman. Cold wind churned her breath into steam. The stranger took another step. Anne's chest constricted as she quickened her pace. Her legs wobbled. She couldn't go any farther.

Waving her arms, she yelled, "Hello there. Wait up! Beautiful morning, isn't it?" Her words hung in the air like smoke. "I'm a tug hooting at an elegant sloop," she muttered.

The woman's shoulders jerked. She glanced up, edged another foot out on the lake as if that were the safer direction, and then stopped, hugged herself, and stared.

Anne, imagining how she might look to someone else, slowly lowered her arms. To catch the sunrise, she'd bolted out of the house in a red down parka, yellow wool cap with a happy face embroidered on the rim, green wool scarf, and purple gloves. At least her red boots matched the parka, and she was warm.

Her sons laughed at her getups but otherwise she often forgot that the young woman she used to be—happily oblivious to other people's opinions—no longer navigated the world, replaced instead by the wrinkled dumpling she'd become.

Age changed her topography, as proved by her shocking image in new photographs. She'd stopped looking at all reflective surfaces since the person staring back at her had become a stranger. From this distance, though, the woman couldn't see her face, only the crazy quilt of an outfit that might give anyone pause.

"I must look like the madwoman of Queenscove."

Anne dropped her walking sticks and held her arms out, hands open, to show she was harmless. "You know it's dangerous out there, don't you?" she bellowed.

The stranger's body stiffened as if only now she realized she was in danger. Glancing over her shoulder at the wide lake opening beyond her, she slid gracefully over the ice back to shore and picked her way across the rocky beach. Without a backward look at Anne or a wave, she sprinted up the wooden stairs that led to the gravel parking lot.

Chapter 2

The minute Tom saw the horse on the straw bed in the stall, its legs beating the air, he knew.

"It's colic," he told the farmer, who stood in the barn with her fists jammed into her vest pockets, her mouth set. "How long have you known?"

She was as much his patient as the horse. He took in her belly puffed out above her jeans, the frayed flannel shirt unbuttoned over her thermal t-shirt, and the down vest that had seen so many days its color had warped from black to gray. Her boots might be a hundred years old, her face twice that. A sick horse might be what pushed her over the edge. He couldn't have that.

She shook her gray head. "Since Sunday." The lines marking her face stood out in the harsh light streaming through the barn's open doors. "Or Saturday."

"Two days ago. Why didn't you call me sooner?"

"Thought it might be gas, or he'd pass it. But he stopped eating."

Tom pressed his lips together. "Biddy, you know better."

The horse's eyes rolled back. His ears twitched.

"There now, boy, take it easy." Tom put his hand flat on the horse's neck and counted heartbeats. *Heart rate elevated.* He soothed the animal and pulled back his lip. *Gums pale with a red ring where teeth meet gum line.* Running a hand over the horse's legs and down over its distended belly, he thought about the human who was already grieving.

Everyone knew Biddy's story. The horses were her pets. She ran a few-hundred-acre farm inherited from her father that included an apple orchard, grain fields, and some fifty dairy cows. Her folks had been in Queenscove for generations, but small farmers had a tough time competing in a global market. In the yard beyond the barn door, two men were fixing the truck. She struggled with competing demands for her money and time. Tom could see how this would go.

"Okay, I'm going to sedate him and give him a rectal to see what's going on, but it doesn't look good. If I find something wrong, we may have to operate. If we're too late, there's a good chance we'll have to put him down." Better to tell her straight out rather than break her heart in small doses.

"I can't afford the surgery, doc."

This was why she'd waited, he guessed, hoping she wouldn't lose the horse, tricking herself into thinking if she did nothing, the problem would resolve itself. His uncle told him Biddy had managed her farm for twenty years without her husband, who took off in his truck for Burlington one gray winter afternoon and never came home. She didn't go looking for him.

Tom's head reeled as his uncle told him her story. Biddy survived everything on her own. Her barn burned down. She lost cattle to mad cow disease. Her boys were wild brawlers always in trouble with the police. The last time, she refused to bail out her youngest son, leaving him to the dubious mercy of the justice system.

Losing the horse might be the final straw for her. He didn't want to follow the thought, but he knew where it went. Hope diminished in long, dark winter nights. Some people let go of everything.

"Okay. We'll try this first," Tom said. "I'll give him a shot for the pain, and we'll watch him. If he doesn't improve, an ultrasound will help us pinpoint the trouble. Think you can get him out to the animal hospital?"

She closed her eyes and nodded. "The boys will help load him in the trailer."

"I'll do everything I can." Tom planned to talk his uncle into a fee Biddy could afford. She wouldn't accept charity.

She half-smiled her assent. They helped the horse to its feet and tied him so he couldn't kick. Tom pulled on the long latex glove that covered his arm up to his shoulder. The horse trembled at his touch. It would be kinder to put him down before he suffered more, but Tom would wait for nature or Biddy to decide what happened next.

Chapter 3

Anne spotted the woman from the lake an hour later, this time seated at a table in the Town Square Café where she bought her morning coffee every day. Her skin prickled.

"There's a reason for this," Anne muttered and shushed Howard's remark about her overactive imagination before he started.

Although she'd showered and now wore the tweed jacket, dark brown wool turtleneck, colorful scarf, and camel-colored corduroy slacks she believed were suitable attire for the owner of a local newspaper, she still felt dowdy compared to the stranger's easy elegance—the leggings and flats, that teal scarf, and the long line of her hair over her shoulder.

Anne touched the short, white hair at the nape of her neck. "God, I'm obsessed, and I don't even know her."

"Anne?" The teenager behind the counter wearing the café's black t-shirt stenciled with the white outline of a steaming cup of coffee grinned at her. "The usual?"

Mildly chagrined at the barista catching her staring at people yet again, Anne smiled back at him. "Oh, yeah, Harry. The usual—a large coffee with cream and two sugars." Remembering Molly was probably already in the office, she added a raisin bran muffin with cream cheese to her order.

She tilted the top of her head toward the woman she was staring at. "Hey, Harry, do you know who that is?"

Harry glanced over at the woman and raised his eyebrows. "Some prof up at the college." He leaned over the counter to whisper, "Not one of mine, though. I think that's Doc Beale, the vet, with her. Why?"

Anne shrugged one shoulder, an attempt at nonchalance. "Just curious." Eyes fixed on the couple, she took a wrinkled dollar from her jacket pocket and shoved it into the tip jar.

As Anne watched, the woman leaned across the table and whispered to the man. His long brown hair straggled out from beneath his black wool cap. A half-hearted beard covered his chin and cheeks as if he weren't sure whether he wanted to grow it or not. She took Harry's word that this was Doc Beale, one of the county's large animal veterinarians. *But they sure don't seem like a match.*

The Doc put his hands on the table, palms up. Anne guessed the woman would slide her hands into his, gaze into his eyes, whisper adoring words, and smile as part of a private ritual. She didn't. Instead, light from the tall café windows slanted across his arms and striped his open hands as the woman crossed her arms over her chest, her eyes in slits as she listened to him.

An entire kingdom was at stake in the look she gave him. Her face was ashen and her lips bleached. Yet even under duress, she radiated beauty. Pulling round stones out of her coat pockets one at a time, she placed them on the wooden table in front of him, building a pyramid to her intention. The man ran a palm over his face and gazed open-mouthed into the exposed rafters of the café.

"Oh, my God. I was right. She intended to drown herself. Like Virginia Woolf."

You don't know that.

Anne already knew being right was no solace. People didn't pay attention to someone else's intuition, particularly if knowing the future interfered with their present illusions or preferred fate. She'd been right before, about Luke and other things, but being right hadn't helped. It never changed the outcome and never made the world better or her happier.

Tempted to walk up to these strangers like a roving oracle and tell them everything always changes, Anne restrained herself. She'd interfered in their lives once. That was her quota for the day. Her mind sped forward into a future that wouldn't happen now—the man searching for his missing wife, his grief when they pulled her frozen body from the lake. *Geez, get a grip.* Best she didn't say anything; they wouldn't believe her anyway.

As she turned away, the woman raised her hand in a half, almost imperceptible wave. A jolt of adrenaline crashed through Anne. *Caught!*

Her cheeks heated. She sucked in her breath and returned the wave with the same restrained gesture and a small smile, hoping to appear sophisticated and only slightly mortified.

You're not fooling anyone, Howard sniped.

Her hands shaking, Anne paid the cashier and gathered up the carry box. The bell above the door dinged as she opened it. The woman's unguarded reflection stared back at her through the café window.

Chapter 4

"Tom, who's that woman?" Indira Anand asked her husband as Anne left the café. "The one who was staring at us."

Tom Beale glanced toward the door. His face broke into a tolerant smile. "Anne Canfield, from the local paper, you know, the weekly. She owns it. Her family has owned the paper forever. She always stares at people, particularly new people, like she's taking an X-ray with her eyes. We're used to it." He shrugged. "Don't take it personally."

"I'm not new."

He laughed. "If your grandparents' parents weren't born here, you're new."

"What's she like?"

"She's, well, let's call it eccentric. On the other hand, her newspaper—that office right across the square—was the only one in the entire state that didn't trash my father." He ducked his head, as he always did now when talking about his father as if to protect himself from an imminent blow. "Why do you ask?"

"I saw her earlier today, out by the beach. She called out to me, but I was too far away to answer." Indira covered her mouth with her hand to stop herself from speaking. *The frozen lake. The rising sun. How the shale blue surface turned gold and then pink.* She could never tell Tom what she'd considered.

"The beach? You were at the beach this morning? That's where you got the stones? What were you doing there?"

"She was wearing the strangest outfit." A peculiar surge of affection for Anne swept through Indira. *She was trying to save me, a perfect stranger.* "I see why people think she's eccentric."

"Yeah." Tom smiled. "And the independent attitude. Which might account for the clothes."

Pain slashed through Indira's pelvis, but she wasn't ready to tell Tom about it even though that's why she'd called him to meet her for coffee. She didn't know for sure what was wrong. Maybe it was nothing. Just because the pain was familiar didn't mean it was *that*. It could be a problem everyone gets—a urinary tract infection or her appendix.

She squeezed Tom's hand. The warmth of his skin brought back the snowy afternoon five years ago when they'd both reached for the same book in a Cambridge bookstore. In a flash of memory, they were back there again. Their fingers touched. A fierce exchange of ions zinged through her skin, up her arm, and across her scalp. She'd trembled and stared at him, inhaling deeply. He smelled like winter.

Tom had pulled off his snow-covered cap, pressed it against his chest, and shook his head like a dog coming inside after a run. He grinned and his blue eyes brightened. He beams, she told herself afterward every time she thought about him, which was every five minutes.

"Remember when we met?"

"I do. Second best day of my life so far." Tom took her hand.

"Second best?"

"My best was the day you said yes."

"Oh," Indira said, recalling his exact words on that second best day.

"I'm Tom Beale from Vermont . . . in my last year at Tufts veterinary school." His eyes clung to her face for balance. "I've got two hours . . . before I have to go back to campus." As if an avalanche were chasing him downhill, he asked, "Would you go to lunch with me?"

"Yes," she said and smiled up at his glowing face.

It was so easy. One word made him happy; one word wrapped her up in the light radiating from him. She agreed to go with him even though she'd already eaten, her mother was waiting for her at home, and he was a stranger to whose invitations she'd been taught to say no.

An hour later, after scarfing down a bowl of steaming vegetarian chili while she clutched a mug of green tea, Tom, oblivious to the din whirling around them in the crowded beanery, put his palms up on the small wooden table.

"You are the most beautiful woman I've ever seen."

Of course, she put her hands in his. His pulse beat against her wrists, and she was sure the universe trended toward rapture.

"We had everything, didn't we?" Indira glanced around at the café where they now sat.

"Why are you using the past tense? We *have* everything."

"I mean, I used to know how my life was supposed to be. What we would do, how we'd do it. I thought we were going to have a beautiful life where everything made sense."

Tom scowled. "We've got this, honey, whatever it is that's bothering you. We've gone through worse together."

So, he did remember the first time, how they waited for days to hear the test results, unable to eat or sleep. How the diagnosis made them mute, turned them to stone, and then she turned to him and sobbed on his shoulder. He held her as if she were so fragile she might break.

Swiftly, her memory shifted to an earlier time when her mind was on fire and only putting words on a page could extinguish it. Tom, writing, and their hope for a child had been her home base, the safe place her imagination leaped from and returned to. That was all she'd needed for life to be perfect. Those early days of absolute certainty were now the altar at which she prayed as if memories were magic incantations that could restore the past.

"Right?" he prodded.

"Right. Of course, you're right." She rearranged the stones on the table so she wouldn't have to raise her face to his.

"What are you going to do with those?"

"I wanted to build an inukshuk on the beach," she lied. "To say I was there."

"Isn't that what you do with words?"

Indira remembered why she loved him.

He slipped on his jacket and pulled gloves over his long fingers. "Honey, I've got to go. Horses to see, pigs to poke." It was his usual parting joke. "See you later."

He leaned over and kissed her, his eyes wary, assessing her like an animal in his care. At the door of the café, he waved, reluctant to leave. How easy it should have been to smile. She just couldn't.

Chapter 5

Anne put the café's cardboard carry box on Molly's desk and pulled out her coffee cup. "Got your muffin for you."

Molly grinned. "Gee, thanks. You didn't have to do that. I would have walked over."

Anne bowed. "Part of the service."

Molly, the paper's receptionist, calendar editor, births-deaths-weddings recorder, occasional feature writer, and more recently social media maven, made a face to say she knew better but that was okay too.

Anne spotted Ozzie—the *Queenscove Journal's* photographer, police blotter, and sports reporter—at his computer with his back to the door but ever alert to a possible four-alarm fire or ten-car highway pileup that might be announced over the police scanner.

Always ready to jump into his ancient Jeep and drive to wherever the next story occurred, Ozzie wore jeans, a quilted vest over a blue plaid flannel shirt, and a blue wool scarf wound around his neck. Black curls squiggled out from beneath the black watch cap on his head.

He was the age of Anne's oldest grandson, and she always had to repress the urge to pet him. Glancing over Ozzie's shoulder as his thumb swiped his phone screen, she saw he was on a social media platform, devouring the world in 280-character bites.

"Ozzie." She waved her hand in front of his screen.

"Hey, boss." He answered without taking his eyes off the small device.

"Ozzie, go up to the . . . the, oh shit, what's it called where kids sit at desks and some professor stands in front of the class and lectures?"

"A college?" Ozzie ventured. He glanced at Molly and grinned. "It's like playing charades." Molly made a face to show he shouldn't joke about it.

14

"What? Oh, college. Right." Anne frowned, worried she'd missed a crucial point in the conversation.

"Anyway, get some color shots of the kids among the Christmas lights and the greenery sale for the lifestyle section, definitely one shot to run off the front page. Make sure everyone you photograph signs a permission slip because . . ."

"Lawsuits," Ozzie guessed after a few seconds of silence. He grabbed his cameras, stuffed a few different lenses in his backpack, grinned at Anne, and took off.

Anne scanned the newsroom for her staff. Two sets of six desks faced each other in an I formation. They were empty and the computer screens were dark. No one was gossiping in the kitchen or standing over the AP ticker. "Where's everyone?"

Molly checked the calendar on her screen. "Out covering stuff—town council meeting, county budget meeting—you know, the town's allocation, senior daycare center funding. The governor visited the Ag Center. Before you ask, Ozzie already got a shot of the Gov talking to a cow. Might work for the front page. I put one up on our Facebook page and already it's got two hundred likes. Sadie's double-checking her notes with a source for her story."

"That story's going to win her an award," Anne said. "She's probably already shopping for a new job at a bigger paper."

Molly tilted her head and scrutinized Anne's face. "You're in an interesting mood today."

Anne stared out of the windows at the front of the office a beat too long. "What do you know about a newish female instructor at the college?"

Molly consulted the ceiling. "Nothing. There are usually one or two new ones every few years or so. Got a name?" She brought her eyes down to Anne's face. "Is it important?"

"I don't know. I don't know her name, but I'm curious about her. Can you find information about their new instructors without making a five-alarm fire out of it?"

"Sure. I'll get right on it."

That's my girl, Anne thought, although Molly was sixty at least, and it was wrong to think of her as a girl because of feminism. They had worked together for thirty years, but somehow Molly didn't seem old. Age was relative, Anne decided; the older you got, the younger everyone around you seemed. Or maybe people stuck in her memory at the age she'd met them and her original impression never changed.

As Anne headed toward her glass-walled office at the back of the open newsroom, Molly waved a piece of paper. "I got the list of local births from the hospital."

"Great. Go ahead and type them in for this week's paper," Anne called over her shoulder.

The satisfying sound of fingertips striking a keyboard followed her through the open space. She liked Molly's no-nonsense attitude. The woman could also spot a typo a mile away and regardless of the season always had a charming bouquet of fresh flowers on her desk that brightened the entire office.

Anne unwrapped herself and dropped her hat, scarf, gloves, and jacket on the visitor's seat. She plopped into her high-backed, open-weave chair and removed the top of her coffee cup to breathe in the aroma. The smell of good coffee stimulated the brain. She was as sure of that as she was of anything.

Long ago Anne figured out she wasn't a genius. Like her town, she wasn't fancy or powerful, only what was essential for living a decent life. Her best bet for success was by being useful. Being content with one's lot might be the definition of happiness, she thought, and gave herself a gold star for her wisdom.

She preferred experience to be arranged like inches of type set on the page in an order that made sense, one paragraph leading to another. Miffed when life buried the lede, Anne wanted essential information headlined in bold, subheads in small caps, with the nut graph in italics, so the point of the story was clear right away. She hated having to root around in a welter of details for the unexpected fact that might ambush her.

From a desk one hundred years older than she was, Anne had led the paper through every technological revolution since the waning decade of the twentieth century. These days adapting to constant change drained her as much as trekking in the Himalayas. Regardless, she was determined to implement whatever the next necessary innovation was to keep the paper relevant. That was her job as publisher, and if she weren't the fourth-generation publisher and editor of the local paper, who was she?

No one, Howard said.

"Shut up, Howard."

To the short list of things she hated, she added the way her dead husband relished whacking her with the unvarnished truth exactly as he'd done when he was alive.

Anne had always planned to die at work the way her father had, although he'd died too young of a heart attack at sixty-three. After a long night of wondering where he was, she discovered him in the small parking lot behind the newspaper office—head back, mouth and eyes open, hands locked onto the steering wheel of his car—shocked by his encounter with death. She sank to the ground, gripped her knees, and keened until a state trooper found her and drove her home.

Forty years on, a pang still shot through her whenever she spotted him standing at a stall just ahead of her at the farmer's market or leaning over to examine a headline in a stack of newspapers. Her heart would speed up as she quickly threaded her way through the crowd, calling out, "Pop!" He'd turn toward her. It was never him.

Now that she was a relic and didn't intend to die at all, her kids wouldn't have the same experience. If she could hang in there long enough, someone would invent a way to transplant her brain into a younger body so her sons wouldn't have to peel her fingers off the keyboard after rigor mortis set in. The fact that none of her children wanted anything to do with the paper made her despair. They saw it as grunge work with little return for the effort. Nothing she said changed their minds.

The paper was always your pet project. You didn't have to do it. No one else cared.

"It's your fault, Howard, putting all those fancy ideas in their heads." Most days, she hated Howard and his hoity-toity attitude toward her family's legacy. On bad days she wanted to shoot him, even now that he was dead.

Unless one of her grandchildren declared an interest in the paper, she would have to sell the business. That was the smart thing to do before the paper went bankrupt, but she couldn't bring herself to look for a buyer. She couldn't gird herself for the humiliation that would follow her or the loss she would feel saying goodbye to people she'd come to think of as family.

But if she didn't sell it, the paper would die with her, and all these people she cared about would lose their jobs at a time when newspaper jobs were getting harder to find. Paralyzed by this dilemma, Anne told herself she had time to figure it out.

Now that she was thinking of something else, Anne suddenly recalled meeting the woman from the lake. They were introduced at a cocktail party for new faculty at the college three years ago. Admiring the young woman's unabashed pairing of teal and purple, Anne had thought, *Prana*, as their hands met. *Such energy.*

Anne typed *new faculty at Queenscove College* into the paper's online search field and within seconds a list of articles appeared on the screen. She scrolled through them until the face of the woman at the lake beamed back at her: Indira Anand, instructor of creative writing, the same face reflected in the window of the café door this morning. Anne stared at the image. *But her light's gone out.*

She clicked the next link. The year Indira joined the college faculty, she married Queenscove native Thomas Beale, large-animal veterinarian, and son of Charles and Amanda Beale. A photo of the glowing bride and groom headed up their wedding notice. Tom Beale looked like he'd swallowed the sun.

Charles Beale's name sounded vaguely familiar. Anne searched his name and read the *Journal's* top news story about the man who had served as county state's attorney for a decade until two years ago when he was imprisoned for fraud and corruption. She didn't recall him at all. A shiver of fear gripped her. Even reading about him now didn't jog her recall. He'd been erased from her mind as if he'd never existed. Anne closed her eyes and tried to breathe evenly to suppress her panic about forgetting one of the most important people in her county. Part of her job was to know everyone.

Beale's current residence, the news story said, was the Northwest State Correctional Facility where he was serving the second year of a five-year term. *What a fall from grace that is.* The state prosecutor and a judge had made an example of him: no one in Vermont was above the law.

A wave of empathy engulfed her as she clicked on photographs of Beale stoically walking into the courthouse. His conviction must have humiliated his son. That must be why Tom dressed the way he did and why he didn't shave or cut his hair. He was in mourning just as if his father had died.

A parent's death could shake a grown child's world, but what if that parent turned out to be entirely different from the idol the child loved? All certainties would fly out of the window, including his sense of who he was. It didn't matter how old the child was. *How would my kids deal with my mistakes?*

Anne held her hand up in the STOP position. "Don't say anything, Howard."

Nothing made sense if you considered it too long. She'd once been stymied by the word "let" while reading a new law passed by the state legislature. "Let this be true," the document began, as if before those words were written, something else was true. Could truth be changed by demanding it?

Anne shook off the willies and walked to the front office to refill her empty cup. No matter what machine she bought for the office, the coffee was always mildly revolting and made her tongue feel like cardboard etched with metal. But caffeine was caffeine, and she needed a jolt of energy. She poured the brown liquid into her cup and stood motionless for a few seconds, watching the steam rise.

Her son, Freddy, said she was mellowing, but she doubted that. Age would probably make her more herself, not less, as she abandoned the camouflage of lipstick and civility she'd donned in a doomed attempt to be socially acceptable. *What a colossal waste of time and effort that was.*

Molly glanced up from her screen, eyes wide. "What's up?"

"I'm going to dive into the first installment of Sadie's story." Anne wandered back to her desk.

Sadie's big story, a series in five parts about the effects of Vermont's death with dignity law, would put her small family newspaper in the big guys' league. The reporter had outdone herself. Picturing herself sipping cheap champagne and beaming with pride at press association banquets as Sadie accepted first-place awards for her series, Anne forgot what she'd been worried about as she mentally flipped through her closet to select what she would wear to the award ceremony.

Chapter 6

On the twenty-minute drive from town to the college, Indira barely noticed the scenery that once made her catch her breath. The four-street village square surrounded by acres of meadows, orchards, and tilled fields, the mountains and woods, the light reflecting off the lake, used to transport her to another planet as far from her crowded Boston home as Pluto was from Earth.

In Queenscove, four cars waiting to get through a four-way intersection was rush hour. Coming from the pressure cooker of a big city, she'd expected the town to be a safe place where their lives would be as serene as the environment. This tranquility was the canvas on which she would paint her stories, but when everything went wrong all at once, the landscape hadn't saved her. If she'd done what her parents had wanted, would the future have been different, or was this her destiny no matter what path she'd taken?

Indira checked the time on the car's dash. Her class started in half an hour. Today's three classes plus office time spread out over six hours were her one long day each week. She used to relish feeling completely used up for a worthy cause. If only she didn't feel so jaded and old right now.

She braked at the stop sign a block before the college, absorbed in her thoughts, and forgot she was driving until the man in the truck behind her leaned on his horn. She jerked, startled by the sound, and jammed her foot on the gas without checking for oncoming cars. Her car bolted into the intersection.

In the next second, impossibly loud screeching shook her. She slammed her foot on the brake and froze. Her hands gripped the steering wheel as the car juddered to a stop. She held her breath, throwing one arm in front of her face as if that would save her. Her backpack tumbled off the passenger seat, her phone slid off the tray, and a gray car skidded to within inches of her driver's side door. Indira closed her eyes and waited for the impact.

"What the hell are you doing?" A woman with a red face, eyes blazing, screamed at her from her outside the window. "Didn't you see the stop sign?" The woman pointed to the sign, put her hands on her hips, and stamped her foot.

The truck behind Indira honked again in annoyance because now her car was blocking the intersection. Unshed tears made Indira's eyes heavy; her heart hammered against her chest. "I—"

"You what? Are you blind? Didn't you see me? You could've killed us both!"

"I wasn't . . ."

"Well, do you speak English or what?"

Indira let go of the steering wheel and leaned back to look at the woman. Blonde hair, gray eyes, pale skin, no lipstick. Attractive, in fact. Her teeth were quite regular. She was wearing a blue cashmere sweater over a white cotton turtleneck, a long gray wool jacket, and gray slacks. Little pearl earrings hung from her ears. Indira saw all this before she could speak.

She rolled down the window. "I'm sorry. I wasn't paying attention—"

"Damn right, you weren't paying attention."

"Is your car damaged? Are you hurt?"

The woman gave her the death ray stare, as Indira's brother used to call it when their mother used it on them.

"No, my car's not damaged, because I braked in time and swerved." She turned in a circle and put her hands on her head. "That's not the point," she yelled. "You scared the shit out of me. I could've killed you."

Indira thought she caught a whiff of alcohol on the woman's breath. That couldn't be. It was barely nine in the morning. "Are you sure you're not hurt?"

The driver of the pickup truck behind Indira walked toward them. "Do you need help?" he called out.

Indira and the woman stared at him. "We've got it handled," the woman said and signaled with her arm for him to drive around them.

"Can you at least pull your cars to the side so people can get through?" he asked.

"No," the blonde said and waved him away. "Go around us."

The man appeared shocked. "What the?"

Indira admired the way the blonde stared him down as if she were accustomed to keeping people in line.

He stomped back to his truck and glared at them as he passed on the right shoulder.

"Men," the blonde said. They both laughed.

"I'm Indira Anand." She held out her hand to shake hello. "Do we need to call the police? Should we exchange insurance information? In case you're hurt, you know, whiplash. Sometimes it shows up later."

"Laura Morrow. There's no need. You shouldn't drive if you're distracted."

"Thank you, sorry, I . . ."

Laura turned abruptly and went back to her car. She backed up and waved as she pulled around Indira.

Shaking, Indira pulled into a faculty space in the lot and leaned her head against the steering wheel. She sat there for a few minutes to get herself together before she grabbed her briefcase and walked up the cement stairs of the brick arts building and into the classroom. She wasn't in the right mood to teach. She should have canceled the class. Before things got worse, she had to find the courage to tell Tom what was wrong. Then she had to go to the doctor. She had to be a grown-up, whether she was ready or not.

Indira opened the classroom door and donned a smile for her students. *Everything that happens is good material*, she reminded herself.

Chapter 7

Trudging home from work in the twilight with light snow still falling, Anne obsessed over how she had completely forgotten Charles Beale, the state's attorney about whom the paper had reported for ten years. Dozens of stories, requests for quotes, clarifications of fact, confirmations of rumor. She must have shaken his hand, watched him at trial, talked to him on the phone. All gone. If she couldn't remember him, what else had she forgotten? Life suddenly seemed much more precarious as if her certain memory of people and events framed who she was. Though this wasn't the first time she'd lost track of someone important.

Last week she forgot about Howard for a few hours, erased him as if she'd never been married, and signed all the paychecks *Anne Canfield*. He even stopped talking to her. She'd only remembered him when she glanced at the driver's license in her wallet and saw the name Morrow with her face on the card. For a few minutes, she was sure someone had stolen her identity.

She'd called Molly on the intercom. "Tell me my name."

"Anne Canfield Morrow," Molly said without hesitation.

"I think my random-access memory is full." She shook her head to tip its interior mechanism back into alignment. "My content retrieval system is corrupted. The same things keep repeating, old information isn't accessible, and new information doesn't load."

Molly laughed. "Don't worry, Anne. I'm your external backup hard drive."

That wasn't reassuring. After all, she didn't spend every waking hour with Molly. And Molly was no spring chicken, either.

Preoccupied with these thoughts, Anne didn't notice her left foot juddering against the frozen path and then dragging as if it had forgotten how to walk. She pitched forward and her right leg failed to step out in time to catch her. After a split-second mental blackout, her brain shifted into high gear.

Throw away the sticks so you don't poke out your eyes, her mind bellowed. *Put out your hands to stop the fall.*

Her knee hit, then her hip. *Don't whack your nose.* Anne caught her fall with her forearms surprised she remembered to put her arms out in front of her. Sprawled on the ground and unable to move, she gasped at the inexplicable abruptness of it, the throbbing pain in all her limbs, and the shock that her legs no longer behaved as expected. Was it possible to forget how to walk from one second to another?

It was already dark. She wanted to whimper but that wouldn't achieve anything. "Come on, get up," she urged her body. "Stop coddling yourself. No one's around to help you."

You always were a klutz, Howard said.

"Oh, yeah? Now you show up. Where were you when I needed you?"

Anne assessed her situation. Her sturdy walking sticks were an arm's length away on either side of her. She reached for them with her fingertips and pulled them closer, feeling a spurt of triumph when she grasped the sturdy rods in her palms. Her phone had tumbled out of her jacket pocket but lay within reach. She picked it up and checked the time. Six p.m. Glad the phone was still working, she stuck her fingers in her left pocket and found her house keys. What a relief, no groping around in the dark necessary.

"Nothing to do but sit up and see if anything's broken."

She pushed herself into a seated position and surveyed the damage. "Torn pant leg but no blood. That's good." Gingerly, she ran her hand over her knee and shin. No sharp bone protruded from her skin, although her knee hurt like hell, and that couldn't be good.

She sat on the ground for a minute or two longer, her head shaking. "I've crossed the line into old age." The realization stunned her.

Don't be so surprised. You did that a long time ago.

"For God's sake, Howard, that's not the encouragement I need right now."

Pulling herself up on her walking stick, Anne clambered to her feet. She put weight on her leg and though the pain in her knee shrieked, she discovered she could hobble. She took three tentative steps. It wasn't far to the house. No longer trusting her balance, terrified she would fall again and not be able to get up this time, she stumbled home.

Porch lights in the distance welcomed her. She scanned the rambling stone and clapboard house with its three chimneys, reassured her home was still the treasure she believed it was. Lights illuminated the inside of the house. Freddy's truck was in the driveway. She pictured her son's curly red hair, green eyes, strong hands, and her heart eased. If she could make it home, she would be safe. Everything would be the way it was supposed to be.

Chapter 8

With constant pain now throttling her body, Indira surveyed the ten enthusiastic faces in her senior creative writing class, her last class of the day.

These students were waiting for her to say something intriguing. She was the catalyst, supposed to set their synapses blazing, and the last thing she felt was brilliant enough to be the spark to ignite their genius. Even the thought of the performance required to deliver the lecture exhausted her. She didn't have the necessary emotional bandwidth to stimulate an earthworm, much less provoke people to write sizzling stories.

All eyes were on her. For a second, she relished their adoration, still thrilled by the fact that they wrote down what she said. Her egotism amused her. What did she have to tell them that they didn't already know? *Maybe I could tell them they don't know they know.*

"Okay. Writing prompt. Fifteen minutes, then we'll read your work and critique."

They readied themselves, shifting in their chairs, pushing back hair, swallowing. She marveled at how well-trained their imaginations were. Competitiveness shone on their skin like sweat as they slyly surveyed each other at the starting line.

"Your character has been told she's going to die. What happens next? What does she want, how does she appear, what does she remember and feel, who does she talk to, what does she say and do? Show us the place. Use all the senses. Move us. Blow us away."

A few gasps, a few smiles, and heads lowered, shoulders hunched, all ten of them began scribbling in pencil or pen or tapping away at their laptop keyboards as fast as they could. Some of the responses would be brilliant. She might learn from them. They might teach her how to get from here to wherever she had to go with dignity. Indira crossed her arms and stared out of the classroom's wide windows.

Two years ago, almost to the date, the doctor had said, "You're not pregnant. Your ovary is enlarged. We need to run some tests." Three body blows. She left the office reeling, clutching the doctor's orders for a blood test and sonogram.

For a week, she wept during the day when Tom was at work and paced the living room in the middle of the night, waiting for the results as fear consumed her. The biopsy. The long needle. Her unabated shuddering. When the doctor said epithelial ovarian cancer, in the dispassionate tones of a newscaster, Indira couldn't hear anything after that, the roaring in her ears was so loud.

She'd tried to be calm when she told Tom, but she hadn't been able to stop shaking or block the sobs that mangled speech. His head had jerked back as if she'd punched him. He gasped and gathered her into his arms. They stayed like that for hours, sitting on the couch, taking turns weeping. He didn't offer any platitudes. He was just there, holding her hand when it mattered.

Three months after surgery to remove one ovary and fallopian tube, the oncologist had declared her cancer free and even held out the possibility of pregnancy. "You have a ninety percent chance of surviving five years—the same chance for life as everyone else."

She and Tom had taken that as an all clear. Now, this pain meant that she had fallen into the dark, narrow crevasse of the ten percent who wouldn't live five years without a recurrence.

Indira had watched her grandmother die from ovarian cancer, covering her ears with a pillow in the middle of the night to muffle the sound of her cherished Nani's screams. She couldn't go through that and wouldn't put Tom through that. There had to be something she could do.

Where is my courage?

Checking her watch—two more minutes—Indira glanced around at her students. The faint odor of the carpet's rubber backing nauseated her. Nervous intensity buzzed in the quiet room. Her favorite student coughed into her hand, announcing she was ready. Most of the others were still immersed in their work.

Indira glanced at her text messages. Three were from Tom.

Are you feeling better?

How are your classes today?

What's for dinner?

He cared about her. He was trying to tell her she wasn't alone.

Chicken piccata, she texted and made a mental note to stop at the market after class for the ingredients. Her mouth watered in advance, savoring the complex flavors of chicken, artichokes, sundried tomatoes, lemon juice, and capers sauteed together in olive oil. Her stomach grumbled. She should have eaten that blueberry scone at the café.

Indira paced the classroom, a way of preparing the more thoughtful students to stop like snapping her fingers to wake them from a hypnotic state. Her back to them, she gazed out at the beach and the now snow-covered path to the center of the cove. She inhaled the chilly air again, saw Anne Canfield wave her arms and yell, and almost smiled.

And then with no warning, memory perched her in a white tissue smock on the edge of the paper-covered table in the doctor's office as if the exam were happening at this moment. A chill radiated outward to her limbs. Indira put her fingertips on her lips to stop their quivering.

This was not supposed to happen. Her parents had raised her to expect the best of everything. She was supposed to go to high tea with her daughter on Saturday afternoons just as she had done with her mother. Her son was supposed to crawl into his grandmother's lap to read a book. Her mother would stroke his soft curls and rub her nose against his. She was supposed to love Tom until she was white-haired and feeble and could barely eke out a smile of greeting. She pictured their gnarled hands entwined.

That wasn't so much to ask of the universe. She wasn't trying to be queen of the world. What great harm had she done to the world in a previous life that karma would punish her like this? It was outrageous that random cells multiplying without reason could colonize her body like invading vandals. If only her fury could burn them out of her body.

Indira faced the class. Her vision blurred, her face got cold, her nausea intensified, and her knees bent. She crashed to the floor. When she opened her eyes, she found herself cradled in her favorite student's arms. Indira managed to say, "Time's up" as the paramedics entered the room.

Chapter 9

The last place Anne wanted to go was to the doctor, but her knee was swollen beyond recognition, pain throbbed through her leg in all directions, and Freddy insisted. "We'll get it checked, Mom. Probably nothing's wrong, but just in case."

Doctors were a necessary evil. The only good thing about old age was that the alternative was worse. It was clear to her that dreadful things were going to happen no matter how often her electrolytes were adjusted.

"You know, if I were a car, the mechanic would fix or replace whatever was broken. But for us humans, after doctors check the fluids, kick the tires, and flick on the lights, all they can report is that I'm low on this and high on this other."

"Yes, Mom." Freddy bundled her into the car.

"I'm not taking anything that hastens the inevitable."

"Okay, Mom."

Anne knew he'd heard her theories about genetics as destiny and the body as a self-healing mechanism often enough to know her position. "I'm still in charge here."

"Yes, you are." Freddy helped her into the doctor's waiting room.

Her doctor was her old doctor's son—same gray hair, same small bald spot on the top of his head, same gray eyes behind the rimless glasses—who now ran the local urgent care facility. A few decades ago, when he took over the practice, she'd thought he was twelve. Now, he was older than his old man had been when he retired. *How did that happen? Where did all those years go?*

"Ticker's fine." Dr. Woodley always gave her the good news first. "You bashed your knee pretty good. X-ray shows you cracked the patella and pulled some ligaments, but you'll live." He scrutinized her face. "I'm assuming you don't want surgery." He smirked at his little joke.

She had often quoted him the statistics on unnecessary deaths in hospitals caused by opportunistic infections following surgery and was mildly cheered to see he remembered.

"I'm going to give you a soft cast and instructions I know you won't follow. Take ibuprofen for the pain." He helped her stand up. "Close your eyes."

Oddly, she did what he said without question. An eternity passed as she fell backward into a lemon-scented black hole.

The doctor put his hand on her back. "Okay. Open your eyes and sit back down." He held her elbow while she found the seat. "I'm concerned about the tremor in your head and hand, Anne." He peered into her eyes. "Seems more pronounced than before."

Anne held her cheek to comfort herself. "Stress of coming here to see you triggered the cortisol cascade effect. Also, I fell, so there's that." But Woodley calling her by her first name scared her more than his words.

He raised his eyebrows and didn't laugh. "There's also an issue with your balance. I'm sending you to a neurologist, and I want you to get some tests."

"For what? For my hand? I didn't hurt my hand."

"No. For your brain."

Anne laughed, thinking he was joking. "There's nothing wrong with my brain. I didn't hit my head."

She didn't tell him how the sudden disconnect of her feet from her brain had stunned her. They had flown out from under her without her volition. Her brain was keeping secrets from her, and she didn't know what her body would do next. Old age was a horror film in which the main characters made all the wrong decisions as the ax murderer steadily crept up behind them.

Anne didn't plan to tell anyone about these sudden revelations. Telling her children would doom her to fifteen years of sitting in a rocker on her front porch, bused mid-day to the senior center for a rousing game of dominoes and a lunch of spam sandwiches on crustless white bread with apple sauce on the side, watching the world go by without her. Everyone in the county would forget her even before all the cells in her body gave up ingesting, excreting, and replicating. That must be where the whole idea of zombies came from—the walking dead of the not-yet-gone but completely erased.

Her sons, with the best of intentions, would sell the paper in the blink of an eye for a few measly dollars or just fire everyone, close the doors, and count themselves lucky to be out from under it. What would happen to Molly, Ozzie, and Sadie? The thought of all those generations of effort and all that history forgotten broke her heart. She couldn't let that happen.

"We'll start with an MRI." Woodley scribbled indecipherable words on his small prescription pad. "You can get it over at the hospital in Burlington. And I'll call Dr. Arnold and warn him about you. He's a good guy. You call him and get an appointment."

He wrote the doctor's name and phone number on another piece of paper, then scrutinized her face again. She squirmed, disconcerted by his looking at her square in the eyes twice in one visit.

"You know what?" He patted her shoulder. "I'll have Barbara make the appointments for you. She'll let you know when they are."

"It's old-timers, doc."

Anne wanted that to be true, but the second Woodley suggested a problem with her brain, she knew he was right. Anyway, that's what Howard had always said—something was wrong with her brain. The old poop would feel vindicated now, which was really annoying.

The doctor wrapped the soft cast around her leg and fastened the Velcro straps. "When you get your medical degree, I'll listen to your diagnosis. Meantime, see Dr. Arnold." He handed her two small paper rectangles and pre-printed instructions about taking care of her leg in the cast and walked out of the room.

In the waiting area, Freddy rose from the chair and rushed toward her, his large hands held out to catch her if she fell as she hobbled through the door. Anne couldn't deal with the fuss. "I'm fine," she told him and took his arm. "Don't make a big deal out of it. Let's go over to the Old Brick Store and get take-out."

Freddy leaned over, kissed Anne's cheek, and held the door open for her for the first time in decades.

Chapter 10

The receptionist at Tom's veterinary clinic blinked rapidly as Indira walked through the door. She yanked her fingers off her keyboard as if she'd been shopping online, coughed, and stood. "Oh, Mrs. Beale. I wasn't expecting you."

Indira smiled to show everything was fine. "Sorry to startle you, Patsy. I should have called before I came. Is Tom still here? He isn't answering his phone." Her voice sounded brittle to her, overly conscious of itself in the quiet room. "And please, call me Indira."

A low moan came from behind the reception desk. Indira's eyes widened. "Who is *that*?"

Patsy chuckled. Her gray curls danced. "A cow in labor. She started early and she's having trouble. We're watching her remotely. Pretty cool, don't you think? We've got streaming video from the barn and all. Doctor Tom set it up. There are text alerts so the docs can run out to the farm if her heart rate accelerates beyond the normal range. We've got all the bells and whistles." She wiggled her shoulders as if her body couldn't hold her delight in the practice's advanced technology. "Want to see?"

"No, thank you. Next time. Would you page Tom for me?"

"Oh, of course. They had an emergency procedure," Patsy said. "They're just done now. I'll buzz him, no problem." Patsy pushed the intercom key on the phone on her desk. "Mrs. Beale's here, Doctor Tom."

Doctor Tom. I'm in a rerun of a 1950 sitcom. Indira wandered around the waiting area, noticing equine magazines, framed color photos of blue-ribbon farm animals on the walls, and a small woman in torn jeans and a quilted vest huddled in a corner chair. Indira glanced at Patsy, whose eyes telegraphed sympathy.

The woman's pale face turned to Indira. "Are you Dr. Tom's wife?"

"I am."

"He saved my horse, my Mr. Henry." A small sob escaped the woman. "He woulda died, otherwise."

"Oh, I'm glad. You must be so relieved."

The woman wiped her face with her hands. "He's a good man, your husband. A good man." She pulled a crumpled tissue from her pocket and blew her nose. Indira nodded again, feeling completely helpless, and turned away.

Tom had proudly escorted her around the five-acre facility the first time she'd visited. The veterinary center included two paddocks, a surgical building, an acupuncture wing, a therapy pool, and a stable. She recalled her husband boasting that people brought their horses here from all over the state and sometimes neighboring states, but she had only the vaguest idea of how they ran the business, of who did what and how. She should have paid more attention to the stories Tom told her.

An award-winning pig winked at her from a framed photograph. Centered on one wall was a poster-sized image of the staff with Tom and his Uncle Bruce, all wearing blue scrubs, grinning, and waving their hands as if it were their best day. She leaned forward to read a framed magazine article with vivid photos that raved about the animal hospital's innovative treatments. She hadn't realized the clinic was internationally famous.

A door swished open and her husband in scrubs, blood splattered across his top with a powder-blue shower cap over his hair, mask lowered beneath his chin, and feet encased in paper booties rushed toward her. He kissed her cheek before she could back away from the blood on his clothes.

"Sorry I was incommunicado, honey. Are you okay? This is twice in one day. I didn't expect you." He grinned cautiously and Indira caught a glimpse of the man she married.

She glanced over at Patsy. "Could we go into your office?"

"Sure. What's going on?"

Indira waved her hand and walked down the corridor ahead of him to the open door of his office. Tom never lingered in his office longer than ten minutes. He could have eaten off his desk. Except for his laptop and a framed photograph of them on their honeymoon, the desktop was clear. With all the clinic's records digitized, Tom could retrieve his patient notes from the system or read papers about the newest surgical techniques and treatments on his tablet. No need for a messy desk.

She shouldn't have been surprised. Her husband was meticulous, a character trait that had always charmed her. The careful arrangement of cooking utensils in their kitchen drawers and his Wellies, rubber clogs, and muck boots lined up in the mudroom between the garage and the house beguiled her. Of course, those were the days when everything he said or did captivated her. It was strange how the very things that had enchanted her now made her want to scream.

Indira sat in the ergonomic chair at his desk, and Tom perched on the shining walnut top. He pulled off the disposable cap and booties, removed the mask, bundled them into a ball, and tossed the ball into a special trash container.

"Tell me what's so important it brought you here."

Indira heard the worry in his voice now that they weren't performing for anyone. She was overreacting. Tom sensed something was wrong. It was her secretiveness that separated them. She put her fingertips on her chest to ease the pain.

"I have to go back to the doctor. The gynecologist. I called her today. The symptoms I had two years ago are back." She couldn't tell him about fainting in class. It would be like admitting failure, although that didn't make any sense. Her body wasn't working the way it should; it was defective, she was broken, and somehow that was her fault.

Tom's face paled. "So that's what this morning was about." He shook his head. "You don't know it's that."

Like her, he couldn't bring himself to use the C-word. Cancer. The word blinked in the room between them as if it scrolled across a twenty-foot-high electronic billboard. He stroked her hair. "You might be pregnant this time."

Indira closed her eyes. "I know this feeling." She put the palm of her hand on her belly over her remaining ovary. "My appointment is Wednesday, two days from now. I'm anxious about it. I'm afraid of what the doctor will say." Her voice trembled and she struggled to control it. "Will you come with me?"

"Wednesday." Tom consulted the calendar on his phone. "I've got surgery. Can you make it another day?"

"Tom, please. I don't want to go alone."

"Reschedule your appointment. I want to come with you, but I can't do it on Wednesday. Any other day works."

"How can you not understand?" Indira was close to tears. She peered at his face hoping to find the way to persuade him. "Wednesday's the only time the doctor can see me. It's an emergency appointment. If I don't take this time slot, she can't see me for weeks. I'll have to go to a stranger. She shoehorned me in because of my history. Please. I need you to be with me."

She saw him set his face, the thin line of his lips saying no for him and hated herself for pleading with him. Saying yes to her should be as natural as breathing.

"Honey, I want to be with you, but I can't. It's delicate surgery. Bruce can't do it. The horse will die if I don't operate. It's a new patient, a referral. They're coming from out of state. There are too many moving parts to reschedule it."

A chill crept up her legs from her ankles. "This is *your wife's* emergency, not some horse's."

"Be reasonable. You won't die on Wednesday."

She stood and put her hand on his chest. Trying to hold back tears, throat constricted, she squeaked out, "I don't want to be reasonable. I *want* to be irrational. I'm terrified of what the doctor's going to say, and you don't care."

He gripped her shoulders. "Indira, for God's sake, of course, I care. What's gotten into you?"

Her lips were stiff, and she could barely speak. "What's gotten into me is that I've got cancer, and I'm afraid I'm going to die. Is that clear enough for you?"

He put his hand out to stroke her face. "You don't know it's that."

The chill reached her face. How could he be so condescending? She stepped away from him and adjusted her purse strap on her shoulder. "Okay. If that's what you want, I'll go alone. I'll let you know what the doctor says."

He leaned in for a kiss as if they had sorted out the problem. She turned her face away, and Tom kissed her cheek.

"I can already taste that chicken piccata."

He was trying to cajole her. Infuriated, words she couldn't say stuck in her throat, Indira darted out of the building to her car. She couldn't go home now. She certainly wasn't going to cook for someone who thought a horse was more important than his wife.

Roaring in her ears kept her from thinking. She couldn't persuade her husband to be with her when she needed him. He'd rather save some animal. She was on her own. Tom could make his own damn dinner. She sped out of the parking lot and swerved onto the road going in the wrong direction.

Driving aimlessly for a while, Indira wound up at the ferry crossing. She drove her car onto the boat and on the other side of the lake, found a small café in Essex, New York, a place she'd never been before. She ordered dinner there, pushing her food around on her plate with her fork, surreptitiously watching the four other weeknight diners murmuring as they ate, silverware clinking against their plates, feeling the ping of her loneliness at every sudden laugh. It was absurd to take umbrage at other people's happiness, but she did.

On the last ferry back to Vermont, Indira stood next to her car in the frigid night air watching the boat's white wake glow neon in the moonlight against the ink-black water. She would ask her mother to come with her to the doctor's appointment. Waiting for Chandra to pick up the call, she tested the words she needed to say. "I might have . . . I have ovarian . . ." Her throat swelled. "This is the second . . . The surgeon will remove . . ."

Her face twisted. She couldn't say the words to herself. How could she tell her mother what she needed if she couldn't speak? Indira ended the call without leaving a message and muted the phone so she wouldn't hear her mother's call back.

She couldn't bear to tell herself she had cancer again. She couldn't form the words, "I will never have a child," much less tell her mother she had an illness that could kill her. Anyway, she could be wrong. Tom might be right—it wasn't cancer. Her reaction was out of proportion.

She needed to get herself under control, but all she had to hang onto was hope that he was right, and she was wrong, and that seemed like so much counter-intuitive hocus pocus.

Eyes closed, with the ferry's engine vibrating beneath her feet, she imagined her mother pacing the spacious living room in her Beacon Street home, her voice running the scales of her disbelief, and demanding Indira come home at once to see a real doctor. Her mother's tears, the drama, and her voluble concern would overwhelm Indira so that she couldn't think.

She could hear her father rolling out a list of specialists' names. "I know people. With my connections, I can get you in tomorrow." Second opinions and alternative diagnoses. He would talk louder and louder as if more sound proved he was right, as if decibels could dispel heartache. If sound could dissolve cancer, she'd go home to her parents in a minute. But there were no miracle cures for ovarian cancer. She would tell her parents when the surgery was over, as she had the first time, and they could do nothing about it.

The moon rode high in a cloudless sky. Indira gripped the railing and stared at the water surging away from the boat's hull. The lake was right there below her. It would be so easy to slip over the side and disappear.

Two years ago, when she'd announced to her parents that she planned to move to a tiny Vermont village and join the faculty of Queenscove College, her father reacted as if she'd signed up to be the first passenger on a trip to colonize Mars. He clutched his hair, exclaiming, "How can you go so far away? Who lives out there? You should be near us. You're our only daughter."

For as long as she could remember, her family had lived in the brownstone on Beacon Street. Her mother's commute was a flight of stairs down to her pediatric practice on the ground floor. In their circle of friends, no one ever left the area except for prestigious postings in Palo Alto or Princeton.

"It's only a four-hour drive, Dad," she'd said. "Not a big deal. And I'll have a salary and time to write. It's beautiful there and the air is clean." She hadn't yet told them she hoped to marry Tom. Her strategy for managing her parents was one shock at a time.

Her father had sputtered his objections. He wanted her to get a doctorate and teach at the university where he held a faculty post. Teaching, he often told her, was a worthwhile profession, unlike scribbling. He wanted to introduce Indira to his colleagues as his daughter, the doctor.

In her father's personal astronomy, his star rose higher and shone brighter with every degree his children acquired. Her brother was a physician. Somehow, it was incumbent on her to make her father happy.

Indira wiped the spray off her face. Her hands were ice cold, and the throb of the engine made her dizzy. Turning away from the rail, she hurried inside the ferry's enclosed deck and took a seat far from the windows.

The night she'd told her parents she was moving, Indira's mother waved her hand, making her husband disappear from the dining room—a trick Indira wished she could learn. "Ignore your father," Chandra said. "I believe in you, in what you're doing."

At their weekly afternoon tea at the Taj Boston the following Saturday, nestled in comfortable chairs upholstered in rose-colored fabric embroidered with multi-colored flowers, Chandra had ordered without consulting the menu. Beginning when Indira turned twelve, no matter how busy the family was, the hotel's high tea was their retreat, the place where her father and brother would never barge in with their outsized demands for Chandra's complete attention.

The waiter laid the tea table with hand-painted porcelain cups, sweet cakes, and tart sandwiches on a tiered tray, white linen napkins, and gleaming silverware. A flower arrangement of pink and white peonies looked delicious enough to eat. Indira, from long habit, unfolded the large napkin across her lap, and held her teacup in one hand and a bite-sized cake in the other. She inhaled the sugar in the air, the spice in the chai, the heady aromas of women's perfumes, the starch in the waiter's tuxedo shirt, and relaxed.

"Writers conjure truth." Chandra had said in the soft tone she used with the worried mothers of sick children. "They summon beauty with mere words. They inspire fear. They make you weep and laugh. They create new worlds." Her mother's voice was confident and sure. This was the voice that stitched together Indira's hurts, read her to sleep, and celebrated her successes. This was the voice she trusted.

Chandra set down her cup and leaned across the table to touch Indira's hand with her fingertips. "Art is true power, more important than facts, more terrifying and dangerous than knowledge of diseases or math. Writers are like physicists piecing together in exquisite detail the equation that explains everything."

Indira picked up her mother's hand and kissed it. "Clearly, I got my fondness for words from you."

Chandra smiled. "This is a good thing you're doing. I'm proud of you. Eventually, you'll teach at Harvard or Princeton and your father will be happy."

Her mother's expectation that she could spin a world into being out of nothing was terrifying, but she cherished the encouragement. Having someone believe in her and acknowledge her talent was both overwhelming and necessary. But after the publication of her first novel, when Indira stood in front of small groups of people and talked about her work, she felt as if she were an imposter and someone else had written the book. Words stuck to the roof of her mouth. She answered questions, hearing her voice form sounds that were meaningless to her.

After each event, as people shook her hand and expressed their admiration, she had no memory of what she'd said. Releasing the words into the air erased them from her mind. Each day propelled her farther from the work she loved. Ink dried in her pens; the cursor blinked on a blank screen. She felt like Gretel, desperate for crumbs that would lead her in the right direction, but birds had eaten all the words. Marrying Tom, she'd convinced herself, was the way to find her way home. Was she being punished now for choosing the wrong path?

The ferry's hard, plastic seat pressed against her thighs. The engine throbbed. Indira surveyed the five other passengers returning to Vermont on the same boat and wondered if they were paying a high price for their journey. Were they fleeing an angry spouse, a lost job, or going home to find solace? Perhaps they were just as lost as she was.

When the sound of the engine stopped, and the boat lurched and bumped against the dock, she returned to her car and waited her turn to deboard. Checking her phone, she saw Tom had texted her several times with increasing urgency.

"Cow in breach. I'll be late."

"Too bad I'm missing that chicken piccata."

"I'm home. Where are you?"

"Indira, did the car break down? Are you in trouble?"

"Call me."

Tom was asleep by the time she arrived home. Just as well. She didn't want to explain why she'd disappeared without a word. She knew she was getting even with him for his callous disregard for her feelings and knowing that made her feel small and petty. *God, I'm so confused.*

Indira lay down next to him and listened to the quiet, snuffling sounds he made in his sleep. The alarm clock read 11:00 P.M. *Was it only this morning that I walked out on the lake? It feels like a century ago.* She closed her eyes and saw that wild woman, Anne Canfield, waving frantically from the beach.

Chapter 11

After a quick meal his mother only picked through, Freddy helped her upstairs. He stood in her bedroom, clueless and worried about what to do next, but she shooed him away.

"I'm okay, sweetheart. I'm so glad you were here to help me. Don't keep what's-her-name waiting. You should go on home now." She hobbled over, hugged him, and kissed his cheek.

"You should know her name by now, Mom. It's Laura. We've been married for twenty years."

Anne made a face, and he couldn't help himself. He laughed.

Walking into the dining room, Freddy interrupted Laura taking a long gulp from a silver flask, her head tipped back, eyes closed as if she were kissing a lover. A flare of fear raced through him. Her sneakiness reminded him of Luke, his lying, stealing brother, and how he betrayed everyone.

"What are you doing?"

Laura jumped and stuffed the flask in her large cotton carryall. She adjusted the straps on her shoulder and shook her torso. "I'm just hanging out waiting for you to be done with her." She cast her eyes around the room. "But I was thinking I would call an antique appraiser to inventory your mother's stuff and estimate its value in case . . ." She glanced away from him. "In case, you know, the worst happens, and we have to liquidate the household to pay for Anne's medical expenses."

Freddy put his hands on his hips and glared at Laura. "She has healthcare insurance." He walked over to her, pulled the flask out of her purse, opened the top, and sniffed. "Gin. When did you start this?" He handed the flask back to her. "Anyway, we can't do anything about the house. I don't have power of attorney."

"What? You're the only son close by."

His face reddened. "Sam's the executor of her will. Just because I have a key to the house doesn't mean you and some stranger can go through Mom's home and make an inventory of her stuff. It's got to be illegal. And it's weird that you want to. Anyway, she's not going to die."

"Everybody dies, Freddy. Even your mother."

He turned on his heel and stomped out to the back porch, returning with an armload of cut firewood he dumped into the box near the kitchen woodstove. Freddy had performed this chore for his mother every winter since it became too hard for her to wield the ax.

As a kid, he had watched her chop wood, mesmerized by the rhythm of her swing and the crack of the log as the heart of it split open. It was one of his favorite childhood memories. His mother did it perfectly. With one whack, she cleaved the log in half and then half again. Not everyone's mother could do that. The memory of it was like an antique coin he could take out of its case, polish, and admire without ever intending to trade it for cash. Now, his mother didn't even have the strength to walk home safely. His breath caught in his throat, and he coughed to release it.

Laura slouched into the kitchen, stuffed her hands in her jean's pockets, and puffed out her pale cheeks. "Well, somebody's got to take care of things and your brothers are all too involved in their own lives to care."

When she made this face, Freddy thought she looked like some poisonous fish living in the deepest, darkest recesses of the Mariana Trench. The sneaky greediness that leaked out of his wife with some frequency wasn't her only annoying behavior. He hated the way she sniped at him in public and made him feel like an idiot, particularly in front of his brothers.

After twenty years, he was having second thoughts about the whole institution of marriage. He'd been thinking this way for ten years if he were honest with himself. He wasn't alone in questioning his marriage to Laura. He knew his brother, Arne, had an ongoing bet with Rob that he wouldn't last five more years. Rob, the more conservative brother, guessed fifteen. Freddy didn't think he would last that many months, but he hated the idea of being the only Morrow brother who got divorced. If his brothers could figure out how to keep a marriage going, why couldn't he? Maybe their wives hadn't turned out to be monsters.

What happened to the pretty, joyful woman he'd met in a Burlington bar, the woman who used to smile at him in the morning and kiss him before he brushed his teeth? She disappeared, replaced by an angry harpy who didn't even try to be happy. And now she was drinking. He told himself it wasn't his fault, but the absence of happiness left him feeling hungry all the time, and he was too much of a coward to change his situation. Being a coward made him sad and angry. He was a proper mess, as his mother would say.

Freddy put down two layers of kindling in the woodstove so the fire would start faster when his mother came down to the kitchen in the morning. He scanned the kitchen to see what else he could do in advance and spotted his wife peeking into his mother's money jar. "Laura! Jesus. What's gotten into you?"

Laura put the top back on the ceramic jar. "Lighten up. I thought there were cookies in there."

Freddy bent his head and twisted it to get the kink out of his neck. "She's not dead yet. She's upstairs sleeping because she fell tonight and had to go to the doctor. It's weird that you're counting her cash. Stop acting so strange."

"I wasn't counting it, just checking to see if it was there in case it's needed."

That his wife was an insensitive liar was not a surprise, but the idea that his mother would die suddenly and soon was incomprehensible. His mother was old but not that old. "You're wrong, Laura, just plain wrong. Mom has at least another fifteen years before she gives up the ghost."

Anyway, his mother couldn't die. She was like the Green Mountains. She'd always been there and would always be there whenever he wanted to see her. What did his wife know about anything? She taught kindergarten.

Clearly, he was having a mid-life crisis. He'd gone home to talk to his mother about whatever was going on with him—why he was mopey, angry, and at loose ends all the time. He wanted to ask his mother why his wife didn't love him, and, more importantly, why he didn't care. Instead of that conversation, she'd scared the bejesus out of him when she showed up on the front porch with her face crushed and vacant. She'd looked the same way when the police informed her about Luke. In one minute, she'd gone from normal to crumpled on the floor like an empty potato bag.

He'd worried then that she would never be herself again, that she'd always be a zombie, barely going through the motions of living. But she had come back to life, and that gave him hope. Whatever she was going through couldn't be that bad. He glanced around the kitchen he grew up in—the sunshine yellow walls, white wood cabinets, black and white tiled floor, and the sturdy oak table in front of the bay window facing the lake. This was his mother's domain and he needed to protect it. It was his job to stand up for his mother.

He whirled around to face Laura. "When did you start carrying a flask and sneaking drinks? I want you to stop."

She opened her mouth to rebut him, to make him wrong the way she always did, but Freddy walked out of the kitchen door before he could hear a word.

The door of the old barn the family used as a storage shed creaked on its hinges as he pushed it open. Smells of rust, gasoline, and mold assaulted his nose. He batted away a curtain of spider webs, flipped on the electric lantern that hung near the door, and went inside.

His mother never threw away anything, just moved it out to the shed. Assorted broken riding mowers sat where they had been abandoned. His father had always claimed he would fix the broken ones, but instead, he'd bought another one to mow the three acres around the house. As long as Freddy could recall, his father, the philosophy professor, had never fixed anything.

An old leather yoke Freddy's great-grandfather used to throw over a horse's neck to till up the back garden hung from two large nails against the back wall. Next to the yoke was an ancient wooden sled that must have been old when his mother was young. If Laura was interested in antiques and not just goading him, she should explore the contents of the shed. Who knew what mouse-nibbled treasure hid in those old chests lined up along the back wall. He wouldn't tell his wife about the black snakes that nested out here. If she was going to snoop, she deserved whatever fright she encountered.

Freddy lit a cigarette—a vice Laura would scold him for if she discovered it—and settled down onto the black plastic seat of the newest mower. These days, a succession of neighbor kids rode their bikes over to the house every week and mowed for his mother. But until Anne was in her mid-sixties and caught herself driving blithely into a tree one afternoon, she had mowed the yard.

As a teenager, Freddy used to sit on the porch and watch her floppy cotton hat wobbling on her head as she bounced around on the tractor seat making neat rows and corners on her green lawn. He asked her why his father didn't do the mowing like other fathers.

She winked at him. "Pop's allergic to fresh air. Besides, why should he? Whatever a man can do a woman can do."

She claimed she liked doing it. Mowing gave her three hours away from everyone's demands, and she could think her thoughts. He hadn't understood. Mowing smelled of work to him and in those years, like his father, he had been allergic to arduous work. His mother knew that, and she never asked him to help.

Freddy didn't tell Laura how hard his mother's fall hit him. It felt impossible that one minute she was striding into his third-grade class with a tray full of frosted cupcakes for his birthday and the next she was a wrinkled gnome, four inches shorter, eyes half-closed, with white hair.

Thinking about it made his throat cramp, and he coughed to relieve the strangling sensation across his throat. He should call his brothers and let them know. His mother would never tell them anything was wrong. She liked to pretend she was invincible. He was the one she confided in, the only one who had stayed nearby, and that meant he had to make the call.

He took three long drags on the cigarette and decided to wait until there was something to tell. No point in getting his brothers wound up in advance, particularly since telling them would be hard. He would never forget the day he told them about Luke. He'd called Sam, his oldest brother, first. Every time he tried to say Luke's name aloud, sobs clogged his throat, and he couldn't speak.

"What's wrong, man?" Sam asked. "Is it Mom, is she hurt?"

Hearing the panic in Sam's voice didn't help. Freddy took a few heaving breaths and wiped his face with the side of his hand before he could speak. "Not Mom. Luke. Luke's dead."

"Our Luke? Our brother is dead? How can that be?"

"Yeah, Luke." Freddy only knew what his mother told him in spurts as if each word were stabbing her in the gut. "He overdosed." The words made him feel like a failure.

Sam gasped. Muffled sounds came from the other end of the call, and Sam's wife, Marie, her voice tight, said, "We'll come right away. Tell Mom we're on our way."

Thinking about it now still made Freddy want to cry. Death was crap. It should be abolished. He walked out of the shed and put his cigarette out in the driveway. Recalling how his mother always snapped at him for leaving cigarettes on the ground, he picked up the butt and threw it in the small metal coffee can left over from when his father used to stand outside the kitchen door and knock ashes out of his pipe.

Freddy wandered through the house until he found Laura sitting at his father's desk rifling through the drawers. As far as he knew, his mother hadn't touched anything in the office since his father died five years ago.

He glared at his wife. "What are you doing in my father's stuff? What's gotten into you?"

Laura glanced up, her gray eyes wide, her mouth open as if her husband were the last person she expected to see. She waved a file folder. "Your father had an apartment in Burlington, for like fifteen years. Did you know about that?"

"How the hell should I know that? What are you doing?"

Laura shrugged. "You wandered away. I didn't have anything else to do. Anyway, the file was just sitting here in his middle desk drawer . . ."

"You opened his desk drawers? It's none of our business what's in there. Let's go. I'll come back tomorrow and see if Mom needs anything." He turned to walk out of the room. Laura rustled papers in the folder as if to get a rise out of him. It worked. He could feel anger clawing its way up his back and onto his shoulders. His face heated.

"You coming?"

She shoved the file back in the drawer, grabbed her purse off the floor, and marched defiantly to her car.

"He had a savings account," she yelled across the driveway. "Your father. He had a savings account that didn't have your mom's name on it. He had a savings account with someone else. A woman named Margaret Morrow. Did you know about that?"

Freddy noted the triumph in Laura's voice like she'd won some competition. He jumped into his truck and drove off. She would keep going on this subject now that she'd started, holding his father's secret over his head like a weapon. Like he cared. It was ancient history, whatever it was. He drove slowly, putting off the moment he would arrive home, the last place in the world he wanted to be.

Chapter 12

The hospital radiology waiting room was lined with straight-backed, pebbly blue fabric chairs set arm against arm as if sick people wanted to be whisper-close to the stranger sitting next to them. The room reeked of cold sweat. Anne squirmed in her chair unable to get comfortable.

Pamphlets on corner tables described in gory detail how people's bodies betrayed them. The walls boasted posters that reminded Anne of air raid drills they'd practiced in grade school—the cold linoleum floor, metal lockers at their backs, arms over their heads to stop the A-bomb from killing them. Even at ten, she understood the futility. *It's all mumbo-jumbo.*

She distracted herself from her fear by thinking about the woman at the lake. Her online search had turned up Indira's debut novel, published when she was twenty-four. Short-listed for prestigious awards, the novel received rave reviews, and the author was lauded with predictions of greatness. *How did she ever wind up here?*

Anne read the opening pages online and then consumed the e-book in one sitting. She'd never read anything like it. Indira wrote as if she were inventing language, each sentence opening a new wonder. The image of Indira standing on the frozen lake as the sun rose shimmered in front of Anne as if the whole episode were happening right now. Her eyes stung at the thought of the world losing all that talent. Everyone thought Anne was a cynic, and yet someone else's misery could shatter the flimsy shell of her skepticism. *Maybe I'm wrong about why she was out there.*

She looked around the waiting room to dispel her sense of foreboding and spotted another poster of disaggregated portions of a human leg. Anne repressed a snort. "How on earth is that helpful?" Her head felt fuzzy as if she were allergic to the images and words on the poster.

I told you there was a problem with your brain, Howard said.

"Be quiet for once, Howard."

The drive to Burlington had made her anxious. All the other vehicles were too close, the lanes too narrow. Everyone was moving at the speed of light. Anne worried she would miss her exit, or someone would cut her off. There wouldn't be any parking spaces. Some careless driver would sideswipe her car in the parking lot. She should have asked Freddy to drive her, but Laura would have made a fuss about his being a mama's boy.

It bothered Anne that her relationship with her geographically closest daughter-in-law was this prickly, but she couldn't help that. The woman flat-out annoyed her, constantly triggering her mama bear instincts with the way she belittled Freddy at every family gathering, questioning all his statements and actions. Even the sound of Laura's voice got Anne's hackles up.

Anne had watched Laura double down when Freddy even mildly objected to her behavior, talking over him as if he weren't in the room. His wife challenged his opinions, interrupted him when he told stories about his work, changed the subject, saying no one was interested in that stuff, and turned the conversation to her exploits—which truly interested no one. She turned Freddy, who used to be the funniest storyteller of all of them, mute, and the rest of the family watched in dismay.

People needed to say what they thought, they needed to talk about their day or their hassles and successes at work, their ideas, and dreams, or they bottled it up and got antsy and rebellious. One thing Anne learned from being a mother to teenagers was that silence was a sign of trouble. It definitely wasn't golden. Howard's snide opinion that no news was good news—a way of sneering at her devotion to the paper—was wrong.

Surveying her fellow patients in the waiting room, Anne spotted Indira Anand entering the room. *I was right.* Something *was* wrong with the younger woman. Indira gazed back at her and tapped her fingers on the empty seat next to hers in invitation. Without hesitating, Anne got up and moved to the chair.

"Hi, I'm Anne Canfield. We met . . ."

Indira smiled. "Yes, I remember," she said. "I asked Tom about you." She didn't say who Tom was, as if she expected her new acquaintance to know him. She didn't say her name either, as if Anne would know that too.

Anne sat in the designated chair. "It's weird, isn't it? I feel like I knew you from somewhere else before I met you," Anne said. "And not a wave hello at the farmer's market or the polite meet and greet at the college."

"I feel that way too," Indira said. "Is that odd?"

"I think we knew each other in a previous life." Anne raised her eyebrows, hoping Indira believed in the same outlandish ideas.

Indira nodded. "You know how once in a while you see a stranger crossing a street and your eyes lock as you pass each other, and a tremor goes through you, but you never met them before?"

"Yes, I do." Anne felt as if she were a plucked harp string, the sound reverberating through her entire body. "Like we're from some long-lost clan disbursed across the globe by catastrophe and now we instantly recognize each other tens of thousands of years later."

"That's it, exactly!"

"And there's something we're supposed to do together."

They laughed briefly at their wild speculations, but their surroundings quickly sobered them.

"What are you here for?" Anne asked.

"Ultrasound. On my ovary. You?"

"MRI with contrast. Brain."

Anne reached over and squeezed Indira's hand, momentarily freed from her solitary dread by talking to someone who understood her. She waited to see if her new old friend would confide more details, but the younger woman only stared at her hands.

This wasn't the place to probe or confide. Biology was personal. Even doctors doled out revelations about the state of the body one finding at a time, which was oddly preferable to knowing the truth all at once.

It was like reporting an ongoing story, Anne decided. Doctors supplied only the facts as they stood today without adding any commentary. Tomorrow, there would be different facts. Everything changed every day, the smallest alteration rippling through all other events, reshaping them.

"I read your book last night," Anne said to break the tension. "I loved it. Kept me up all night."

Indira's face brightened. "Oh, I'm delighted to hear that."

"I particularly like how your main character found her own way out of her dilemma instead of being saved by someone else." Anne tried to be careful about how she phrased her opinion. She didn't want to seem like an idiot to this brilliant author when they were getting acquainted.

Indira nodded. "Yes, when I finally realized that's what had to happen, it seemed important to me too. Like a lesson for us mortals."

They sat in silence. Anne's mind drifted to Sadie's series. "What would you do if your son told you he wanted to die?" the reporter had asked her when she'd pitched the idea. "Would you help him?"

"God, no," Anne said. Her head shook of its own accord as if she agreed and disagreed with her memory.

She glanced at Indira, who was studying her hands. No matter how successful someone's life appeared from the outside, an incoming tide of trouble might tumble them over and over on the inside until they were nothing but particles of sand.

Even if she wasn't a superior individual, as Howard had often reminded her, Anne had always thought of herself as sturdy enough to deal with disasters. But when they came, she'd discovered she wanted to hide away with the thousand good books she hadn't yet read, hunker down inside the family homestead that had withstood blizzards for a century, and never venture outside again.

The nurse called Indira's name. She rose and walked away without saying anything but at the door she paused, looked back at Anne, and waved.

Anne waved back and smiled, hoping to encourage her new friend. The door shut, and she closed her eyes to wait her turn. In the background, machines hummed and banged as if the world were having trouble turning on its axis.

Chapter 13

At the technician's instructions, Indira lowered the top of her pants. Warm gel spurted in a blob on her skin, and a probe pressed against her abdomen. The technician rotated the wand, pushed down, watched the image forming on the screen.

Indira didn't watch, instead she closed her eyes and breathed deeply to fend off the pain. Squiggly white lines on a black field meant nothing to her anyway. She couldn't understand what they revealed. If Tom was with her, he could have held her hand and distracted her with stories about horses and cows. He would have made her laugh, but he wasn't here.

The night she said yes to Tom—the fifth time he'd asked her to marry him, all previous times during their six-month courtship being too off-the-cuff and unserious—she couldn't wait to show her mother the amethyst and diamond ring he put on her finger. She tilted her hand back and forth under the chandelier and the diamonds winked. Chandra raised an eyebrow and said nothing for a few moments. The raised eyebrow said everything.

"Isn't it beautiful, Mom?"

Chandra rose from her chair. "Who is his family?" She paced the dining room, her expression the opposite of delight.

"They're lovely people. His father is a lawyer, the state's attorney. His mother is involved in charity organizations. She does the annual craft festival. Their family's been in Queenscove for generations."

"Queenscove. Whoever heard of such a place." Chandra pursed her lips, and Indira recognized her mother's way of holding in her icy disdain. "This marriage is beneath you. You're too young to make such a decision, and you don't see the obvious pitfalls. You are an artist and he is . . . what? Beneath you, really. It's too soon, and your father and I don't know him. You should stick to your writing and not divert your attention to things you cannot control like a relationship with some man from God knows where."

"Mom, *I* know him. Don't be such a snob. He's wonderful. Caring, smart, attentive, funny, down to earth, everything I want." Indira searched her memory for attributes that would impress her mother. "He believes in my work as you do. He listens to me."

Chandra closed her eyes. "You should save this passion for your writing, but I won't intervene. You should have someone who's prime minister material, at least, but you'll see. You have nothing in common with him, with his family. Remember I warned you." She swept out of the room, and Indira had felt a chasm crack open her chest.

"Ms. Anand," the radiology technician said, "I'm going to talk to the radiologist. He'll want to see this immediately. Wait right here."

Indira nodded. She wiped her sticky abdomen with the tissue the technician handed her. This was a repeat of the last time she was here, exactly what she had dreaded. She stared at the ceiling to avoid trying to decipher what the image on the screen meant.

On her wedding day, her mother had kissed her cheek and fastened a gold heirloom necklace around her neck. "Let there be spaces in your togetherness," she whispered.

Indira backed away from her mother. "I'm not giving my life over to Tom if that's what you mean. I'm not surrendering my autonomy." Even if she wanted to sink into his flesh and become one being with him, she'd done no such thing, or only for brief, rapturous moments. "You're the one who wants me to surrender my life—to you!"

Chandra's eyes opened wide, her cheeks flamed. "You misunderstand. I meant it as a benediction."

Indira picked up the bouquet of red roses and gold Calla lilies. Sadness pulled at the edges of her lips. "I know what you meant. Why are you spoiling what's supposed to be my perfect day?"

Chandra's silence would have been enough of a response to make her point clear, but she cleared her throat and said, "I wanted better for you" before she bustled out of the dressing room.

When the ache in her heart eased, Indira walked out of the dressing room. The red silk sari whispered around her legs and made her feel like Parvati, the ancient goddess of love and marriage. Chin high, she walked down the stairs to the flower-bedecked hotel ballroom her parents had rented for the wedding. Gold threads in the sari's lush embroidery glistened in the bright sunlight flowing through tall Palladian windows.

At the foot of the stairs, her father blinked rapidly and held out his hand to escort her. The assembled guests breathed out, "Ah," banishing her new doubts. Tom, standing under a bower of flowers, stared at her, beaming.

When she reached his side, he leaned over and whispered, "I knew you were the most beautiful woman in the world the first time I saw you."

Her skin tingled. "I love you."

"Ms. Anand," the radiologist said.

Indira opened her eyes.

"I've called your gynecologist. We've found a problem. She's making arrangements for you to remain in the hospital." He put a hand on her shoulder. "They're scheduling surgery for tomorrow. You can wait in the lobby for your room assignment. They'll do the intake tests today. Your doctor will call you shortly."

The exact words she'd been expecting all day came from the radiologist's voice reeking with excessive kindness. Now that he'd confirmed her fear, she wanted to run away and hide, to find someone who would make it all better. But no one could change this, nothing would make it disappear, and running away wouldn't help. Indira had never felt more alone.

Chapter 14

Lips imitate Morse code's dots and dashes, Anne thought as she watched Dr. Arnold's mouth. It was a wonder anyone ever understood anyone.

"The MRI identified a tumor in the left hemisphere of your brain," Dr. Arnold said.

Anne heard, "Humma humma brain."

As the doctor talked, she imagined a Hollywood song and dance number complete with music and klieg lights. Wearing green scrubs, surgeons catapulted over the patient on the table in an operating room. Scalpels winked in the spotlights. Accompanied by nurses doing hand-springs, surgeons sang a cappella through their masks, "There's a tumor, we found a tumor" to the melody of some Wagner opera theme in an Elmer Fudd cartoon.

Her brain was working overtime to distract her. She should have brought Freddy with her. It wouldn't be easy to tell him this news. What do you say to your child in this situation? "I'm going to die from a brain tumor, sweetheart."

Anne's eyes blinked: message received.

"Have you been experiencing headache, nausea, vomiting, or drowsiness? Dr. Woodley told me you had an episode of weakness on one side of your body." He pointed with his pen to Anne's leg in its black, supportive sheath. "Any memory or speech difficulties? How is your vision? Are you seeing double?"

She shook her head. "Not so I noticed. I've been a little tired, and sometimes things get blurry, but no one's said I'm more incomprehensible than usual. Of course, they wouldn't." She wasn't going to tell him sometimes she couldn't remember her husband ever existed.

Anne tried to smile but she couldn't break through the tightness in her cheeks, the heat radiating up from her throat, the quaking in her belly. This conversation terrified her, and she shouldn't have done it alone. Where was Howard when she needed him? Then she remembered. Howard was dead. "Well, you wouldn't have been any help anyway."

"I'm sorry?" The doctor looked mildly dumbfounded at her comment, but he ran through her entire medical history, including the car accident two years ago when she banged her head on the steering wheel, the window, and the gear shift, resulting in a concussion. She'd lost track of what lane she was in, panicked, hit the gas instead of the brake, and collided with a Jersey barrier.

The prior injury didn't matter, he said. They didn't know what caused this tumor. The past was irrelevant, and the future was more precious as it slipped away second by second the longer the doctor talked. She watched his mouth, impatient with her inability to understand what he was saying.

Finally, Anne blurted, "What do you mean exactly?"

"Okay," Arnold said and started over. "The MRI shows you have a mass in your left temporal lobe about the size of a baseball." He slid a large piece of film up on his light wall and the inside of her brain vibrated there, exposed like a small animal accustomed to living in the dark.

"I got that part." Anne shivered with indignation.

He pointed to a large white circle. "That's the tumor. It's been growing there for a while. The mass is pressing on the parietal and occipital lobes as well." He waited for Anne to digest this information.

She choked on her own saliva and coughed. Whatever parietal and occipital meant, she couldn't remember and probably never knew. Her mind spit out the words perineum, trilobite, and lobular, although she didn't know if that was a word. *It should be a word.*

"Wouldn't I have noticed this before?"

"Human brains are good at rerouting mental tasks. We generally don't notice this cancer until something fails, like when you fell for no reason." He swiveled slightly on his stool and fixed her with a serious gaze. "So, we'd like to have a rummage inside your brain."

He smiled and Anne decided she liked him. "For a biopsy?"

"Yes, and to remove every bit of the tumor we can get to."

Howard had always said something was wrong with her brain. How awful that he was right. "Why don't you take out all of it?"

"Sometimes cancer cells are tangled up with working brain cells. We try to leave you enough to get around on."

The doctor was joking with her. Maybe this wouldn't be too awful. "When do you want to do the surgery?" She expected him to say she had a few weeks before the surgery, time enough to set up everything at the paper, tell the kids, get used to the idea.

"Two days from now. I've already checked with the neurosurgeon. I want to admit you tomorrow for pre-op."

The timebomb of this diagnosis exploded. Anne mumbled, "How long will I live?"

The doctor cleared his throat. "Median life expectancy after surgery, chemo, and radiation is thirteen to fifteen months," he said in his no-inflection doctor voice. "Some people live longer, some less."

"And if you don't do the surgery?"

"Weeks. Months. Impossible to tell."

"What happens first?"

"You'll probably lose your sight, then speech, then your ability to ambulate."

Anne squared her shoulders. "Well, we better get cracking. I have stuff to do."

* * *

"Anne said we should carry on," Molly told the newspaper staff assembled quickly for the impromptu meeting.

"We know our jobs. Wilbur's going to come two days a week to edit and lay out the pages. He also knows our printer and distributor. He said he's had enough retirement anyway. He's glad to come in and help out for a while."

Sadie, doodling on her pad, glanced over her shoulder at Molly. "Think she'd let me interview her? For my story."

"Jesus, Sadie." Osborn pulled his cap down over his eyes and tucked his chin to his chest.

"Well, you know, firsthand account of what it's like to get this news and have a death sentence hanging over you and have to decide what to do. Powerful stuff."

Molly swiped at the corners of her eyes with the side of her hand. "She's already decided what to do. She's going to live. And *we* have enough to do without getting into side issues. She said she wants to run the first part of your death with dignity story off the front page with a jump to the inside double-truck next week. Is it ready?"

Sadie's face brightened. "Been ready for five weeks." She tapped her pen against her pad. "Wow. Anne wants to see it in print before she dies. That's impressive."

Molly rolled her head around on her shoulders to relieve the stress of dealing with the younger generation. "Let's not count her out yet, Sadie. She's tough. Ozzie?"

Osborn pulled up his cap. "Yeah?"

"She wants you to be the editor of the sports section, you know, make the assignments to all our correspondents, make sure their copy is in, edit it so it's decent, and keep doing the photography. You'll get a slight raise. We'll list your name in the pub box as sports editor. Can you do it?"

Osborn's face turned red and his eyes filled. He closed them. "I can." He leaned over, picked up his backpack, and headed to the door. "Need a short break. I'll be back." He closed the door softly behind him.

Sadie sat on Molly's desk. "What's your new job, Mol?"

Molly faced the reporter and steadied herself. "She made me managing editor." She watched Sadie. "We good?"

"No problem," Sadie said and went to her desk to polish her story about a woman who was fighting for the right to die.

Chapter 15

"Tom."

Indira's voice over the phone—toneless and too quiet—hobbled Tom's breath. He pulled the truck over to the side of the road, took the phone out of its cradle, clicked off Bluetooth, and held it to his ear. The movement was instinctive. No one else was in the truck. He needed her voice in his ear as if she were whispering to him at night in bed.

"Yes, babe."

"Tom, there's a mass, on the other ovary. My remaining ovary."

He heard her catch her breath. He held his own and waited while the world spun. Everything lost its color. The air stopped moving.

"She said the ovary was 'engulfed.' Could that be right? It's the size of an orange." She gasped. "My ovary. It's as big as an orange."

Tom wished she had waited to tell him in person. He wished he had gone with her for the doctor's appointment. He should have gone. What was the matter with him? Why didn't he listen to her? If only she hadn't put this mountain of separateness between them. Or he'd done that. Whichever way it happened, he wasn't there with her and couldn't hold her in his arms, couldn't wrap his hands in her silky hair, and tell her it would be okay. Anyway, he didn't know if it would be okay, or how to make it better. His arms ached from the absence of her.

"The doctor wants to do the surgery right away. Tomorrow. She wants me to check into the hospital now for the pre-op stuff."

He needed to be calm for her. He was supposed to be her rock and he had already let her down. His mind was screaming *this is the second occurrence. It's only two years since the first. This is bad.* He couldn't let her know his fears. He wanted to be strong, and he didn't know how to do that.

"I'll get some of your things and come right over. I'll cancel my appointments and be there in an hour, max."

"Tom."

She used his name as if it were an ancient key to a vault full of treasure. No. He had that backward. She was the treasure. A shiver ran through him. He was supposed to be with her, that was the promise he'd made when they married, the promise he broke. He gripped the steering wheel.

"Tom, the doctor says they'll have to take out my uterus." Her voice broke. "Because of metastasis."

He imagined her sitting in the hospital reception area in one of the tan fake-leather chairs with chrome arms, leaning over, her face shielded by her hand, weeping into the phone. Strangers walking by would be careful not to gawk.

His lips froze. "I'll be right there, honey, I'm coming right now. I'll be right there. Stay on the phone. Talk to me."

"Tom, I can't. They're here for me." She clicked off.

Tom made a U-turn. He should have been paying attention. He had to make up for that, starting now.

Chapter 16

Freddy's older brothers, Robert, Arnold, and Sam Morrow, plus their wives piled assorted coats, hats, and scarves on nearby seats to keep strangers away. They sat in a semi-private U in the hospital's waiting area, faces glued to phone screens, not daring to meet each other's eyes.

The brothers had nothing to say. They'd choked on dinner last night, and their usual jokes fell flat. Even their wives had given up polite conversation. Silence was safer, otherwise, their slow-boiling anxiety would flare into fights no one would win, and that no one cared about anyway.

Freddy wished he'd never told them his mother was having brain surgery. The idea alone made everyone a little crazy. He could've done this vigil on his own and told them what was up afterward. Slumped in the comfortable chair, he kept his hand angled against his brow to avoid the glare from any of his siblings.

"At least Pop had the good sense to die from his heart attack right away. None of this drawn-out drama," Arnold, the accountant, blurted into their silence. He rubbed the back of his neck and folded his arms across his chest, defiant in advance of his brothers' inevitable attacks.

Rob considered his knees and peeked at his wife. "Jesus, Arne," he said. "What the hell's the matter with you?"

Arnold jumped up and paced. "It's not like Mom's some spring chicken. We should be prepared." He glanced at his wife who frowned at him and shook her head. He waved her off.

"How old was Pop when he died?" Sam asked.

They all stared at the oldest and, by family decree the smartest brother, astonished he didn't know off the top of his head.

Freddy slouched farther down in his chair and rested his head against the brown leather back. "It was at the end of the year that Luke died. Pop was seventy. Five years ago."

Heads swiveled to consider Freddy. "God, how do you remember shit like that?" Sam asked.

Freddy shrugged and closed his eyes. "You sound like Mom, Arne." His skinny, jean-covered legs stuck out into the space like a hurdle on a track.

His brothers laughed, Arne's face reddened, and Freddy felt sorry for him. Being like their mother was the last thing any of the Morrow boys wanted, but they didn't want to be like their father either. Having fought so hard for his independence and suffered for his difference from his brothers, Freddy thought he had a leg up in this respect. He wasn't like any of them.

Laura licked her lips. "As long as we're speaking candidly," she said from her perch on the couch, "does Anne have a will?"

Sam, the family's lawyer, squinted at his sister-in-law. "Candidly? Yep."

Freddy winced, hoping his wife wouldn't embarrass him. He bet she'd been nipping from her flask when she went to the bathroom and her tongue was loose.

"Well?" Laura tilted her head, her chin pointed in Sam's direction. "Did she split everything evenly among the brothers? Because I'd like the silver if no one else wants it. You can take the value of it off our share of the cash."

They stared at her. In the ensuing silence, she stood up, moved some coats, and chose a different seat farther away from the Morrow brothers. Freddy regarded his wife with disbelief. He wanted to shred her. "*You* don't get squat," he wanted to shout. His throat burned as if he had swallowed scalding tea. He buried his face in a tissue instead and blew his nose for cover. Laura's comment died in the room without a response.

Arne shook his finger at Freddy. "You should have told us sooner."

Freddy's face heated. "Yeah? Like before I even knew about it?" He rubbed his neck where the label on his plaid flannel shirt rubbed against his skin. "I told you as soon as I knew."

"This isn't anyone's fault, Arne," Marie, Sam's wife, said. "No one could've predicted this."

Aghast at their mother's shaved head and her pallor, the Morrow boys needed to blame someone. Last night, she made jokes about her new punk hairstyle—half of her white hair shaved off—and teased them, but she wasn't herself. They read the fear in her eyes, pupils wide and hungry for their faces. The woman who'd weathered everything except Luke's death with icy calm was frightened. That was unacceptable. She was their barometer, and if she was afraid, they should all be afraid.

To console themselves, they recited what she used to say: "Life is tough. People die. That's how it works." But being stoic wasn't enough in the face of their mother's mortality. Freddy's insides quaked. She couldn't die, he wasn't prepared. It was too soon—that was the bottom line. He expected her to live forever.

As they left her room the previous night, Anne hugged each son in birth order and said, "I love you." To Freddy, she whispered, "You're the best thing that ever happened to me."

Freddy scratched his nose to avoid anyone seeing the tears in his eyes.

Anne squeezed each wife's hands. "Take care of my boy," she said. The wives agreed those words were scarier than anything else. Anne would never have relinquished the care of her sons to anyone unless she was sure she was going to die.

Freddy wished his brothers hadn't come. Why couldn't they have found an excuse like they usually did? He could have waited this out on his own. Watching their faces, he realized they felt as crushed as he did. Like him, they didn't know what to do with all of their feelings.

He could figure out how to build anything anyone wanted—a homey 10,000-square-foot house or a spacious-feeling 900-square-foot dwelling. But people were too complicated. Even if you thought you knew how they went together, you were wrong. *If humans had designed people, the resulting being would never have made it past day one.*

Sam's wife, Marie, touched Freddy's knee. "I'm going down to the cafeteria," she said. "Want a coffee?"

"Thanks, Marie." He glanced at his watch. They had hours to go. "I'll take a cup. Large with cream and sugar." He leaned forward to pull his wallet out of his back pocket.

She smiled and held up her palm. "My treat."

Freddy watched Marie walk toward the bank of stainless-steel elevator doors and adjusted his opinion of her. She was wearing old jeans and a sweatshirt. Her Frye boots might have survived her adolescence. Even though she was a partner in a law firm, she wasn't hoity-toity the way Laura had always said she was. He hoped Marie wasn't being kind to him because his wife was such an embarrassment.

He stole a glance at Laura and saw she was sleeping, her head tilted against the chair's high back, her mouth open, snoring slightly. He checked his brothers, who were watching him, and grinned. They grinned back at him.

Slowly, for the last ten years, like arsenic in his morning coffee, Laura had implied his siblings and their wives were snobs, poisoning him with her jealously until he'd taken her word for it. Early on, she'd convinced him she was the smart one in their marriage, that his impression of his family must be wrong. "They all look down on you," she insisted, "because you work with your hands."

When Rob announced his promotion to full professor at the private college where he'd taught for years, Laura had said, "History's a dead subject. No one cares." When Arne's wife was pregnant again, Laura said she already looked like a cow. Freddy never told her about the size of Sam's bonuses.

"Why can't you be happy for them?" Freddy asked.

Laura shrugged. "Why should I be happy for them? Where were they when we lost our baby? All I got from them were some lame texts and emails."

Freddy had no answer. Ten years ago, Laura had miscarried at six months pregnant, and the loss devastated them. He'd already imagined taking long hikes with his son. He could feel his hand on the boy's silky hair and had pictured the delight on the child's face each time they saw each other. Freddy imagined hoisting him into the air, the tickle fights, the child's giggles, and those tiny feet in his hands. He could feel his son crawl into his arms, the weight of his sleeping head against his chest. His heart made room for the baby, and then there wasn't one, only this huge emptiness inside him that nothing could fill.

Laura had been alone when it happened, and nothing he did after that mattered. His yearning for the child didn't matter. His grief. Whatever he did to try and make her happy again was never enough. Laura picked at that scab every day until she drew blood.

Two hours later, their mother's patient advocate entered their circle. "Your mother is out of surgery and doing well." The brothers stood simultaneously. The patient advocate motioned with her hand for them to sit back down. "In an hour or so, we'll let you in one at a time to see her in recovery, for five minutes each. Sons only."

She gave each of the women a warning glance. "She's heavily sedated and we don't know yet if she'll be able to talk. She may not recognize you. Don't press her or make her anxious." Her face performed a practiced smile, lips pressed together, cheeks puffed, and the skin around her eyes crinkled. She wasn't going to tell them anything else.

Speechless, the brothers exchanged glances.

"Does this work for you?" She nodded to show them what they were supposed to do.

Mouths holding in questions they couldn't ask, they moved their heads up and down in unison.

"Which one of you has medical power of attorney in case we need to make end-of-life decisions?"

Rob blanched and raised his hand. "That would be me," he mumbled. "Robert Morrow."

She wrote Rob's name on her chart. "Does she have a DNR?"

Rob glanced at Sam, who shook his head, confirming what they all remembered about that awkward afternoon a month after Pop died when their mother told them about her will and the various documents related to caring for her if she were brain dead. They'd thought then she was being silly.

"No," Rob said. "She doesn't. She wants to be resuscitated."

The woman's mouth dipped down at the corners as if she disapproved of their decision. They had failed some unstated test related to healthcare economics. She jotted a note on her form, pivoted on her heel, and walked away. They shrugged.

Freddy decided Rob was a good pick for the medical power of attorney job. He took forever to make up his mind about anything. He wouldn't rush to pull the plug on their mother. He nodded at Rob to show his solidarity, and his brother bowed his head, sank into a chair, and covered his face with his hands.

"You see Mom first, Freddy," Sam said.

Laura stared at him. Freddy touched his own cheek and discovered he was weeping.

Chapter 17

The warmth of Tom's hand wrapped around hers. Electronic bleeping pierced her sleep, and light seeped through the blinds. Indira opened her eyes. She was alive. Her husband sat next to her hospital bed, his face half-buried in the blanket, sleeping. She watched his chest expand and contract. Her gaze lingered on the perfect dark crescent of his eyelashes against his cheek and the blue vein pulsing in his temple.

"Tom."

He stirred and tightened his grip on her hand.

Her throat hurt. Tubes stuck out of her everywhere. She inhaled the crisp smell of bleach and the sour odor of sweat. A heavy blanket of pain lay across her pelvis. Threads of pain fringed her thighs and belly. The surgical team must have run over her with a tank. Fatigue kept her plastered against the bed, but she wanted to jump up and run as far away from here as she could.

Instantly impatient, she closed her eyes as Tom caressed her face and stroked her head. "What did the doctor say?"

He kissed her hand. "They're doing the biopsies now."

"Plural?"

"Yes. They want to see if the cancer metastasized to other organs."

He was using doctor words. It must be bad news. *They'll try to break it to me gently.* But there was no gentle about this. Being a woman was the central fact of her identity, and the doctor had neutered her. All the children she would never bear, hold in her arms, kiss, or croon to. The loss in Tom's eyes reverberated through her.

He tried to smile. "We can adopt."

"You can't fix this, Tom."

Indira faced the curtain and closed her eyes, falling into the welcoming black hole of another pulse of morphine through her I.V. line.

In a dream, she found Tom—pale, wounded, and wearing sack-cloth—standing barefoot in a stone bunker. Beige travertine blocks lined the floors and walls. In the distance, music played. Bars of sunlight slid into the space through a small window.

Outside, waves sighed against a beach. She wrapped her arms around her husband, placed her palm on the back of his neck, and rested her face against his cheek. Their limbs moved in perfect unison as if they had trained all their lives to dance like this.

In the distance, she heard the boom of the world breaking apart piece by piece like ice on the lake in early spring.

Chapter 18

It was a million steps from her hospital bed to the patient lounge at the end of the hall. Anne didn't count them, but she knew a million when she saw them. Knew it from the tension between muscles and ligaments in her legs, the slow grinding of balls in joints, the bend of her knees, the slap of feet in those ridiculous suction-padded socks against the shiny linoleum floor, and the rattle of the rollers on the I.V. stand she gripped in one hand.

The frigid air in her nose and her sweaty forehead alerted her to her body's struggle. At first, it had taken an hour to push the walker all the way to the lounge. She'd dropped into a chair gasping like a beached whale. The nurse had brought her back to bed in the wheelchair. By today, the ninth time she'd walked the corridor, she was a pro. Now it was part of her daily routine. Sometimes modern medicine worked, but the sooner she was out of the hospital, the better. Tomorrow, she would go home.

The nurses and doctor were impressed with her progress. When she yelled, "Get the hell out of here, leave me alone," they grinned and eye-balled one another. Anne wondered if she was saying what she thought she was saying. Was she speaking gibberish or garbling her sentences? It would be embarrassing to be funny when she didn't intend to be.

When she asked about this, the doctor said, "Whole sentences. You're speaking in whole sentences with the correct nouns, pronouns, and verbs in the right places. It's a good thing. We're very proud of your progress."

Anne thought about all the times her mother had told her to be quiet when she was young. "A nice girl is seen but not heard." Her mother alternated that instruction with "Don't curse, honey. It's so vulgar."

Anne had determined she would never be a nice girl. She'd practiced. "Fuck, fuck, fuckety, fuck," she said to her bedroom mirror in a variety of tones and inflections, relishing the feel of the bad word in her mouth and

70

the satisfaction it gave her to defy her mother. She had never expected anyone would be glad to hear her bellow at them. They must be making allowances because she had brain cancer—because she was near the end.

"I'm having none of this," she declared out loud to anyone in the lounge with her. "I'm getting the fuck out of here and going home."

Except for extreme fatigue, she didn't feel different from the day she'd walked into the hospital, which was odd since the doc had extracted a baseball-sized chunk of cells from her brain with a knife. If anything, she could see more clearly. They had scoured out her brain and words now found their way to her lips more easily instead of racketing around in her head like a pinball in a game played by an extraterrestrial with four hands.

The doctor had given a name to her tumor. "Glioblastoma," he said as if it were as common a thing as pigeons or French fries. He warned her about the scheduled chemo and radiation. "The treatment might knock you out a bit," he said. "Someone needs to stay with you at home. I don't want you to be alone or try to drive."

Her options were limited. She didn't want a stranger in the house, someone she would worry was stealing her money. Freddy was the only son she could stand being with for longer than two days. She adored them all, but the others were so well defined that they took up too much space. They had opinions and habits. Their wives would want her to do things their way, and she didn't have the patience to accommodate them and hated the idea of doing anything anyone said she should do. It had to be Freddy, but not with that wife of his. She had to do something about keeping Freddy's wife away.

Her glee at surviving the surgery ebbed after a week. In the mirror was a woman who had aged fifty years in five days. The sickle-shaped scar on the left side of her head was impressive. She watched the kids' eyes dart away from it as if wisps of cancer might seep out from under the black staples holding her scalp together. It was the rest of her face—flattened and white as a hospital bed sheet—that frightened her. All her light had gone out when they opened her head.

In the lounge, Anne sank into the club chair and stared out of the window at the bare tops of trees surrounding the hospital. Someone slowly collapsed onto the sofa near her. She turned to assess her companion and saw Indira, as bleach-faced as she was, press a small pillow against her stomach, chin down and shoulders hunched as she eased onto the seat.

Grief welled up in Anne's chest followed fast by fury. *They got her. They got her as if she were a doe some fool shot out in the woods, against the rules, for the sheer glee of killing a magnificent being.*

Indira raised her face and smiled wanly. "You're the last person I expected to see here in one of these stunning gowns." She touched the blue cotton shift they both wore. Her I.V. drip was slightly faster than Anne's. Her hair had lost its shine.

"Oh, God, I'm so sorry," Anne whispered.

"I want to die," Indira said, her voice as calm as ice.

Anne had heard those words before, in that exact tone, from Luke when he was nine. They made her shudder. Whatever she'd said then had been wrong. Best to say nothing now. Instead, she hauled herself out of her chair and eased her body down next to Indira on the sofa. They sat together silently, staring out over the trees, their IV towers standing sentinel until the nurse came for Indira.

After she settled into the wheelchair, Indira turned to Anne. "Thank you for hearing what I said and for not telling me I'm wrong about how I feel or what I should do about it."

Indira reached out her hand, and Anne clasped it. In the next second, she was gone and the room cooled.

Chapter 19

Tom buckled Indira's seat belt and covered her legs with the wool blanket she always kept in the car in case a snowstorm stranded her in the middle of nowhere. He ran around to the driver's side and climbed into the Jeep.

His wife was wounded. All his careful plans—the emergency flashers, boots, water, poncho, blanket, and energy bars in the go kit in the trunk—hadn't kept her safe. Pain rippled off her in waves. He concentrated every instinct, every bit of training he had to figuring out how he could help his wife heal. He wasn't thinking about tomorrow, next week, next month, or next year. He could only focus on one hour at a time.

"Okay, babe?"

"Let's just go." She closed her eyes.

He turned out of the hospital parking lot and headed toward home, thinking he'd already done something wrong. Fear nudged out reason and distracted him. He couldn't do things in the right order or keep track of what he'd been thinking. Glancing at her to make sure she was okay, he saw she'd turned to stone. How would he get through to her?

Hope was essential in any healing process, and Indira had lost all hope. He promised himself that he would pour himself into every minute and prayed that if he did that hour after hour, she'd recover. He'd always been the pragmatist in their partnership; she was the optimist. Now they had traded places.

Tom had stocked the pantry with her favorite chocolate truffles, filled the log bin on the deck, and made sure they had an ample supply of green tea and honey. His mother had brought over the homemade chicken soup Indira liked. All he needed to do was reheat it.

The doctor said Indira could eat soft foods and progress to solids in a week. She might have indigestion as a result of the surgery, and there would be some pain as she healed. "Try ginger ale," she suggested. The pharmacy would deliver the serious pills.

He imagined her tissues knitting together, blood pumping through them, and the skin repairing itself cell by cell. If he could visualize it, it would happen. He didn't want to think about the other things the doctor had told them before she released Indira from the hospital, but he couldn't help it.

Tom's hands had gripped the chair arms as the doctor explained that Indira's surgery two years before might have accidentally accelerated the cancer's spread. Her cancer was now at stage three-A. It had affected her remaining ovary and fallopian tube, infiltrated her uterus and related lymph nodes, all of which the surgeon had removed, but it had already migrated to nearby organs.

"The cancer might have been released like a virus into Indira's blood-stream, and then hijacked cells in other organs for its own purposes," the doctor said in that perfectly reasonable voice that made Tom want to scream. He wanted to sweep everything off every surface in the room. He needed walls to cave in, window glass to shatter, and the room to shake from the bomb the doctor dropped on them. And he needed to be calm for Indira's sake.

Indira had stared at the doctor in disbelief. Tom squeezed his eyes shut to control himself. There'd been no place to put his fury. He needed to get control of himself, or he wouldn't be of any use to anyone.

"We found tiny deposits of cancer cells in the lining of your abdomen," the doctor continued in that neutral voice intended to imitate compassion. "But even though the cancer has spread, given your age and general good health, with the appropriate treatment and luck, you have a forty-five percent chance of surviving five more years." She smiled at Indira as if she were presenting her with a medal for combat bravery.

There was more but Tom stopped listening. Deliberate deafness was the only way to remain calm, but despite his intention, his brain absorbed the information and stored it away while he stared at his knees.

A forty-five percent chance of survival was better than none at all. Five years was a lifetime, as long again as all the time he had known Indira. It was an eternity. He would fill it with everything good in the world and make the time left to them mean everything. She'd die happy. A bell gonged in his skull and the sound vibrated down his spinal cord. His throat clogged and his eyes felt heavy. *She can't die, she can't die.* He refused to allow himself to even think that was a possibility.

Indira's parents were supposed to arrive tomorrow. Everything had happened so fast, there'd been no time to call them before the surgery. During the operation, Tom sat in the waiting area with his head in his hands, trying to remember how to pray, and forgot her parents existed. After, when she'd made it through the operation, Tom had called to tell them about the surgery and let them rail at him.

"Why didn't you call me before?" Indira's father shouted. "We could have brought her to Boston for a second opinion instead of leaving her to those backwoods butchers in Burlington."

Below his bluster, a sob hovered in the older man's throat and Tom forgave him. Like Tom, he wanted the prognosis to be wrong. He hoped he could scare the cancer away with the right sounds in the right order at the right volume. If only that were true, Tom would repeat those words over and over for the rest of his life.

In the background, Indira's mother wailed, her voice reaching a crescendo and falling into whimpers, over and over, a tide advancing wave by wave that would engulf all of them. Tom didn't care if he drowned in that pain if that's what saved his wife.

He expected Indira's parents to blame him for her illness. He blamed himself, the universe, God, fate, and any random collision of atoms in space. Chandra had always intimidated him, the arch of her eyebrow, the diamonds of her perennial broach winking at him as she gestured. If Indira died, nothing would matter, including what his mother-in-law thought of him. He didn't tell Indira how her parents reacted to the news, understanding why she hadn't told them herself.

He had wasted two years of his marriage in a funk over his father's iniquity, the humiliation of the trial and incarceration, thinking he could put everything on hold while he made his peace with it. His priorities had been all wrong, but he could make up for his absence now. The present moment was what mattered: the fact that his wife was still alive, out of the hospital, sitting next to him in the car, and going home.

Tom turned his head to tell her. "Sweetheart . . ."

Indira opened her eyes. "I'm not going through chemo and radiation. I'm not doing it."

"Indira, we don't have to talk about that today."

"I'm telling you. It's not a discussion. I'm not doing it. I'm not going to make myself miserable so when it's over I can die thinking I was heroic." She hugged herself. "I'm not heroic and my body is not a battlefield. This isn't a war. I'm not going to fight. The cancer is going to win anyway."

"Babe . . ."

He wanted to say gentle, reassuring words that would soothe her, but she shifted in the seat and watched out of the passenger window as they passed bare trees soldiering across empty, snow-covered fields.

"That whole terminology is ridiculous," she continued, still facing the window. "Who can fight genetics and biology?"

She seemed to be speaking to the snowy hills in the distance. "The doctors are going to kill my cells to fight death. It's absurd." She glanced at him. "I want to be prepared for when it gets impossible to bear. I'm going to ask the doctor for the medication to end my life. It's my right."

His face chilled. He studied her: she was dry-eyed as if she'd said they needed to buy toilet paper. Her breathing was normal. Her too-pale face was almost tranquil. She was certain.

Neck stiffening, Tom slowed the car so he wouldn't accidentally drive them off the road. He didn't want to have this conversation now, or ever. He had sworn to do everything possible to prevent her death. He would say anything to keep her with him. "I think we should wait to talk about this. Until you're healed from the surgery and feel more like yourself."

"I will never feel like myself. My self has been irretrievably altered and is being altered cell by cell as I sit here. I am not the same now as I was a year ago, last week, or five minutes ago."

Her voice was hard, curt, and sounded like an old woman's sharpened to a fine edge by time. "The treatment plan is to cut, poison, or burn parts of me. It's monstrous. Why not put hot coals on my stomach or cut a hole in my head to let out the bad juju? That's not living. You should understand. You euthanize animals that are in pain and dying, don't you?"

Tom's hand jerked on the steering wheel and the car careened across the two-lane road, skinning the two feet of snow piled up on the shoulder. He steadied himself and brought them back to the right lane. His breath came in spurts. He wanted to close his eyes and give in to his sobs. His hands trembled on the steering wheel.

"You're not an animal," he whispered. "You're my wife."

Indira was quiet for a few miles. Tom pulled the car into their driveway. Tires crunched on the snow-covered lane. He drove slowly up to their mid-twentieth century house with the wall of windows at the back overlooking the lake. He hoped Indira would remember their elation when they found the place and that it would remind her of all they had to live for.

They'd bought the property after she said yes, when they imagined four children running through every room with grandparents chatting companionably in front of the wide stone hearth in the living room. Tom had pictured standing at the window wall, his arm around Indira, watching the sun set behind the mountains across the lake. He'd imagined walking into the house after work and finding his wife looking out at the lake—her favorite pastime. Indira would put her arms around his neck and tilt her face up for a kiss. The image faded and their wonderful house seemed cold and empty. He cut the engine and gazed at her. Words were insufficient.

She put her hand on his thigh. "I do love you."

He closed his eyes and sighed.

"Tom," she said. "I need you to help me."

Tom covered his face with his hands. "No, I can't do that. Don't ask me to do that. No."

Chapter 20

After the hospital reek of death and disinfectant, Anne's house had never smelled so good to her. Everything was in its right place. A fire in the wood stove warmed her as soon as Freddy opened the kitchen door. The old grandfather clock in the front hall ticked out its customary beat. Through the bay window was her favorite view of the lake and the mountains beyond.

Freddy removed her coat, scarf, and hat while she stood still like a child who didn't know how to do these simple tasks. Weak-kneed, she clung to his arm and made her way to the comfortable chair he'd placed near the woodstove in the kitchen.

"Smart boy," she said, patting his hand. He tucked a blanket around her legs. Laura handed Anne a cup of coffee, her face looming into view for a second as she leaned over. The coffee smelled delicious. Hospital coffee was undrinkable. Anne sniffed the brew greedily and leaned her head back. When she opened her eyes, it was dark outside. Someone had taken the cup out of her hands.

"Want something to eat, Mom?" Freddy asked.

"I could eat a cow." She grinned at her son.

Freddy matched her grin. "One cow coming right up."

"Aren't you eating?" Anne asked.

"We ate already, Anne," Laura said, patting her shoulder.

"When did you get here?"

"I was here when you got home."

"I don't remember that. What time is it?"

"It's almost six," Laura said. "You've been asleep for two hours."

That sounded like an accusation to Anne, as if she'd broken some rule. It was easy to annoy Laura. She couldn't have this woman staying with her. Her sanity wouldn't survive Laura's minute-by-minute instructions and her quick frown of disapproval when anyone failed to conform. That tactic might work with five-year-olds, but it drove Anne crazy.

I'd have to kill her. Anne didn't bother to repress the smile provoked by her thought and peeked at Freddy, whose face had the same sour-milk aspect hers must have. She congratulated herself on not saying her thoughts. Or at least she didn't think she said it.

"I'm going to stay with you for a while, Mom," Freddy said. "At least through the chemo and shit, till you're better and can do things for yourself. My foreman will supervise the jobs at work. He's a steady guy, and I can trust him."

He glanced over his shoulder at his wife. "And Laura won't be staying here. She needs to be at the cabin where all her class prep materials are. Those kindergarteners will eat you alive if you don't have something planned for every five minutes."

Anne watched him tilt his head and nod toward the door like a sheepdog nudging a lamb to get her moving toward the gate.

"Right. Sure." Laura put on her coat and gloves and gave Anne a peck on the cheek. "I'll be back tomorrow after school to check on you two, see if you need anything." She wrapped her gray scarf around her neck and pulled on a gray wool hat.

"Good plan." Anne wondered about the odd medicinal smell coming from Laura.

Freddy said, "Great."

Laura stopped with her hand on the doorknob. "Oh, by the way." She peered at Anne over her shoulder. "Is it okay if I go through the stuff in the shed? I'm searching for old-timey things to show my class."

Anne shrugged. "Sure. Lots of old-timey stuff in there." She couldn't recall what she had squirreled away, but it couldn't be anything valuable. Even if it was, she didn't mind sharing those old artifacts of a time gone by with little kids. "Have at it."

Laura gave them her practiced keep-away smile and walked out of the house. Anne waited a few seconds to see if her daughter-in-law would pop back to kiss Freddy. *They're so disconnected.* When the car started, Anne wiped her brow with the side of her hand. "Whew."

Freddy raised his eyebrows at his mother, and they giggled like hysterical conspirators almost caught in the act.

"Is there a problem between you two I should know about?" Anne asked.

"Not one you didn't know about before." Freddy busied himself at the stove, put the medium-rare steak on a plate, and brought it to the table.

"Is she drinking?"

When Freddy said nothing, Anne noticed salad in a small bowl, flatware, and a glass of water had magically appeared on the table. *I'm not all here.* The first taste of steak made her whole mouth water as if to remind her humans were carnivores. *Living in the moment won't be all bad.*

She managed three bites and pushed the plate away. "It tastes delicious but that's it. I'm full. Save the rest for tomorrow. We'll have steak salad." She smiled, hoping Freddy would notice she could plan for the future.

Freddy rinsed her plate and glass and put them in the dishwasher. For a few seconds, Anne confused him with Luke, glowering at her the first time he'd squared off with Howard and headed out the kitchen door.

Howard had blocked his way, putting his sturdy body in front of the door.

"Get out of my way," Luke mumbled, his teeth clenched.

Howard and Luke had been the same height with the same long nose, thin lips, jutting chin, and hazel eyes, but Luke was the width of a reed. When his hands balled into fists, Anne saw her son as a physical threat for the first time. Nothing she could do would stop or protect him.

"Where are you going at ten on a school night and who are you going with?" Howard asked.

"None of your business."

Howard's face turned red. "It *is* my business. You live in my house. I feed and clothe you. I put up with your insolence. It's a simple question. Where are you going? Just answer it."

"Fuck you, old man. Technically, it's Mom's house. And all of a sudden you care what I'm doing. Where've you been for the last ten years?"

A week before, Anne had found a crumpled brown paper bag stamped with a Burlington head shop logo in Luke's sock drawer. She'd waved the bag at Howard. "The boy's doing drugs."

Howard smirked. "Someone gave him the bag, and Luke thought it made him look cool." His face wore that expression of disdain she hated.

"Jesus, Howard. Wake up. The kid's doing drugs right under your nose. If this were any of the other boys, you'd have lectured him blue with your personal responsibility catechism. He's way past recreational drugs."

Howard had responded with an extravagant shrug. Now, suddenly, he gave a damn.

"I'll do any fucking thing I please." Luke's eyes narrowed to slits. "With anyone I want. And you can't stop me, old man."

Howard's face contorted. He grabbed Luke by the shoulders. "You—"

Luke wrenched himself away, eyes blazing. "Leave me alone, or you'll regret it," Luke whispered under his breath as he slammed out of the house.

Howard stared at the fragment of his son's shirt left in his fist and grabbed the edge of the kitchen counter. "What the hell?"

"You never cared about what he did before. Why now?" Anne asked.

"He took money from my desk."

"Ah, so now when it's too late, it's not imaginary anymore." She could still feel her incandescent fury searing her veins.

"Mom? Mom."

A warm hand grasped her shoulder. Anne blinked and stared at Freddy. "Oh, sorry, honey. I got lost in my thoughts for a minute."

"You were staring into space. For a long time, way longer than a minute."

"Do I get a special beanie with pinwheel blades on top to wear so everyone will know I'm a space cadet?"

Freddy laughed as Anne hoped he would and helped her upstairs. Tomorrow, she promised herself, would be better than today.

Chapter 21

Indira examined her hands as the doctor talked. This morning she cut her nails, surprised they had grown so much in the six weeks since her surgery. *Odd that cells continue to replicate when in my mind I'm already dead.* She was in limbo, the space between alive and dead, the bleak waiting room of an eternal nothing. Waiting made her angry. Her body's betrayal made her angry. That she had to endure all this chatter made her angry.

She raised her eyes to watch the doctor. A small, black mole dotted the doctor's left cheek, and a simple gold necklace peeked from beneath her white coat. This person dressed every morning, put on jewelry, ate breakfast, greeted her colleagues, went into her office, and day after day told doomed women they were dying and should get their affairs in order. How did she do it? How did she observe all that anguish and keep going? She must have a good therapist.

A list of causes for adrenalin-spiking alarm equal to the words "you have end-stage cancer" leaped into Indira's mind.

Your house is on fire.

A tsunami alert bleats on your cell phone.

An earthquake rumbles beneath your feet, or the thunder of an avalanche shakes the walls.

Your four-year-old runs out into the street in front of an oncoming car.

A phalanx of bombers fills the sky.

People run. It's the normal human impulse. Run, scoop up your child, save your life, leave everything else behind. She had no child. What would she take with her?

Her honeymoon photograph on the beach in Tofino—the one with them perched on a hunk of black volcanic rock jutting out from the sea, the clear turquoise Pacific Ocean lapping their toes, sea anemones blooming on the seafloor beneath them. Arms around each other, faces open, eyes shining, buoyed by every atom of life floating around them, this was the happiest time in her life. She would take that photo. What more could she carry in her bare hands?

"Ms. Anand? Indira?" The doctor prodded the silence around them the way a child might poke a small creature caught at the edge of the sea.

Indira stared at her hands again, the bones in them clearly delineated. She had shed ten pounds in the last six weeks because consuming anything except ginger ale caused severe pain in her abdomen. Her face looked like sand-washed porcelain, unrecognizable in the mirror.

Her prana was gone, dissipated into the air when they opened her belly. Indira closed her eyes and pictured the wake of the ferry as it rushed across the lake, waves pulsing over the water's surface, diminishing as they reached the shore. How far would the wake of energy she'd left behind her as she moved through life before the surgery take her?

"What happens when our chi is gone but we're still walking around?"

The doctor smiled gently. "That's an intriguing question."

The steady flurry of snow against the office window calmed Indira. "I would like a prescription for the medications that allow me to die with dignity when I'm ready."

The doctor sat back in her chair and folded her hands together on top of the desk as if she needed to invoke a higher power to answer. "You realize with chemo and radiation you may live another five years. We should start the treatment regimen as soon as possible."

Stay calm, Indira told herself, but the instruction didn't work. Her pulse thrummed in her temples. "May is the operative word, isn't it? Five years is not a guarantee. It's the outside possibility. Meanwhile, this treatment will poison and burn me. I'll be sick to death, wishing I were already dead. Yesterday, I read an article that said radiation treatment destroyed a cancer patient's heart. I choose not to undergo such barbaric treatments."

The doctor leaned forward, her chin now above her hands. "Even without any treatment, you may live longer than you expect. A recent paper revealed that a few women in stage three, particularly otherwise healthy young women like you, lived for ten years after diagnosis. We don't yet know why."

All Indira's attempts at calm flew out the window. "What kind of life are you offering me? Five or ten years of not knowing if each day is the day I collapse in agony, not knowing when to say goodbye to my family so I can do it without writhing in unbearable pain." Her voice rose. "You're saying under miraculous circumstances no one understands I might live to be thirty-seven. Do you expect me to think that's some kind of gift? That I would have only half the number of years I should have."

Indira gazed out of the window, grasping at anything to ground herself, to not scream. The scent of apples and cinnamon came from somewhere in the room. In the hallway, a voice on the PA system paged a doctor. The wood arms of the chair were smooth under her palms. She swallowed, trying to get her voice under control.

"Wasn't there another paper suggesting chemo after breast cancer surgery didn't extend life for more than three months if at all? After all these years, all those women tortured, the medical community now strokes its collective chin wondering if chemo is effective. None of you know what you're doing. I need to control my own fate."

In the exam room, the doctor told her the incisions were healing nicely. All physical indicators pointed to recovery from the surgery. Doctors amazed her. They could lop off your arm, examine the sutures, touch the skin to test for inflammation, and say it was healing nicely. They saw the body as discardable diseased parts and missed the human entirely.

"Vermont law says I have a right to manage my death if I have a terminal disease."

The doctor bowed her head for a second, then lifted her chin and looked straight at Indira. "Not quite. You must be within six months of your death to receive the prescriptions. You are not. You're healthy, other than the cancer which we have removed. If you take the treatment I recommend, you could live years more. I can't, either by good medical practice or law, give you the prescriptions now. We can revisit this subject in the future if you want."

Heat flared in Indira's face. She stood. "It's *my* life. If you won't help me, I'll find someone who will. And if none of you will, I'll just stop eating. That should do the trick."

Ignoring the doctor's proffered hand, she stormed out of the office. Tom was waiting for her in the reception area. She took three deep breaths to cleanse herself of her resentment toward the doctor. On the upside, Tom would be glad a medical professional agreed with him.

Indira considered the request she wanted to make. He had already made clear this was too much to ask of him. She closed her eyes and sighed, knowing she would make it anyway. When she pushed open the door, he glanced up, his eyes full of her, only her, promising anything except the one thing she wanted.

Chapter 22

Anne's scalp itched. The chemo and radiation made her tired and nauseous, but she couldn't sit in front of the fire and vegetate. Every day of this enforced isolation made her think she would die of boredom instead of cancer. She paced, tottering from chair to sofa to chair, muttering about fate, brain matter, and doctors.

"I need to do something to save the paper. I'll go crazy if I sit here and do nothing."

"Cranky much, Mom?" Freddy leaned over and kissed her forehead. All evil thoughts flew out of her brain. It was a cliché, but her son was the best medicine.

When she couldn't stand another millisecond of impending doom, Anne called the office. Molly answered in her customary way. "Queenscove Journal, Molly speaking, how can I help you?" Her voice made Anne smile.

"Molly, I have a new vision for an online magazine, a way to generate more subscriptions. The hell with relying on advertising. We can save the paper even if social media is gobbling up all the ad dollars."

Anne could see the whole magazine laid out in front of her as if it were already real. She saw the masthead, the fonts, and page after page of words and images. Mostly images. Large, screen-sized, in glorious color. It sizzled; it sang. They would have links to podcasts and video interviews, something interactive. Everyone would want to read it. The whole state would talk about it. They'd win awards, and she'd be the toast of the town at conferences.

She tried to explain to Molly what she imagined. "We can do this. I'm sure of it." But the words to describe what she saw escaped her. Frustration made her sputter.

"It takes up the whole screen. Big pictures. One paragraph of text and then you turn the page and there's the story and people can click into it and see video or hear the interview. We can have theme music. Polls. Comments. Stuff like that. The reader will feel like she's right there, like it's happening in front of her."

"That sounds interesting," Molly said.

Interesting was the place where all new ideas went to die. Molly was trying to be nice. Anne understood her motives, but she wanted Molly to see what she saw, to be excited about the possibility. It used to be so easy to get people to do what she wanted.

Annoyed that she'd lost the ability to command, Anne snapped, "You're not listening to me!" Her cheeks heated. "I'm trying to tell you my vision. Why don't you understand?"

Anne hated the answer scrolling across her mind like a giant ticker in Times Square. *Because you're sick, because you're dying, because you're already irrelevant.* That sounded like something Howard would say.

"It won't replace the paper." Anne tried to keep the testiness out of her voice. "We'd still do the weekly print pub. But we'd create a separate online space for a Sunday special, do more arts and lifestyle stuff, play up the high school sports more with features about the athletes, and not have to worry about space or page count because we wouldn't print it. Think of the trees we'll save! People could share our articles on social media. It would build digital readership, subscriptions."

"Uh-hum," Molly said.

She'd hurt Molly's feelings; she shouldn't have yelled at her. Bumbling around her kitchen trying to find the right words to explain her idea, Anne realized no one had mopped the floor in a while and then forgot for a minute where she was and what she'd been thinking.

"You were saying." Molly's voice was kind. "It's a whole new product with more content?"

"Yes." Anne relaxed. Molly did understand. She hadn't failed to express her idea. "Yes, we'd have to hire four writers, a graphic artist, more photographers, a videographer, a tech person or two, and an editor. We'll need more servers to handle the traffic and a cloud contract. We'd need some advertisers to pay for it. But it would make the paper relevant again and, and . . ." The words she wanted escaped from her grasp. "That's important. So, . . ."

She couldn't describe why this new project was vital, why it mattered. If she couldn't persuade Molly, her personal cheerleader, she wouldn't be able to convince anyone.

Frustrated, Anne said, "Send Wilbur over tomorrow. I'll tell him about it, and he can do a few mockups so you can see what I mean. You should both come over and have lunch with me."

Silence from Molly. In the background, Anne heard the buzz of reporters talking to each other, a squawk from the scanner, the whoosh of the office door opening and closing. Someone's phone rang. The paper was going on without her.

Stunned, she stumbled into her chair. "Look, I've only lost four raviolis worth of my brain, and I feel energized and full of ideas." Anne laughed. The whole cancer thing invading her brain seemed absurd, like something the doctors had made up for their amusement.

"I'm so glad you're feeling better." Molly's voice was cautious. God knows what she heard from the town rumor mill.

"Don't worry. I'm going to beat this thing." Anne put her head in her hand. "Hey, I'm sorry I yelled at you. I shouldn't have."

Molly sighed. "No worries. We're running part three of Sadie's story tomorrow."

Molly intended to make her feel better—the great editor had worked on an important story. Things were proceeding as they were supposed to. But that was all past tense, work Anne had completed before the surgery.

"Yeah. That's terrific. Can't wait to see it in print." She didn't need pity; she needed a challenge.

"I can bring you a proof."

"No, don't need it. I trust you. I'll see it when the paper lands in the box at the end of my driveway. It's a solid story. The letters in response to the first two installments have been great. I want to talk about my new idea."

Anne wondered if Molly's hesitation was about seeing her with a scar on her head. She was queasy, although that seemed out of character.

After all, Molly had visited her in the hospital. When Anne opened her eyes a day after the surgery, Molly was sitting next to her bed. She held Anne's hand, told her what was going on at the paper, and made her feel connected to the rest of the world.

Freddy entered the kitchen while Anne was on the phone and asked if she wanted a cup of coffee. "For sure," she whispered. Watching him make the coffee, Anne realized she didn't know what day it was. "What day is today?"

Molly coughed. "It's Wednesday, February 8, two p.m. in the afternoon, two feet of snow outside and more coming tomorrow."

Anne glanced out of the kitchen window and saw nothing but white all the way to the mountains on the other side of the lake. Even the lake's surface and the sky were white. *Skiers must be happy.* "Okay, so tomorrow's deadline. Not a good day to meet. How about Saturday? Come for lunch. Luke will make a delicious meal."

Anne peeked at Freddy and realized she'd called him Luke. His face reddened. She waved her hand in front of her face to erase her mistake. "I mean Freddy."

Molly agreed to Saturday. Freddy brought Anne's coffee cup over to the table, leaned over, and kissed the top of her head, forgiving her for the heinous blunder of thinking he was his black sheep of a brother.

"Hey," Molly said. "I found out some stuff about the writer, Indira Anand, you asked about. Want to hear it?"

Anne had forgotten she asked. It was so long ago, she felt like she already knew Indira, heart to heart, even though they'd only met three times for a few minutes each time. But she said yes to assure Molly her effort was important.

"So, her first book was a wild success," Molly reported, "short-listed for the National Book Award. She has a two-book contract with one of the big literary fiction publishers but so far, other than a few well-placed short stories, nothing new."

Anne nodded and remembered Molly couldn't see her. "I thought she might be something special."

Molly cleared her throat. "Also, students give her high marks on the annual faculty rating. The school is thinking of offering her a full-time, tenure-track position next year. That's from inside the Academic Dean's office. Do you want to do a feature on her and the book?"

Not knowing if Indira wanted anyone to know she'd been ill, Anne dodged the question. "You've got great sources, Molly."

That was all the information Anne could bear. An image of Indira depleted and grieving at their last brief encounter in the hospital appeared in her mind. The young writer might not have another year. Dizziness took Anne and the world grayed out. She closed her eyes. "See you on Saturday."

She took a sip of the coffee Freddy put in front of her when he took the phone from her hand.

"She has so much to live for, I can't let her die. I have to do something."

Freddy touched her shoulder. "Who are you talking about, Mom?"

Anne fluttered her fingers in front of her mouth. "Thinking out loud, sweetie. About saving the paper. Nothing to be concerned about." She stared out of the window at the lake covered in snow and remembered the son she didn't save.

After Luke ran away, when she was still pretending everything was normal, she'd found a late rent notice for an apartment in Burlington among the bills on the hall table. Her heart leaped. Her son wasn't far away after all, and Howard was helping him. Her husband hadn't said anything because he thought she wouldn't approve. She and Howard were often at cross purposes, particularly about Luke.

She waited until dinner to ask Howard. "Are you putting Luke up in an apartment in Burlington?"

Howard reared back in his chair and swiped his lips with his napkin. "What? No. Where'd you get that idea?"

"From the late rent notice for the Burlington apartment."

Howard's face went red then white. His chest heaved. "You opened my mail? You have no business opening my mail."

Anne put down her fork. "Well, by mistake. I'm not mad if that's what you're doing. I'd rather know Luke is safe instead of living in an alley somewhere."

Howard rose from the chair so swiftly it tipped over, clattering on the tile floor. He leaned over to right it. "I don't feel good. What did you put in the stew? You put rosemary in the stew. You know I can't stand rosemary." He ran out of the kitchen and slammed the bathroom door.

She heard him retching then water running in the sink. His footsteps went from the bathroom to his study. The door closed; the lock clicked. Anne sat at the table watching the sunset. Her mind kept returning to one question. Why, besides taking care of one of their children, would Howard rent an apartment in another city?

After a week, her natural curiosity had gotten the best of her. The address was imprinted on her brain because of Howard's outlandish reaction. She drove to Burlington and found the apartment building. It was only half an hour from their home. None of the names above the six buzzers at the entrance to the three-story brick building were familiar. She surveyed the street. This wasn't a bad neighborhood—the buildings were in good shape, the gutters were free of garbage, and ornamental trees and shrubs enhanced the entrances. Howard must have wanted a refuge, a place all his own where he could go to think, but his name wasn't on any buzzer. And he hadn't told her about it.

Anne shook her head at her naivety. If the place wasn't for Luke, there was only one reason her husband would have an apartment—he had a mistress, someone he cared enough about to provide housing. Not a casual fling. Nor short-lived. All the breath in her body rushed out. She closed her eyes and tried to reason with herself. Her knees buckled and she sank onto the concrete stoop, lowering her head to her knees to stop her head from spinning.

A young woman about Luke's age came out of the door with a backpack slung over one shoulder. She eyed Anne sitting on the steps, faked a smile, and walked off, her wavy brunette hair flouncing as she strode away. *That could be her. That young thing could be Howard's lover, a student in his seminar.* Anne pulled herself up and dashed back to her car. Halfway home, she pulled over to the side of the road and vomited. That done, she had rummaged in her purse, found a crumpled tissue, wiped her mouth, blew her nose, and got back on the road.

Anne opened her eyes and oriented herself in her kitchen. She checked her phone to make sure of the date. It was now, not then. Howard was dead. Whoever he had shacked up with had moved on. And

Freddy was nowhere to be seen. She got up to search for him and tripped over her own feet. "Freddy," she called out as she caught herself against the counter.

Freddy strode through the kitchen door, his arms full of firewood.

She grinned at him. "For a minute there I thought you'd left me."

"Don't worry, Mom." He dropped the wood into the box. "I'm not going to leave you."

Anne sighed. "I was thinking how the truth leaks out in strange ways."

Her son smiled at her and took her back to the chair. "At some point, what you don't know doesn't matter anymore, does it?"

"I don't know about that. Doesn't the truth always matter? Like a tree, and the sound it makes falling in the forest even if no one hears it."

They laughed and Anne forgot to warn him that what you didn't know always comes back to bite you.

* * *

On Saturday, at the stroke of noon, Molly and Wilbur showed up at Anne's house with Wilbur's warm bread fresh from the oven, Molly's mixed berry pie made with preserved fruit, and a pair of striped, fingerless, wool gloves. Anne tried on the gloves and rotated her hands around in the air.

She laughed. "Very colorful. Where's the rest of them?"

Molly put her hand on Anne's shoulder and leaned down to scrutinize her face. "It's so you can type outside if you want. You can sit by the lake even when it's cold and type on your laptop. Write your editorials."

Anne's face showed her confusion. "Why am I going to type out there?" She glanced out to the lake as if the answer lay on its still frozen surface covered in two feet of gleaming white snow.

Wilbur and Molly exchanged glances. "Your editorial?" Wilbur said. "You've done one every week for thirty years until the surgery. We figured you'd want to resume it now you're recovering."

"There's nothing wrong with my legs," Anne said. "As soon as I'm done with this frigging chemo and radiation, I'm coming into the office. I've been gone too long as it is."

"Hey," Freddy said, "I made Mom's vegetable soup from scratch. It's delicious if I say so myself."

Freddy served up bowls of soup for each of them. He sliced the bread and put out sweet, local butter on a blue dish. Putting a pitcher of iced tea on the table, he kissed his mother on the forehead. "I'm going to chop more wood. Back in twenty minutes."

Within a minute, they heard the satisfying thwack of the ax splitting the heart of a log. Anne sighed. "He's very good to me."

Molly patted Anne's arm. "You deserve it. Now tell us about your idea for a digital weekend edition."

While they ate, Anne tried to describe her vision for the new content. "I want it to be modern, visual, exciting. You know, like the *New York Times Magazine*, *Vanity Fair*, and *The New Yorker* all rolled into one, only we feature all local art, places, events, and writers. We use color graphics, snappy writing, and even video. You know, all the sizzle."

"Sounds expensive," Wilbur said to his spoon and sucked soup into his mouth.

Anne shot him a withering look. "Are you saying it can't be done?"

He shook his head. "I'm saying it can be done for a lot of money. Right now, you're running with an editorial staff of six and a half plus an old codger, a dozen stringers, and two salespeople. What you're talking about requires full-time professionals."

Anne leaned back in her chair, spoon forgotten halfway to her mouth, and contemplated Wilbur. "There are all those talented kids laid off because their papers went bankrupt, or the owners are cutting newsrooms from three hundred to thirty reporters. Don't you think they want work?"

Wilbur sighed and stared out at the lake. "Yes, they do. But there's a reason they're laid off. No one's reading the news anymore so no one's paying to put advertising in papers and as a result, there's no money to pay their salaries. But even without that problem, where's the start-up money to put all this in place going to come from?"

"My trust fund from Mom. I haven't dipped into it at all."

"You'll burn through a million in six months if you're going to hire another five full-time people plus buy equipment and cloud space. You'll need more office space to house them. Think you'll be able to pull in the millions in advertising to support their salaries and compensation long term? People can get the *Times*, and every other major outlet, online already. Why would they read a new product from the *Queenscove Journal*? You'll never make a profit."

Molly put her hand on Wilbur's arm and shook her head. "No need to be so blunt."

Anne grimaced with annoyance. "They'll read it because it's relevant to their own lives," she said to the window, her face tight. "Familiar places. People whose names they know, who they might run into at the farmer's market."

Molly buttered a slice of bread and took a bite. "Don't you want to leave your kids a legacy?"

Anne scowled at her. "They don't need the money. They're adults. They have their own lives."

"Your grandchildren might need some money."

Freddy threw open the kitchen door and carried in a pile of split logs, loading them in the bin near the woodstove.

Anne's face was blank. "I forgot about them." She closed her eyes as if she were surrendering to the enemy. "How many grandchildren do I have?"

Freddy glanced at his mother and washed his hands in the sink. "Six, Mom, you have six grandchildren."

"Oh, right. Howard, Nora, Rena, Osborn, Sally, and Richard, but not in that order."

Freddy tilted his head. "Osborn works for you, Mom. Arnold's son is Joe."

"Thanks, honey." Anne smiled at her guests. "See, I'm not off my bean."

Molly removed the bowls and sliced the pie, putting generous pieces on Anne's hand-painted blue plates. Anne ignored the plate Molly placed in front of her. She was far away, seeing images they couldn't, that they'd never see.

When she finally regarded Molly, her tone changed. "How lovely you look. You have a halo around your head like an angel. I never noticed it before."

Anne glanced at Freddy to check if he noticed Molly's halo and saw he had tears in his eyes.

Chapter 23

Laura was elbow-deep in a wooden chest with leather straps and metal buckles so old it might have traveled across the Atlantic Ocean with the original Canfields six generations ago. Scrunched against the back wall, she found three chests containing what she assumed were the discarded artifacts of the family's life. She would rummage through the rattan and metal chests after inventorying the contents of this one.

The only light in the barn entered through the open door. Freddy said there was an electric lantern, but she couldn't find it in the shadows. As with everything Morrow, you had to know the secret first before you could participate. All these special signals and words the kids had made up when they were young and still used today totally pissed her off.

Maneuvering through the unnatural dusk and a veil of cobwebs, Laura pushed away a painting tarp, two wrenches, a coil of rope, and a length of hose that at first sight she thought was a black snake. She shrieked and jumped backward, tumbling over an old wooden rocking horse. When her heartbeat slowed to normal, she took a few swigs from her flask to refresh herself, rubbed her arms, and laughed.

She set aside the rocking horse, the first of a group of items she wanted to bring to her class. The Morrows would never know she took it; nothing in the shed had any value to them. All of it would wind up in the county dump when Anne died. They wouldn't miss the few things she happened to keep, and the rocking horse would look great in her front room. She wondered how long it would take Freddy to notice it was there.

Her hand hit a small tin box. She pulled it out of the chest and pried open the lid. It brimmed with green paper money. One of the Morrow boys must have stowed his little fortune from a paper route out here thirty years before and forgotten about it.

She pulled out two of the notes and held them up to the dim light. The bills didn't look right. This was play money from some long-abandoned game of cops and robbers. She imagined the boys had been called into dinner, stashed their loot, and never retrieved it. She brushed one bill against her jeans to remove years of dust.

Printed on the bill with the date August 1862 were the words, "Will pay the bearer one dollar." The other side of the paper said, "legal tender." Laura put her dusty hand on her heart. Could these be real paper greenbacks issued by the bankrupt United States during the Civil War and later taken out of circulation? They must have originally belonged to Anne's great-great-grandfather. If so, they were worth something. Laura put the tin in the growing pile of found treasures she planned to take home with her.

She didn't question her motives. Anne had deprived her of the admiration she deserved and she was going to take whatever she found to make up for that slight. She'd never expected her mother-in-law to love her like a daughter, but Anne should at least have accepted her as a member of the family. She'd been married to Freddy for twenty years. How long would it take before she was one of them?

The Morrows were so la-de-dah because of the paper, because Sam was a lawyer, because Howard had been a professor, because they had so much money they never even thought about it. Even if she no longer wanted to be part of them, their refusal to include her was infuriating.

Her fingers closed on another box in the jumble of things in the chest. This one was wooden. She yanked it out of the chest and shook it. The contents chucked against the sides of the box. Laura dusted off the top with the edge of the tarp and sat on the seat of the riding mower. Gingerly, holding the box as far from her body as possible in case a living creature or the skeleton of one of the boys' long-dead hamsters rattled inside, she lifted the lid. In the box was a stack of letters tied in a bundle with a faded green ribbon.

She rubbed the stamp of the top envelope with her thumb. The postmark on the letter addressed to Anne at the newspaper office was Burlington, Vt. December 22, 1977. Without hesitating, Laura opened the top envelope and pulled out the letter.

My darling Anne, the letter started. *I am nothing without you.* The letter was one page long. Laura scanned down to the end. It was an agonized farewell, signed by Colin.

Who the hell was Colin? Wasn't Freddy born in 1978? Was Howard not Freddy's father? The questions piled up as she examined the postmarks on all thirty letters in the stack. Half of the envelopes were unopened. She'd opened the last one first, and then she needed to know what was in all of them.

By the time she read the letters, Laura knew the secret Anne had kept from her family. She felt guilty at first, peering into the old woman's past uninvited, and then delighted that she'd discovered the flaw in her mother-in-law's character. Anne was a liar and a cheat, and Laura was vindicated for hating her. How delicious that felt. And then she was sad for no reason she understood. Eventually, glee dominated. She'd found a cudgel to hold over the old crone, and she intended to use it.

In the dim barn, Laura did a little goal dance as dust motes swirled around her. This was the hidden treasure she hoped to find. She needed to mull over what she wanted in exchange for what she knew and find the right time to make her demand. Soon though, it had to be soon. Anne was fading, even if she didn't know it, and any day now the sons would take over all decision-making. If Laura waited too long, she'd miss her opportunity.

Seconds later another thought struck her like a revelation. *Of course, like mother, like son.* Infidelity must be a genetic trait: Anne cheated on Howard, and Freddy must be cheating on her. And Howard had been unfaithful to Anne. She was sure of that, even if no one else knew about his infidelity. Those documents she found in Howard's desk had another woman's name on them. No married man has a bank account with a woman besides his wife unless they're having an affair. Freddy got the infidelity gene from both sides. When she confronted him, she should use that word Howard liked: ergo. She had proved her case.

It was like the sun rising. These new facts illuminated everything. That's why Freddy had behaved oddly for the last few years, and his cheating was why she didn't trust him. Freddy had someone else he cared about, and he was hiding it, sneaking around, lying to her about where he was. He was spending all of his attention on another woman. That's why he was emotionally unavailable, why she didn't get pregnant again, why he didn't give a shit about her.

And his mother was complicit. Anne had known all about his affair and was protecting him. Laura's brain sizzled with vengeful schemes. She would find out what was going on with Freddy, and then she would take her revenge.

Chapter 24

Indira sat in the high-back chair close to the fireplace. She was always cold these days and heat radiating from the sparking logs comforted her. From here, she could see through the wall of windows to the lake and the mountains beyond it. The view was her refuge.

She had girded herself for this conversation with her mother and couldn't wait any longer. Her father and Tom were out doing errands. This was the only time they'd be alone. Her mother deserved to know what she intended to do and to have a chance to express her emotions unedited by her father.

A wave of love for her mother—for the million kindnesses and acts of devotion lavished on her all these years—broke over her. Her throat swelled. How could she leave her? Indira closed her eyes as if not seeing would make her anguish easier to deal with. She missed her parents as if she'd already gone away and would never see them again. Half of the time her stomach hurt from homesickness for her childhood, the other half from yearning for a future she'd never have. Some days she was close to being ready to let go of everything, even herself, and be at peace, but she wasn't there yet, and she needed to prepare her mother. That was only fair.

Chandra snuggled back into the oatmeal-colored couch, leaning against purple and teal silk pillows sighing under her weight. "Are you in pain, my dearest?" She put her feet up on the round, purple ottoman, sipped her tea, and regarded her daughter. "We need to fatten you up, darling. You've lost so much weight since the surgery."

Indira knew her mother wanted to hold her, and yearned to say, "You are my best creation," as Chandra had said every day of her childhood. When she was small and her mother brushed her hair and helped her

99

dress, Chandra would say, "You are the world to me, my dearest. You are such a joy."

The words embarrassed Indira when she was a teenager, but she thought of them fondly now. At sixteen she used to hold her mother at arm's length and declare, "I'm my own creation." Her mother would smile, indulging Indira's adolescent omnipotence. The comfort of her mother's words was too much to bear now. She pulled herself away to protect herself from sadness.

"I know you want to tell me something," Chandra said. "I'm afraid you're going to tell me you're leaving Tom. I hope not. I didn't think much of him at the beginning when you met him. He's a shaggy dog of a man, but he's a strong, calm, caring husband—exactly what you need."

Indira smiled at the image of Tom as a shaggy dog. He'd like that. She took a sip of her ginger ale. "I'm not leaving Tom, Mom. I'm leaving all of you."

Chandra paled. Her hands came up to her face and she held her cheeks as if to keep herself together. "No. What are you saying? Where are you going?"

"I'm going to die, Mommy. You know that. That's where this cancer leads, even if I went through all those treatments."

The catch in her throat stopped her from saying anything else. She tipped her head from one shoulder to the other, but the sense of a noose tightening around her neck didn't let up. "But I'm going to do it in my own time when I'm ready."

"I don't understand what you're saying."

"I'm saying that Vermont law allows me to pick the time I die if I have a terminal illness." Her mouth was dry. She took another sip of soda. "I'm going to invoke my rights."

"But you only had the surgery two months ago."

Indira averted her face. She wasn't going to argue with her mother.

Chandra stood, spilling her tea on her pants. The cup and saucer clattered onto the wood floor. Her hands flew out into the air. Her mouth opened and from it came a sound Indira had never heard her make—a keening, wild, circling sound like singing, a sound that wound itself around her, filling her ears, and reaching its tendrils into her heart.

Chandra fell to her knees in front of Indira's chair and wrapped her arms around her daughter's waist. She put her head in Indira's lap.

"Do not tell me this, do not. I can't bear it. I won't let you. I didn't carry you in my womb for nine months, I didn't dream about you for years before that, I didn't hold your hands when you took your first step or hold my breath the first day you walked into school by yourself, to have you take your own life."

Indira stroked her mother's thick hair, recalling the feel of it in her hands when she braided it as a child. She bent and kissed her mother's forehead. "I love you, Mommy, but this is my life. And my death. I have a right to do this when I want."

Chandra raised her head and stared into her daughter's eyes. "You do *not* have that right. I gave you this life. I cherished it. Only God, or nature, or whatever it is, can take it away."

Indira shook her head. "I remember when Nani was sick, screaming from her bed, over and over, for hours. Screaming and screaming. I had to put a pillow over my head. I saw your tears, how you wept day after day taking care of her. I won't let that happen now. I can't bear the idea of such pain. I won't put Tom through it. There's a saner way."

Chandra took Indira's hands in hers. "My darling, that was long ago. There are medicines now to keep the pain at bay. We can take you to good doctors. You don't have to do this. I can't understand why you're doing this." Chandra's lips trembled.

Indira wiped her mother's face with her palms. "Nature, as you call it, *is* going to take my life, and in the process give me months of agony. Why should I endure that? Such agony doesn't improve any of our lives."

Chandra lowered her face. "You don't know what will happen. Perhaps there will be a miracle and you'll live a long time. I've read about such things. But even if there's not, each day you're alive is a wonder. There's such beauty in the world, and in you. My brilliant, beautiful daughter, you don't even know yet what you're capable of."

"I know I'm capable of dying."

Chandra struggled to her feet and put a hand on Indira's head. She bent and kissed her daughter's cheek. "No. Something will happen. You'll see. The universe will point you in the right direction. I'm certain." She staggered out of the room as if she were trying to find her way in the dark.

Indira hugged herself and stared into the fire. An image of Anne Canfield standing on the beach, arms raised in warning, came to her.

Chapter 25

Determined to make the best of her time alone with Anne while Freddy ran to the market, Laura rehearsed what she wanted to say. She would only have twenty minutes or so. She wanted to make them count.

Normally, Freddy kept her away, making her uncomfortable when she showed up after school. "You don't have to be here," he said. "No point in you having to watch Mom fade. It's depressing."

Freddy's behavior made her want to scream. Mr. Goody Two-Shoes so concerned for his mother's welfare. Butter wouldn't, and all that shit. He must have thought he was fooling her. She understood his motives better than he did. He couldn't bear to be in the same house with her.

He could have his separation. She didn't care. Their marriage was over. She understood that now. They only had to complete the formalities, and she'd be a free woman. Free. The idea made her feel she'd lost twenty pounds and won a marathon it was such a relief. But she wanted more than being free. She craved retribution, compensation for all those years of putting up with him, with the whole damn Morrow family.

Laura put the letters she found in the barn on the table, fanning them out like fancy napkins at a buffet. She'd read them over and over until she knew some of the lines by heart. When she was at work, she kept the stash of letters in the glove box of her car to make sure Freddy didn't find them by accident if he dropped by the house to get whatever junk he wanted.

She needed to act soon, to use the letters for leverage for whatever it was that *she* wanted. Anne was dying—that was a fact even if the rest of the Morrows were still in denial. She'd lose her chance to get what she wanted from Anne if she waited too long.

Anne was in good spirits today. Some woman from her office had visited her—Molly she said her name was. They sat out near the lake in the Adirondack chairs and talked for an hour. Laura could see Anne was fond of Molly, and their friendship made Laura's stomach hurt, a sure sign she instantly hated the woman.

She watched them through the kitchen window—how they leaned together, their heads only inches apart, like people posed for a silhouette portrait. Why wasn't Anne like that with her? She burned to drive a wedge between Anne and that stranger for no reason other than that she existed.

Sometimes, when the kids were engaged in quiet play in her classroom, Laura daydreamed about publicly snubbing all of Anne's friends and children before they could spurn her. She could feel their looming disapproval of her as if she were entering a town from which there was no exit. The thing that drove her crazy was that in the space of what seemed like a minute, she'd gone from beloved kindergarten teacher to Freddy's wife to a nearly complete mess and nobody in his family gave a damn.

Molly brought Anne back into the house on her arm and settled her into the chair in the kitchen. Anne's eyes sparkled, and her cheeks were pink. The early spring air refreshed her, not her friend, Laura thought, finding some relief in her spite.

She waited for Molly to leave and handed Anne a cup of tea. The cup shook in Anne's hand, and she put it down on the table. Laura plunked herself down in the chair across from Anne. "You seem to be doing pretty well today."

Anne picked up the mug with two hands, leaned forward so her chin was over the table, and took a sip. "I am. What's this stuff on the table?"

To Laura, Anne's mind seemed as sharp as ever. Blind in one eye now, her balance so bad she couldn't walk around unaided, Anne still didn't beat around the bush. Laura grudgingly admired her for that trait, not that any of that mattered now.

Laura took a sip of tea she had laced with gin. "I always liked that you were a straight shooter."

"And you're telling me this now because . . . ?"

Laura raised her eyebrows and shrugged. "You're dying?"

"Ha! Of course. Well, go ahead and get it over with. Say whatever it is you want to say. Now's the time."

"Okay. You had an affair. You were married to Howard, you already had three kids, and you were fooling around with a stranger behind everyone's backs." Laura lifted her chin and wagged her shoulders, triumphant that she had challenged the Queen of Hearts, as her mother called Anne, and lived to talk about it.

Anne jerked away from the table as if Laura had pinched her. Tea sloshed from her cup. "Where did you get this idea?" She put the cup down on the table with shaking hands and blotted her shirt, pants, and the table with a napkin.

"Don't deny it. These letters from Colin." Laura pointed to the envelopes arrayed on the table. She picked one up and shook it in Anne's face. "The ones you stored in the shed. The letters he wrote you."

A look of incomprehension crossed Anne's face. "What do you mean letters in the shed? I don't understand you."

"Good God. The proof is right in front of you." Laura folded her arms across her chest and shoved her face inches from Anne's. "Colin McDowell, your old lover, he wrote you letters, these letters. Don't give me your addled old woman routine. I know better."

Anne's face puckered in dismay. She closed her eyes and took a deep breath. "So what?"

As if increased decibels could pierce Anne's confusion, Laura bellowed, "The letters to you from someone named Colin prove you had an affair. You tied them up, put them in a box, and hid the box in the wooden chest in the shed. Those letters. That Colin. You had an affair."

Anne's eyes darkened. "Why do *you* care?" She sighed again.

"You lied to everyone. You deceived your husband. And Freddy."

Anne turned her head as if she couldn't bear to see Laura's face another second. "Freddy? What does this have to do with Freddy? He wasn't even born yet. It happened before *you* were born. It can't possibly matter to you."

"It does, though."

"Why?"

"Because it'll matter to Freddy when I tell him."

Anne touched her scar. "Why would you tell him?"

"He needs to know his mother isn't a saint. It'll help him grow up. That's one of his problems. He's a mama's boy. He never grew up. You always protected him." Laura raised her arms in a wide shrug. "Besides, if he's not Howard's son that would matter to him."

"Freddy is a wonderful man," Anne said. "Why do you want to hurt him?"

Laura's face twisted. "That's what my mother says."

"It's me you want to hurt," Anne said slowly as if she were working out a puzzle. "Not Freddy. You really hate *me*."

"Bingo! Now you get it. If you'd ever paid attention to me, it would have been obvious before." Laura had spent her pent-up fury and felt herself deflating. "You never liked me. You never think about me. You always take Freddy's side. You want him to leave me."

In the silence, Laura understood what she'd said was true. She saw her mother-in-law as competition for Freddy's attention. And she wanted Freddy all to herself, whether she loved him or not. What was wrong with that? She was his wife. Wasn't she supposed to come first in her husband's life?

Anne rested her cheek on her hand. "So, your plan is to destroy my son because I don't like you. That doesn't make any sense at all. Why does it matter to you whether I like you or not? You didn't marry *me*."

"Because, because . . . because you ruined my life."

"That's absurd. How did I ruin your life? I have so little to do with you."

"You didn't give a damn when I lost the baby." Laura's eyes filled. She pursed her lips to keep from sobbing. "You told Freddy it didn't matter."

"You're out of your mind. Of course, the baby mattered. I was terribly sad that you miscarried. I would never say such a thing."

"Yes, you did," Laura yelled. "Freddy told me what you said. The whole Morrow clan didn't care. You all should be taken down a peg or two, so you can see what it's like to live like ordinary mortals."

Anne's cheeks flushed. "I didn't mean the baby didn't matter. I didn't mean *you* didn't matter." She gripped the table edge until her fingers turned white. "You're deliberately misunderstanding. Freddy was distraught. He blamed himself. I was trying to tell him the miscarriage wasn't anyone's fault. You could have another child."

"Well, apparently we can't. Whose fault is that?"

Anne shook her head. "Well, it's certainly not mine! Anyway, we Morrows are plenty mortal. Every crappy thing that can happen to humans has happened to this family."

Laura took several deep breaths to calm herself. This wasn't the way to get what she wanted from Anne. She had always told herself she didn't care whether Anne loved her, but this wasn't about love. She wanted respect and belonging, and Anne had never respected her. The family had never accepted her as one of them.

"I'm exhausted," Anne said. "You should leave now."

Laura grabbed her jacket off the coat rack and slipped it on. "All I wanted from you was to be seen. To have the family include me. You couldn't even give me that."

"I see you for who you are all right."

Instantly, Laura understood she married Freddy not because she loved him but to be part of his family. There were so many Morrows they generated their own electricity like a small self-sustaining city. Her family was tiny—only her, her sister, and her mother. There hadn't been enough sound, movement, or affection in her house when she was growing up. She'd wanted to be part of a pack, to move in concert with them, have a place, join in the laughter, and be the one who made them laugh from time to time. What was wrong with wanting a little applause once in a while?

Freddy lit up when his siblings laughed at his jokes. They put their arms around each other for no reason at all and patted each other on the back. They celebrated each other. That's all she wanted, someone to hug her for no reason other than she happened to be standing next to them. She yearned for someone to appreciate her. Anne did that with Marie. They would glance at each other and laugh at whatever a grandchild said or did. They excluded her because she hadn't added any children to the tribe.

Laura tramped to the door and wrapped her scarf around her neck. "I should have told Freddy first."

Anne's face turned paper white. "Get out of my house!" She rose from the chair and shook her cane in the air. "I'd rather die alone than have you here with me. Get out so I don't have to brain you with this thing."

Laura laughed. She knew exactly how to drive Anne wild now. The old woman would die knowing she had stripped Freddy of his father and gotten even with the whole Morrow clan. Her revenge would be knowing Anne didn't go to her grave happy.

In the car, Laura took a few gulps from her flask to steady her nerves and headed to Burlington. She had unbuttoned her shirt before Freddy's old college roommate, George, opened his apartment door. He took one look at her, grabbed her by the back of her neck, and pulled her to him.

"If this is forty, wow, give me forty every day," he murmured into her ear as he unzipped her pants. She dropped onto the floor and held up her feet. He pulled off her boots and yanked off her jeans.

"You are one amazing woman." He buried his face between her legs.

Laura groaned and chased away the image of Freddy's kind face as he helped his mother into her house. She banished everything that wasn't this pleasure, this moment, and gripped George's long hair.

"I've got a few hours. Hell, they wouldn't miss me for days." She laughed.

George was only the beginning of her plan. Freddy would never be able to hang out with his best friend again after he discovered they'd been screwing. He'd have no one to talk to when he learned his father might not be his father.

She'd tried for years, over and over, to pull Freddy away from his mother, inventing reasons to keep him from being with his family, resisting the tug to come for holidays, birthdays, Mother's Day. She said they needed to make their own traditions. She created bountiful meals and bought piles of gifts. Nothing worked. Freddy always boomeranged right back to where he started, but when he learned his mother had lied to him all his life, that would end it, that would sever his connection to her forever. Laura could almost taste the glee on her tongue.

That desperate afternoon when she'd miscarried, she called him and asked, "Where are you?" expecting him to say he was at the worksite. Instead, he said, "I'm at home."

Well, she'd been at home—their home—and he wasn't there. He was at his mother's house, mowing the lawn for her. Laura screamed at him, "That's not your home! This is your home. Where I am."

George gazed up at her and kissed her belly. "Hey. Where are you?"

Her mind swung back into the present. George was good looking. It was extra titillating and a little evil to have sex with Freddy's best friend. It never would have occurred to George to fool around with her if she hadn't made the first move.

She'd gone to his restaurant in Burlington to confront him about all the time Freddy said he was spending with him, and to catch her husband in a lie. In the mirror behind the bar, she saw her cheeks were red, her eyes bright. Bands of energy emanated from her, but underneath, the hurt she felt was as bad as a stomach cramp. Freddy was discarding her, and even if he didn't know it yet, she knew it. He was shucking her off like a skin he'd outgrown.

When George recognized her, he came over and smiled. "What are you doing here?"

She blurted, "What the hell are you and Freddy doing all the time?"

George leaned against the shining wood bar. "Nothing. We're just hanging out. Freddy needs somewhere to go when you're mad at him. We drink beers, watch sports, and talk shit."

She checked her image in the mirror again. "Does he talk shit about me?"

George lost his smile. "Never."

The minute the word was out of his mouth, she could see he realized never talking about her was as bad as constantly complaining about her, or worse. George leaned back and swept one hand over his long, black hair. "I mean, he doesn't complain about you."

But moderating his comment didn't help. Her face collapsed. Her husband didn't care enough to complain about her. She climbed onto a barstool and put her head in her hands.

The dinner rush was an hour away. Servers in white aprons over black shirts and slacks walked through the candlelit dining area prepping their tables, shooting side glances at the bar. The empty black and white dining room with red carnations on each table and the candlelight reflecting off wine glasses reminded Laura of a painting.

She considered herself in the mirror again—blonde hair, pale face, gray eyes—nearly invisible, a stereotypical kindergarten teacher. She wasn't George's type. George went for wild women, brunettes who knew their own minds.

He put his elbows on the bar and took her hands. "Honey, come by tomorrow. You know I live in the apartment upstairs. We're closed on Tuesday. We'll go someplace else and have a drink. We can talk."

She threw back the double shot of gin he put on the counter and stared at him. Her eyes were wide, her swollen lower lip quivered. He leaned over and kissed her. It was a pity kiss, or he couldn't help taking advantage of her vulnerability. Laura didn't care. She kissed him back as if only he could save her. It was a declaration of freedom.

When he pulled away, she was blushing. "I'd like that." She smiled.

Now, three months later, George was making noises like a trapped dog who had no idea how to extricate himself. Laura wasn't worried. If she could have one affair, she could have another. She had hidden depths. She was the kind of woman who could burn down a bridge and never look back. She was George's type. He should be careful. Everyone should.

Chapter 26

Indira soothed herself with the view of Anne Canfield's home. Its several stone and clapboard additions and garland of old trees, how it spoke of generations of family, continuity, and permanence. Smoke plumed from one of the four chimneys.

Behind the house, sunlight shimmered off the lake. If she closed her eyes, she would hear the water's quiet murmuring as it lapped against the shore. And now, even if she didn't want to, she also remembered Anne yelling in her gravel voice about the weather, sunrise, or whatever it was she'd said on that morning three months ago.

The front door opened, and Anne, swathed in a sweater and shawl with a turban on her head, appeared in the doorway leaning on her cane. She waved exuberantly. Indira parked on the wide circular drive in front of the house, cheered by the welcome.

The women embraced each other gently, mindful of recent wounds, and moved inside. "We always sit in the kitchen these days," Anne said, "but if you want a more comfortable chair, Freddy can make a fire for us in the living room. Leave your boots there."

Indira removed her coat and scarf and hung them on the antique coat rack. She gazed around the house with its bright walls, sun-bleached wood floors, and antiques still in use as she shucked off her boots. An antique grandfather clock with an inlaid scene of a man serenely fishing from a small skiff adorned the hall. It was as if time stood still in this house. "Let's sit wherever you prefer."

A man with blazing red hair and a beard to match emerged from the kitchen wiping his hands on a paper towel. Indira looked up into his face and watched his eyes change colors. His face crinkled into a smile, and he held out his hand.

"Freddy Morrow," he said, taking her hand. "Mom talks about you all the time. This is kind of thrilling. I never met a real live novelist before."

Indira let her hand rest in his large one. "We're often disappointingly average." Heat from his body seeped through her pores and up into her arm. So much life in one body. "It's wonderful to meet you."

Although he was older than she, he had the aura of a younger man breaking out of the cocoon of adolescence. He radiated the possibility that right around the next corner life would offer him unexpected and astounding gifts, and he'd be happy to share them.

Freddy held her hand a few beats longer than polite, then tore himself away and went in search of wherever his mother had wandered. Indira followed him. They found Anne in the living room where she had sunk into her favorite armchair near the fireplace.

"Stay there, Mom. I'll make a fire and bring you some tea." He pulled a hand-crocheted blue and white Afghan off the sofa and placed it across her legs. Anne's striped woolen slippers protruded from beneath the blanket.

Squatting in front of the fireplace, he opened the flue, arranged a few logs, and lit the fire. The room filled with the aroma of cedar. Sparks leaped and crackled in the hearth. Anne smiled at her son. Her face said everything anyone might need to know about their relationship.

A pang shot through Indira—she would never have a relationship like that. It took all her self-discipline not to speak her thought.

Anne nodded in Freddy's direction. "He takes wonderful care of me, doesn't he?"

Indira nodded and sat in the chair nearest Anne. Pain from the surgery was only a memory, but the loss of what she would never have deepened every day. Sorrow grew like the cancer that lurked in her body—silent and patient, a terrorist with a bomb set to go off whenever it wanted.

Physically, she was feeling well enough to go back to teaching. Her stamina had returned. She could focus, a relief as potent as being able to breathe in the air after a two-month burial, but writing was still out of the question. The surgery had erased all the stories she was meant to write. She was blank and empty without a word of her own on the horizon. She yearned for work, to immerse herself in making a sentence, to feel her mind diving deeply into the invisible and retrieving whatever truth was hidden there, but she still couldn't break through the surface of her fury to find the words she needed.

Indira snapped herself out of her malaise and gestured toward the lake they could see from the bay window. "What a beautiful place you have here. The view is spectacular. It suits you."

"Yes, I think so. I grew up in this house. That view is part of my identity."

"Houses, particularly old houses, have their own lives," Indira said. "But I see what you mean. Your environment formed you."

"Right. All those dead cells swirling around, sifting over everything, covering the walls and furniture. They accumulate weight," Anne said. "Do you think dust has a memory? If so, we'd be immortal in a way, all those cells embedded with our DNA that we've shed everywhere."

Indira laughed. "I've never thought about that!"

Anne touched her head. "I've been thinking about collective consciousness—that all human memory remains in the unconscious waiting to be tapped. My husband called it hooey. He always thought my theories—or any theories that weren't his—were ridiculous. But what if it's true and memories are encoded in our DNA so we pass them on to future generations and they learn from them?"

"We're not talking about dust anymore, right?"

"Dust? We were never talking about dust," Anne said.

Indira laughed. "This is the most intriguing conversation I've had in a long time. You don't do small talk, do you?"

Anne waved her hand in the air. "I'm nearly at the end of my use-by date. Got to get everything out on the table. Who has time for small talk?"

"No one, now you point it out."

Freddy brought in blue mugs that matched the color of the sofa. Indira noticed the blues in the paintings on the walls and the rug. Anne had a color scheme and a favorite color. That was a side of her Indira hadn't expected. She had thought of Anne as a clean slate on which she could write her own designs, and that was not the case. It struck her sharply how selfish she intended to be.

Indira observed Freddy watching as she sipped her tea and motioned to the sofa. "It's perfect, Freddy. Did you put honey in it? Why don't you sit with us and talk?"

Freddy's cheeks pinked. "Oh, no, I have stuff to do. I'm making Mom's stuffed cabbage for dinner. Lots of steps. Sam and his wife are coming for the weekend." He backed out of the room, half bowing, never taking his eyes off her.

"I think he's a little infatuated," Anne said. "I don't blame him. This feeling in my chest about you is different from other new friendships. I feel like we were supposed to meet. Like it was destiny. Is that peculiar?"

"Maybe."

They both laughed as if having announced their mutual idiosyncrasies made them happy.

"But that's the way I feel, also," Indira said. "I think when your heart is broken and what you hoped for most dearly is stripped away from you, it opens you to new and different experiences. You see things differently."

Anne stared at her and they sipped their tea in perfect peace as if this moment were all that life had ever promised, and they had all the time in the world to savor simple pleasures such as silence. It was a lesson of sorts. Indira could enjoy the time she had left, minute by minute, and not make any plans.

The idea was beguiling. She could drift away without trying to control her life. She didn't need to produce or succeed at anything. Imminent death gave her a freedom she'd never experienced before. She could let go of striving, hope, effort, and every grand goal. She could just be. The idea almost made her giddy.

Anne put down her cup on the round mahogany table next to her chair. "Let's get to the point. What did you want to talk to me about?"

Unwilling to risk the warm feeling in the room to ask for what she wanted, Indira leaned back in the chair and closed her eyes, as if that would keep her from seeing what she was doing. "I have stage three ovarian cancer. There's a chance I might live another five years, remotely ten, but it could be grim."

Anne was silent.

Indira took a sip of her tea and swallowed. "There's a greater probability I'll die before five years are up. And there will be pain." She sighed and opened her eyes to watch Anne's reaction. "I'm hoping you'll help me exercise my right to die with dignity and be my witness."

Color rose in Anne's cheeks, but she said nothing.

"I know I'm asking a lot," Indira rushed on. "Everything needs to be done the way the law requires so you don't get in trouble. You would have to sign an affidavit and might be interviewed by police afterward so they can make sure we followed the law."

Indira took a deep breath and held it, trying to tamp down the bubble of fear rising in her stomach. She couldn't bear hearing another person reject her plea. "I've read about how to do it. I crush the drugs, mix them with juice, and drink it. You would videotape my doing it to prove you didn't administer the drugs, but there could still be a hassle."

She wrung her hands and shook her head. "I know it's a big request."

Anne held up her hand. "You're right. It is a big request. Aside from any personal thoughts I might have about it, you have a husband and parents. Don't they want to be with you when you die?"

The words flew out of Indira's mouth before she could stop them. "They won't help me. No one will help me." She held down a sob.

Anne examined her hands in her lap, then glanced out of the window, and said nothing.

"I thought of you," Indira continued, "because although you don't want me to die, I thought you'd respect my choice to die with dignity."

"You're right. I don't want you to die, and I might respect your choice but not be willing to take part in it. You don't know I won't mess this up for you. I've already proved I will. At the lake. You intended . . ."

"Yes. I think so." Indira threw her hands up. "I don't know anymore."

Anne regarded her closely. "So, you have some doubts."

"Yes. Other people in my situation have had doubts. I read that one in three people who fill the prescriptions don't use them. I need someone to be with me at the end who will be there for me, whatever I choose, even at the last minute." Indira held her breath and waited.

Anne stared at the mountains across the lake. "I *do* want you to reconsider your decision. We're just getting to know each other. I'm not ready for you to leave. There's something we're supposed to do together, even if I don't know what it is right now. If you want me to help you, you need to give me time to mull this over. It's not something I can decide in a minute."

Unlike Indira's mother, Anne was calm. Her voice didn't rise. Her chest didn't heave. No melodrama. It was hard to believe she had brain cancer. She was more lucid and rational than all the doctors in Indira's own family.

Indira walked over to the window. "I shouldn't ask you to do this." She crossed her arms over her chest, protecting her heart. "But how do I convince you?"

After a minute of silence, Anne said, "It's hard for me to read these days and I miss the sound of a story rumbling around in my mind. I'd like you to read your novel to me, or whatever you're working on now. Not all at once but a few pages each time you visit, like every day. That will help me feel alive and connected to the world."

She grinned slyly, as if she were a precocious child pulling a trick on her parents, then stared at her hands and seemed to forget Indira was in the room.

Indira lowered her head and pressed her lips together. Her chest tightened. Anne's request had nothing to do with what they'd been talking about. *What if she doesn't understand what I'm asking for?* She wasn't the right person. Indira rubbed her forehead with her fingers. Wrapped up in her sorrow, she hadn't fully understood the older woman's state. Their situations were the same; they were both going to die. Yet Anne believed what mattered was not the dreaded future blackout but that she was alive right now.

If only she could shift her perspective to Anne's view of the situation, she might experience some relief from this constant dread. Yet even without being able to do that, she could be kind. That was the point of this visit, the real reason she came without knowing it. Indira squatted next to Anne's chair and took her hand.

"Of course, I'll read to you. I'd love to."

Anne smiled, said, "Then we have a pact," and leaned her head back in the chair. Within seconds, she drifted into sleep.

Indira found her way to the kitchen and stood in the archway from the dining room. Freddy halted his food preparation. Bowls, spoons, eggs, rice, tomato sauce, spices, and cabbage in no particular order she could discern covered every inch of space on the counters around him. Cooking was obviously a challenge for him and yet he was thrashing his way through it for his mother. Indira shook her head in admiration.

"What's your mother's prognosis?"

Freddy's face flushed and his eyes filled. "Not good."

"Does she know that?"

"The doctor told her she has thirteen months to live, max. But if she understands what he said, she's a good actress. She insists when she recovers from the surgery and treatments, she'll be good to go."

"What happens next?"

Freddy put down the red-handled silicone spatula he was using to mix the chopped meat. Translucent leaves of cabbage lay in a heap on an orange plate on the granite counter nearby. Tomato sauce glazed the bottom of a glass baking dish. The next steps in preparing this meal, Indira gathered, were to stuff the leaves and place them in the baking dish.

"Let me help you," she said.

Freddy pulled an apron from a drawer and handed it to her. "The next stage is awful. The doc says it could happen slowly or all at once. Disorientation. Loss of speech, blindness. She won't be able to walk or feed herself. She might have delusions, paranoia, irrational anger, and apprehensiveness. There's a long list." He passed the back of his hand across his cheek.

Indira washed her hands at the sink. "That sounds terrifying."

He handed her a ball of chopped meat and she rolled it into a pliable cabbage leaf, overlapping the ends into an envelope, and placed the stuffed leaf into the baking dish while he watched. He smiled his approval at her technique.

"It's grim. I'm not looking forward to it." His lips compressed into a thin line reminding her of Tom, making her wonder if this is what all men did in the face of insurmountable sorrow.

A tinge of chopped onion hung in the air and made Indira's eyes water. "What's the timeline?"

"Nobody will say. Six months, a year? We go back for another MRI in two weeks. The doc's worried the cancer came back in spite of the chemo and radiation."

They worked in silence until the baking dish was full. Freddy poured tomato sauce over the cabbage rolls and added a stick of cinnamon. Indira washed her hands in the sink and dried them on the towel hanging from the nearby drawer handle. It was good to have work to do, to be useful.

"What do *you* think?" she asked.

"My guess is the cancer never went away. The doc says it's aggressive. I get this picture in my mind of the meanest bullies in school ganging up on my mother." He frowned and fiddled with a ladle, spooning sauce over the cabbage rolls. "I want to kill them with my bare hands."

His honesty startled her. She touched his arm. His face contorted as he struggled not to cry. She wanted to embrace him and take away his pain, but she didn't have that kind of power. There was something she could do, though. She could keep her promise to Anne.

"I'll come back tomorrow. She wants me to read to her. What's a good time?"

Freddy stroked his face, first one cheek and the other, leaving a streak of tomato sauce on his skin. "That's a great idea. This is a good time, in the early afternoon."

Indira reached up and wiped away the sauce on his cheek with the dishtowel. She walked to the front of the house with Freddy, pulled on her boots, and grabbed her coat.

Already incapacitated, Anne couldn't help her. Indira pictured that morning she deliberately walked onto the lake and imagined the spunk it must have taken for Anne to intervene. She owed her something in return, even if it was only her voice calling out across an icy expanse.

Chapter 27

It took all Anne's energy and concentration to walk into the parlor and sit in her favorite chair. She pulled the blanket over her knees and listened to the grandfather clock in the foyer tick. Otherwise, the house was quiet. She could do anything she wanted to do, unwatched. She should fire up the old tractor and take a ride around the neighborhood. That would get people's tongues wagging. She smiled. If she had the balance, she would have danced a jig just to see if she still could.

Then she remembered Laura's threats and her glee evaporated. That mean woman was going to make trouble for her son. She couldn't let that happen. Freddy could never know the truth. This was the one lie she would take to her grave, the lie she'd never regretted telling. Unexpectedly weary, Anne closed her eyes.

Colin materialized right in front of her. "This is the magic no one tells you about." She sighed. "I can conjure people out of thin air."

You're hallucinating. It's a sign of your illness.

"Shut up, Howard. You have nothing to say about this."

Anne had thought of Colin intermittently over the years but here he was—curly red hair and mustache, long-limbed, broad-shouldered, flat-bellied, on a long ramble through New England one spring long ago.

She had almost forgotten being in love, the sensation in her stomach that made her full. How energized she'd been, her delight in everything. "Oh, those thighs." Her eyes had seen more, everything had been brighter. "His hands, his shoulders." She could feel his bare skin beneath the palm of her hand, see the indentation just above his wrist she had to kiss.

She had been thirty-five, floating on air, sleepless, and yet full of ideas. Colin McDowell was not in her father's plan for her. He was the man she was never supposed to meet, the man who would take her away from Queenscove and everything she'd ever known. Her father had constructed an entire didactic regime to keep her hidden from anyone like him.

From the year she turned five, Anne knew she would go into the newspaper business and marry a college professor because that's what her father said to her every day at dinner. "When you take over as editor of the paper, when you find a smart man who teaches at the college, when you have your children . . ." She inscribed his words in her memory.

If she did everything he prescribed, her life would have meaning, she would have her singular purpose and become who she was meant to be. Her father promised. This was the moral of all the stories he told her.

"You will be a useful person, Anne," he used to say. "You're a sturdy woman with a good brain. If you're disciplined and flexible, you will have a comfortable future."

Her father had determined her future just as he had given her half of her genetic traits. His prescribed path stretched out in front of her like a necessary pilgrimage required by his religion before she could think for herself. All her early life, she'd worked to hit the marks her father had set.

When her father sent her to cover a lecture by Howard Morrow, Ph.D., assistant professor at the college who was discussing his new book, Anne realized that this man was the next item on her father's to-do list. She hardly heard what Howard said, standing behind the lectern on the stage, talking about the history of time as a philosophical conundrum without having to consult his notes. He was too smart for her, but, on the other hand, he was funny and handsome in a craggy kind of way. She liked his wild hawk's wings eyebrows ready to carry him off on a whim.

After the talk, she waited in line for a chance to interview him, hoping to get the Cliffs Notes version of what he was talking about for her piece. He had an easy way with each person who approached him. Despite his numinous brain, he was amiable. His head bent, brows drawn together over his nose, he listened intently to each person and responded to their questions and assertions.

By the time Anne reached the front of the line, she hungered for him as if he were a feast and she only had to step up to the table to gobble up whatever she wanted. When she introduced herself and put out her hand to shake his, Howard regarded her for a full second, his pupils dilating, before he said anything. He took her hand, put his other hand on her elbow, and pulled her to his side.

"Don't go anywhere," he whispered, leaning down so his lips touched her ear. "Stand right here. Wait for me."

She stood next to him and waited for him to talk to all the others who wanted a bit of his time. They went for coffee and then to the cabin he was renting outside town. They went to bed and Anne had her first orgasm—a sensation akin to whitewater rafting, spinning down a waterfall in a barrel, and parachuting from five-thousand feet in the air all at once. She woke up next to him in the morning and decided she liked the funky smell they made together.

Long before this moment, Anne had decided that she wasn't much of a catch—a klutz, mouthy, unruly hair, too sure of herself. She put men off with her bluntness and her clear demand for equality. But the way Howard gazed at her when she glanced up from a book or whatever she was writing as if she were the best thing that had ever happened to him moved her. He made her feel as if she were saving him from the arid desert of the intellect.

That look lasted five years. His devotion was gone in ten. Until she met Colin, Anne had never let herself imagine a life outside the box her father and Howard built.

Anne opened her eyes and contemplated her living room. She had a lot to be thankful for. Outside the window, sunlight beamed off the lake. She was grateful for the sweet, deep pool of memory. "Respite, is that the word I want? No. Reprieve."

That wasn't it either. A word about refreshment was what she needed, but she couldn't find the word. "So frustrating."

An image of her grandson glancing up from running his toy cars across the floor rose in her mind. That angel hair, those extraordinary eyes, the perfect mouth, and his silky skin.

"Grandma, I'm hungry," he said.

"Do you want a cookie?"

He tilted his adorable face, auburn curls jiggling with disbelief. "Seriously? Don't you know real food comes before cookies?"

Anne smiled as the memory of her grandson elided into memories of Colin. Colin was dessert before real food. They had spotted each other in town at the Saturday farmer's market. Eyes locked, breath stopped, all other people faded away, just like in the romance novels she refused to read. He walked up to her and introduced himself. He bought a paper and asked if she needed any stringers for a few months while he camped in the state park.

"I want to write like Annie Dillard about the wonders of nature," he said. He needed practice writing for an audience, a way to test the reaction to what he wrote.

Anne suppressed her laughter. The guy aimed high. "I'll give you a shot," she said on a whim because he was so handsome and made her grin with joy simply because he talked to her. "Bring a piece in for me to read. No more than eight-hundred words. If it's good, I'll run it."

She gave him a business card with her name and office phone number on it. His eyes never left her face as he took it. "I cut from the bottom," she called out as he left.

She laughed every time she recollected how his turning around to acknowledge her words, checking her over his shoulder had made her feel warm and undone.

A week later, the most wonderful two-page essay she'd ever read on camping in the Green Mountains was on her desk. She took one sip of coffee and didn't raise the cup to her lips again until she finished reading it. The guy could write the white off a piece of paper.

Since he was camping and only had use of the payphone at the ranger's station, Anne had to wait for Colin to come into the office to tell him she would publish the piece. That afternoon when he walked in, she told him she'd pay twenty-five dollars for each column she ran in the paper, but she could only run one piece a week.

"You won't get rich, but you'll get a byline and clips." *And I'll get to see you once a week.* She didn't say that part out loud. Her beaming face said it for her. She must have been embarrassingly obvious, and she didn't care.

"Deal," he said and grinned at her.

That was too easy. "It's not bad pay for a stringer out here in the boonies, and it's the most I can pay."

That was stingy, but there was only so much lovely writing her readers could take. They preferred news about high school sports, bake sales, what the town council was up to, PTA plans, how the county government was using their property tax, the sailing race results, wool prices, snowpack levels, and reports from the fish and game warden. She didn't tell Colin that either.

The following week when he brought in his column, she took him to her favorite spot on the lake—a wooded cove the tourists hadn't found, and the teenagers had abandoned after being chased off by the police. She thought he would write about it.

They sat on the bank for half an hour without talking, watching the world around them. Dragonflies buzzed the surface of the lake. A breeze made the leaves whisper. Bird calls racketed through the surrounding woods. A green heron flew off its perch and snatched a small fish from the water.

They were the only two people on earth. Her hand accidentally brushed the soft reddish-blond fuzz on his arm as she reached for a stone to throw into the water. The tingle lasted for minutes. "Isn't this all so, so . . . Beyond words," she said to break the intense silence.

He took her hand.

"I'm . . ." married with kids she'd intended to say.

He leaned toward her, their breath mingled, his lips touched hers, and there was nothing to do but surrender. She had no thought but to yield and yield and yield, opening her body to him until every molecule blended with his.

For the next twelve weeks she lived a double life—loving mother and efficient editor most of the day, and the wild, boundary-less self she became when she was with Colin for an hour or two each day. The world lit up for her as he pointed to clouds tinged with gold at the beginning of sunset, the fine veins on leaves that echoed rivers branching across the plains, and the way long grass silvered as it bent to the wind.

"Nature wastes nothing," he said. "What works is repeated across all the individuals in a species and echoed in others. That intricate engineering is the result of endless experiments over millions of years."

Sound became erotic, her ears an orifice into which he could pour himself. He traced the veins on her arm with his finger. Time melted.

They walked in the woods as if walking were a way to penetrate each other, moving until the magnetic force between them drew them into one writhing being.

Every minute away from him was delicious agony. She waited for their time together, anticipating the explosion of energy that blew through them when their bodies pressed together. Every day, as a countermeasure, she reminded herself to be kind to her sons and patient with her husband.

When the time came to go back to graduate school, Colin begged her to go with him. Anne thought about her boys—Sam, Arnold, and Rob. The sounds they made when they played, their skin, and their sweet potato smell. They were part of her biology. How could she leave them? The thought of not kissing them goodnight left her hollowed out and breathless. They were the blood in her veins and her exact nature.

No matter how Colin implored her, she refused to go away with him. "Please understand how impossible this decision is." She tried to explain. "It's like I've found the secret of life. You, loving you, that's the secret. But the rules of the secret are I can't tell anyone about it, and I can't use it for my own benefit."

"You're not making any sense. This can't be what you want."

Anne closed her eyes. She couldn't bear to see him weep. "It doesn't matter what I want." She turned her back so she wouldn't watch him. "I have to live in the real world. I must stay with my sons. You need to go. That's how it is."

He left without telling her where he was going. She was unable to eat, barely able to speak, and prone to bursting into uncontrollable sobs for no reason in the weekly news budget meetings. Molly worried about her. Only a view of the lake and mountains could steady her.

After a few months, Colin wrote, and she was able to function normally again. His longing leaped off the page. She walked out to their spot on the lake and read his letters out loud just to hear his words hang in the air, give them skin, and let them breathe. She wanted to caress them and feel them in her mouth. Her heart quaked, but she didn't write back, and he stopped.

Anne never told Howard about the affair, but her perspective shifted. Colin proved there was more to life than the limitations she'd accepted.

She could expect astonishment, delight, and wonder, just not with Howard. She'd made her choice, though, and the memory of delight would have to do.

Now it turned out that it didn't matter whether she'd sent Colin away or she had stayed in her marriage. Faithlessness left its mark, a fingerprint on the glass of her life that Laura had detected and figured out how to use to hurt her and her sons. The truth would shatter Freddy in particular, and she wouldn't be alive to help him cope. He'd have to find a way to survive it. Laura would do her worst, and nothing could stop her. Unless there was something she could do, a story she could invent that might cushion the blow.

All this thinking made her tired. Anne folded her hands in her lap and leaned her head back. A word danced in her head. "Restorative." That was the one she'd been searching for.

Chapter 28

Laura mentally rubbed her hands to warm them. They were clammy as if delving into Anne's secrets made her uneasy. That was ridiculous. This was the simplest thing she'd done in a while. She took a few gulps of her gin and tonic to steady herself.

It had taken no special talent to find Anne's mystery man, but she hesitated to take the next step. It was one thing to know someone existed, and quite another to intrude on his life. She didn't know how this would play out. Colin McDowell was headmaster at a posh private school in New Hampshire four hours away, practically next door. Five years ago, he'd left the prestigious west coast university where he taught for two decades and moved east to become headmaster at the private boarding school where she found him. That seemed like a demotion to her. He wasn't as perfect as a summary reading of his bio showed.

Laura's fingertip hovered above the phone link on her screen. Contact with Anne's Mr. Wonderful was seconds away. She didn't ask herself what she'd do after the call or what contacting him said about her. She would burn that bridge when she got to it. Right now, it didn't matter that she might not be on the side of the burned bridge that led to a future. She was a lit match. Only the heat and light mattered.

She had formed a complicated plan intended to trick McDowell into visiting Anne unannounced. His sudden appearance would be a bomb that sent them all scurrying for cover. They would back away, abandoning Anne and leaving her exposed and distraught when she was most vulnerable. Accused of betrayal, she would finally understand what it was like to be the outsider. Laura felt a momentary twinge of guilt about this scenario as it played out in her mind, but she let it go. No point in being skittish now. She took a deep breath and, calling the private school's admissions office, asked to talk to Headmaster McDowell about boarding her son there.

"Oh, I'm so sorry, ma'am, but it's too late to apply for admission for this coming fall semester," the admissions director explained. She didn't sound sorry to Laura; she sounded arrogant.

"You know, my son's been at Choate but it's not right for him and we have to go abroad for my husband's work," Laura explained. "It's an emergency and I've heard such wonderful things about your school. If I could just talk with the headmaster and explain our situation . . ."

"I guess it won't hurt to talk to him if you can wait for admission for next term," the woman said.

The acceptance of her lie was delicious. They would call her back. As she waited for McDowell to call, Laura poured herself another drink and rehearsed what her affluent, worried-mother persona might say. Earlier, she'd tried out what she thought was a private school accent but gave up when the sound of it coming out of her mouth made her giggle.

She scrolled through the school's website. The three-story stone administration building that was once a private mansion was massive. In the marble-columned entry, portraits of serious men and women stared down from mahogany-paneled walls. The swimming pool, tennis courts, lacrosse field, and even the huge dorm rooms reeked of money. With every pulse, Laura yearned to let the air out of this pompous bastion of privileged learning.

She had dressed for the call to shore up her new identity just as she would have to meet McDowell in person. Her new white linen pantsuit, low-heeled white pumps, gold necklace and earrings, and blonde hair swept into a bun made her look like a trust fund baby. Even if he only saw her from the shoulders up, she emanated wealth and sophistication. Her colleagues at school wouldn't have recognized her. She positioned herself in front of the great room bookcase beside which she had added a large potted palm. For all this man knew, she came from money. She could be whoever she wanted to be.

She imagined ceiling-high bookshelves lined McDowell's expansive office. There would be two chairs, though not the kind anyone lingered in, arranged in front of his large ebony desk. She tried to see herself as a student called to the office and forced to sit in one of those chairs in front of the headmaster. Laura straightened her back to make it clear *she* wasn't intimidated.

Behind him would be a bank of twelve-paned, lead-glass windows that faced out onto the green quad with its colonnade of evenly spaced birch trees. The school was the epitome of classical erudition and time-lessness. Laura blinked and lifted her chin in defiance.

When he appeared on the screen, McDowell was wearing a short-sleeved, green checked shirt with the collar open—far more casual than she expected. Some women might have found his slightly long, white hair with errant curls irresistible. That white beard made Laura think of Mark Twain for no reason she could explain.

"Nice to meet you, Mrs. Hanratty. Thank you for your interest in our school. Why don't tell me a little about your son?" His eyes seemed to bore into hers.

While she stumbled through polite greetings, Laura pictured McDow-ell in Birkenstock sandals, imagined that his second toe was longer than his big toe, and resisted her strong urge to giggle. She hadn't intended to describe a son she didn't have, but after a second's thought, Freddy would do nicely. If she'd had a boy, he would've been like his father.

"Well, he's a nice boy, affable, and gets along with everyone. He's smart, good with his hands. He might be an engineer. But he's not living up to his potential. He doesn't have any goals. He should excel at some-thing. Anything. He needs to be in a place that will challenge him to reach his potential."

Worried she sounded like a commercial for joining the military, Laura stopped and peered into McDowell's eyes. Did she use the wrong words? A twitch at the corner of his lips said he thought she was lying. Did he run a background check on her before he called to see if she could afford the school's hefty sixty-five-thousand dollar a year fee? The thought spooked her.

"Why do you want him to come to our school?"

"I've heard your graduates go to the Ivies and from there on to decent careers."

"What do you think of as a decent career?"

Laura touched the bun at the back of her head. Her cheeks heated. "Oh, you know. Famous novelists, senators, CEOs, that kind of thing." She laughed to cover her nervousness. She wasn't prepared for this line of questioning. With a start, she realized that if she had a child, if her baby hadn't died before he was born, she wouldn't have cared what he became, only that he was happy. *Destroying his grandmother wouldn't have made him happy*, whispered a little voice in her head she ignored.

"Is that what's important to you? Success?"

"Well, isn't that what's important to everyone? One wants to see one's son do well in the world. Wouldn't you?" She raised her eyebrows and smiled at him. The hairs on her arms stood up. She wasn't fooling him. He didn't take notes or even unfold his hands.

McDowell leaned back in his chair and regarded her, his eyes moving slightly as he examined her face on the screen. "At Grumman Hall, we try to encourage the growth of the whole being. We emphasize the creative arts, reading, writing, dialogue, and independent exploration. I think you may have confused our goals with those of other private boarding schools. It doesn't sound like Grumman Hall is the right school to meet *your* goals for your son." He furrowed his bushy white eyebrows and stroked his beard.

Laura wanted to reach across the ether and smack his conceited face. His whole patronizing attitude infuriated her. He was like them, the Morrows in general, and Anne in particular. No wonder he and Anne had found each other—he fit with them. Snobs, all of them. Now she would have to crush him as well.

Her hands gripped the edge of the table so hard her fingertips turned white. Laura's composure slipped. She couldn't control herself. She took a sip of her drink to get a grip and hoped it would look like water to him.

"I think you know my ex-mother-in-law," she said. "Anne Morrow. You do know her, right?" In her mind, she pictured a bridge bursting into flames.

McDowell sat up in his chair. He put his arms on the desk, his fingertips touching. "You were married to one of the Morrow boys? You should have said so right away. Any child of theirs is bound to be a delight and we would be happy to have him here. Which son did you marry?"

His sudden eagerness disgusted her. Laura squared her shoulders. "Freddy."

This guy was dim. His sudden delight at the idea of being near Anne Morrow's grandchild was pathetic. She abandoned her strategy. It was better to put it to him straight. There was no point in delaying.

"Look. I know you had an affair with Anne, and Freddy is your son."

For a second, Colin looked shocked and then he threw his head back and laughed. Laura's face crumbled. He disappeared from the screen for a moment, and she heard him closing the door. Coming back to his chair, he rested his fingertips on the surface of his desk as if to gather himself together before facing her and then sat.

"Although it's none of your business, I don't mind acknowledging I had an affair with Anne Morrow. Those were the most glorious few months of my entire life. But it was more than forty years ago, and there's no reason it must be a secret now. But, no, to respond directly to your mistaken suggestion, Freddy is not my son."

Laura's blood pressure plummeted. She touched her cheeks with her fingertips. "How do you know that?"

"I asked Anne if he was my son. She said no. I believe her."

The remaining bit of Laura's composure slipped. "So, if you're so smart, do you know she's dying? She's got a malignant brain tumor the size of a grapefruit in her head."

Colin gasped, whether from the news or the way she spit it out. His chair swiveled. "That's enough," he said. "This call is over." The screen went blank.

Ten minutes later as she shook out her hair and removed the expensive earrings she would never wear again, she replayed in her head what Colin had said. "I asked Anne if he was my son. She said no." When did he ask her? If he asked her about Freddy, he *was* in touch with Anne after the affair ended, even after she stopped reading his letters. There was more to this story.

Chapter 29

The drive to Burlington took forever. Anne was cranky and out of sorts as if there were two of her co-existing side by side, the edges not fitting together so that every thought blurred. She hated the city, but she couldn't remember why. Looking at the scenery with one eye as it zoomed by at the speed of light gave her a headache. One working eye caused what the doctor called depth perception issues. She couldn't tell how close objects were to her. Danger lurked everywhere.

She had developed a system for making sure her hand reached the cup on the table or the flusher on the toilet, but driving past other cars on the road made her anxious. She clung to the armrest, trying not to cry out at each perceived near-miss, and hoped Freddy wouldn't collide with anyone.

"Do you think my sight will come back?" she asked to take her mind off the truck Freddy was passing. Its sides shuddered as they passed as if a huge animal thrashed around inside it.

Freddy kept his eyes on the road. He looked tense, and that worried her more. "You can ask the doc that question, Mom."

She had slipped into the cozy blanket of her dependence on him as if it had waited there all this time for her to snuggle under it. Every day, she fought it for a while, telling herself she needed to work. Yet every day she succumbed after making only a token effort at writing her editorial, doing the dishes, or making toast. She'd never realized how long it took for bread to brown. After this appointment with Dr. Arnold, she would go back to the office at least once a week. She would do her work, have a purpose. She was determined to have a normal life.

Yesterday, she called Molly to warn her. "I'm going to come into the office two days a week. One day to write my editorial and the other to read the copy before Wilbur lays out the issue."

131

"That'd be great, Anne," Molly said. There wasn't a smidge of disbelief in her voice. "We miss you."

Anne choked back a sob. She was turning into such a sentimental fool. Being in her work environment would straighten her out and get her to knock off these lazy ways she'd developed since the surgery.

The staff was doing an excellent job, but the paper read as if they were running on automatic. They needed a spark or a kick in their pants. She might be imagining that, and she certainly couldn't say anything to Molly, who was working her butt off to put the paper out by the deadline every week.

For no reason, the thing she'd wanted to tell Freddy all week but kept losing track of flashed into her mind. Anne pounced on it. "If you only have a few regrets about your life, you haven't been paying attention."

Freddy glanced at his mother, his hands gripping the steering wheel at nine and three. "Are you talking to me, Mom?"

Anne nodded. She didn't want to utter extraneous words that would make her lose her thought. "There are instant regrets when the words you never should have said are out of your mouth and can't be sucked back in. Like when I told Luke he was an asshole."

Freddy laughed. "You were right, Mom. He was an asshole."

Anne grimaced. "But those regrets are not as bad as the clench-your-teeth-and-groan kind that come at you in the middle of the night years later when you remember something you did that you didn't think was terrible at the time and all of a sudden you realize it was."

"Like what?"

"I was too hard on Luke."

Freddy grunted, his eyes on the road. "I don't think you were. He stole my money. He stole money and stuff like your car, from you and Pop. And our neighbors. He sold drugs to kids. He never said he was sorry. He didn't care about us."

"Well, how about when I told you Laura was too skinny? I was wrong to say that. I should have been kinder or just kept my mouth shut."

Freddy glanced at her over his shoulder. "That was a long time ago, Mom. And her being skinny was a sign. You were trying to warn me about her, but I was too gaga to see what you meant."

Anne's head wobbled. "I didn't like her, but I shouldn't have said it."

She couldn't seem to get across what she was trying to tell him. "The second I met her the word T O X I C scrolled across my brain in all caps. I worried for you, and I didn't know how to protect you."

She wanted to prepare him for what his wife might reveal about her. Inoculate, that was the word she wanted. If she could inoculate him against Laura's spite and the sharp edge of truth, he would be able to cope, or at least not hate her for the rest of his life.

Freddy reached across the seat and squeezed her hand. "You don't like Laura because she's like you, Mom. She says what's on her mind and wants people to do what she tells them to do."

"Ha! I never thought of that." Anne stared out of the window searching for her original thought. "I think I didn't like her because you were so crazy about her. I resented her for taking you away from me."

"Huh. Don't worry about that, Mom."

Anne clutched the armrest on the door. "Oh, there it is."

Freddy looked around. "What, Mom?"

"What I was thinking about regrets. The last kind, the worst kind, stays with you forever, because you discover too late that if you'd done one thing differently, everything would be better—your child would be alive and happy, your husband wouldn't have died, and you would have made a difference."

Freddy's face was blank as if she hadn't said anything. Maybe she hadn't. Erring on the side of repetition, Anne said, "I don't have any regrets about you, Freddy. I'm so grateful you're taking care of me."

He pressed his lips together. "You told me before, Mom. It's okay. I want to help you."

The car slowed as they arrived at the entrance to the doctor's modern brick building, which looked the same as every other brick building in the medical complex. How were people supposed to know where they were going?

"I'm going to pull up in front, Mom," Freddy said. "I'll help you inside and when you're settled, I'll park. You sit where I put you and I'll come back with a wheelchair." He smiled. "I'll spin you."

Anne grinned, delighted at the idea. "I don't deserve you." She'd already forgotten what she'd been trying to explain and why.

Doc Arnold ran through his regular routine. Anne closed her eyes, held up her hands, opened her eyes, and walked down the hall and back, exhausted by the time he let her sit down.

"Have you been feeling tired, Anne?"

"*Pfft*. Not until you made me do this marathon."

He asked questions she didn't know the answers to, and then he got to the pop quiz at the end. "What are the three things I told you to remember?"

Anne didn't have a clue.

"Noses are red, roses are blue, and you've got a cute little butt on you."

Freddy snorted. The doctor grunted, tilted his head, and said, "Try again."

"Okay. I live at 1800 Whooping Crane Lane in a red house with blue shutters."

That wasn't Anne's address or what her house looked like, but the doctor smiled and typed letters into his computer. She had missed something important and couldn't remember what, and that thought made her anxious.

"I feel good, doc. I'm getting better."

He pulled his rolling stool close to Anne. "We got the results of your latest MRI. We're going to stop the chemo and the electrical field therapy we've been using to try to keep the tumor at bay."

Her heart thumped in her chest. "So, I'm cured?" Anne had a feeling the doctor didn't mean that, but he was a "the cat got up on the roof" kind of storyteller. It took him a long time to get to the punchline. She always wanted to yell at him, "Stop burying the lede!"

Doctor Arnold glanced at Freddy. "It's time to call in Hospice. Are you willing to do that?"

Freddy's face paled. He looked away from her. "Yes," he mumbled.

Freddy understood but Anne didn't. "What do you mean, exactly, doc?"

The doctor pressed her shoulder with his hand and stared into her eyes as if he were trying to connect telepathically. "It means, Anne, the tumor is growing again and there's nothing we can do to stop it."

"But I'm going back to work. I have to go back to work. I have to take care of the paper."

He patted her shoulder. Anne knew there was a time when she would have been annoyed at him, but she couldn't find the word she needed. Was it condensation or Patronus?

She jerked her shoulder away from his hand. Tears overwhelmed her even though she hated crying in front of people. Paternalistic, that's the word. Condescending. Patronizing. "I still have my words, you misogynistic troglodyte."

Neither man reacted. She must not have said that. Without warning, she effortlessly understood what the doctor meant. "How long?" she asked, to show she was still in charge of what happened to her.

Doctor Arnold's eyes flicked to Freddy's face. "Six months, six weeks, somewhere in between. Hard to say. Meanwhile, you might have new symptoms, like sudden anger, a sense someone is watching you when no one's there, unfounded fears . . ."

"You mean I'm going to go fucking psychotic?" Anne heard herself yelling but couldn't stop. "That's what you're saying. Right? I'll be paranoid and delusional. Nothing unfounded about *those* fears. Well, say it, for God's sake! Stop dancing around."

Freddy stood and put his large, warm hand on her shoulder. "Mom." Anne put her cheek on his hand.

Tears knotted her throat. "This can't be how it goes. The newspaper, how will it survive without me? This can't be what happens now." She glanced at her boy. Freddy had caved in, shoulders hunched, clutching his stomach as if he'd been kicked by a horse.

The doctor had given her a death sentence.

This cancer was always a death sentence, Howard said. *You should've been paying attention.*

She shrugged him off and bit her lip to keep from sobbing.

The doctor, unperturbed, wrote on his prescription pad and handed a piece of paper to Freddy. "You call and say I've recommended Hospice. They'll set you up."

Her head shook. "I don't want all those strangers around me. How's that going to help?"

"They'll help Freddy and that will help you." He patted her back and left the room.

In a whirl of movement, she couldn't keep track of, the exam had finished, they left the building, and returned to the car. Freddy was driving and crying at the same time. She hated to see her son cry, lips twisted, cheeks wet, and wished she could tell him it would be okay, but her words were stuck in her throat. Anyway, it wouldn't be okay. She was going to die before she was ready. She was definitely going to regret that. That might be a fourth category of regret—shitty things that happened over which she had no control.

"The paper, I have to take care of the paper. You kids can't just close it. I won't leave Molly, Sadie, and Osborn out in the cold. It's not right."

Freddy reached over and held her hand. "It'll be okay, Mom. Something will happen. Indira said a buyer you know would show up." But his voice was full of tears, and it was hard to believe him.

"When did she say that?"

"Yesterday, when you were napping."

Exhausted, Anne closed her eyes. A buyer she knew. Who could that be? She'd have to go through the list of publishers she knew. There was a directory in the house somewhere. A cartoon image of Sisyphus pushing a huge boulder up a hill popped into her mind. She sighed. This wasn't the time to give up, not yet, but she needed to figure out how to do what was next.

Chapter 30

Colorful abstract paintings on the walls, sculptures and mobiles, potted plants, and comfortable furniture created a sanctuary in the psychiatrist's office. At the very least it was a place where Indira could rest from her relentless battle of wills with everyone. She leaned back in the blue leather chair and focused on being calm.

The psychiatrist, Dr. Young, sat in a matching chair across from her. She crossed her legs and held a pen above the pad onto which she made initial marks Indira assumed were her name and the date. "So, what brings you here?"

"I have a terminal illness." The rasp in her voice surprised her. "And the second doctor I consulted said I had to see a psychiatrist."

She'd already rehearsed this conversation with Tom. "As if," she sputtered telling Tom what the law required of her, "as if I must be mentally ill because even though I'm dying, I want control over my life, and I choose not to have their poison in my body. I have a right to say what happens to me. It's my body. It's this system that's insane."

Her reflection in the dining room window—pacing up and down, waving her arms, hair whipping around her face—looking the way her mother did when she was upset, had stopped her.

Tom came up behind her, wrapped his arms around her shoulders, and kissed her neck. "It's the law, honey. The doctor's checking the box, so she doesn't get sued or arrested." He held her in his arms and leaned his forehead against hers.

She'd ripped herself away from him, even though what she wanted was to fold herself against him and hear him say that everything would be all right. She walked across the room and watched the lake ripple in the breeze, glinting with late afternoon sun. Birds chirped and warbled, distracting her with their sounds. Their jubilance was an affront.

"Everywhere I turn, there are barriers." She locked eyes with her husband. "Why is it so difficult?"

He held his hands out from his body. "Do you think it should be easy to end your own life?"

"Yes. No. Oh, God, I don't know. I've never done this before. Why won't you help me?"

Tom shook his head. "I'm glad there are obstacles. I don't want you to die."

"You want me to writhe in pain? To weep until no tears are left?"

"Of course not." He walked out of the room.

A few minutes later, she heard his car drive down the lane away from the house. He kept putting distance between them when what she craved was intimacy, but she had the uneasy sensation that she was the one driving him away.

What a mess she had made.

The doctor scrawled on the page. Indira leaned forward to see if she could read what Dr. Young wrote, wondering if she simply doodled instead of making insightful observations. Indecipherable hieroglyphs marched across two lines. Indira sat back. She had to find a new way to explain herself.

Dr. Young's face registered no emotion. "What's your diagnosis?"

Indira held her face rigid, determined to emulate the psychiatrist's composure. "Ovarian cancer, stage three A." There. She said it without breaking into pieces.

"And the prognosis?"

"A forty-five percent chance of living five more years. Unless there's a miracle." Her mouth twisted to stop a sob she couldn't prevent. "This is my second occurrence."

"Is this year one?"

Indira squirmed. Her first doctor had said she needed to be within six months of her death to get the prescriptions. "Yes. I had the surgery four months ago."

"Are you getting chemo and radiation therapy?"

"No."

"Why?"

"I think they're torture and won't change the outcome, or only by months."

"What does your doctor say?"

"I should take the treatments."

"And you don't think you'll live to the end of this year?"

"I want the prescriptions so I'm ready, so I can die in my own time when I decide, not because unruly cells multiply over and over until they suffocate everything else in my body and make my life a living hell."

Exhausted, Indira closed her eyes.

"You must be frightened," Dr. Young said without censure or disappointment.

Indira swallowed her tears. "Of course, I'm frightened! I'm also angry. I'm angry at the doctor, the disease, my husband, at everything that strips away my control over my own life. I thought the point of the law was to ensure we could die with dignity. There's nothing dignified about having to beg for a prescription or justify my decision to strangers over and over again."

"Control over our bodies should be a right," Dr. Young said, her voice soft and even.

Indira sighed. This perfectly healthy woman, who couldn't remotely understand what she was experiencing, was going to decide whether she was sane or insane.

Indira leaned forward to emphasize her point. "Look, the law says people who are determined to be mentally ill aren't allowed to take their own lives because they don't know what they're doing. The law implies that a person who wants to die must be insane. It's circular reasoning. The state has decided that people who have died on purpose might have second thoughts after they're dead, and the state must protect them from that possibility."

She spread her hands out in front of her, holding the invisible bowl of her argument. "Being deranged and alive is supposed to be better than being dead. How does that make sense? Who writes laws like these?"

Dr. Young's pen moved across the pad. Her face gave away nothing.

They must practice that bland look in front of a mirror.

Indira plunged ahead. "Isn't dying when you choose it instead of enduring horrible pain and sure death the sane approach when you have a terminal illness? There's no value in suffering that leads to nothing."

Her throat felt scorched, her body emptied of its argument. She leaned back in the chair and waited to see if her reasoning had had any effect on the doctor's decision.

"Do you have friends in the area, besides your husband?"

Indira adjusted her tunic, smoothing the silk fabric over her thighs. "We did before the misery with Tom's father." She tugged on the scarf wrapped around her shoulders and stared out of the window. Everything glistened in the spring sunlight. How still the psychiatrist could be. Her own heart pounded in her chest, her pulse twitched in her forehead, her foot tapped the floor. She crossed her legs the other way.

Haunted by an image of her grandmother writhing in pain, she had forgotten how to be still. Indira missed her own serenity, the sense of trusting her body to do what it was supposed to do. It took all her self-control not to spring out of the chair screaming in frustration and run away. She pictured Anne sitting in her chair, listening to her.

"Yes, I do have a friend, a wonderful woman who loves life and hates the idea that I want to end mine."

"How often do you see her?"

"Every day. We have tea and I read to her."

Dr. Young wrote on her pad. "Is she blind?"

"In one eye, so far. She has brain cancer."

Saying it sounded harsh, like a death sentence. *It is a death sentence.* Indira examined her own hands, her carefully pared nails. Without her wanting it to, her mouth drew down at the corners.

"So, your friend is someone else who's dying," the doctor said. "Is she going to exercise her right to die?"

Indira laughed at the idea of Anne yielding one second of life she didn't have to. "No, she's not. She's a spitfire. She wants to live right up until the end. She says she has too much to do."

"How do you feel about that?"

"Sad. She doesn't believe she's going to die, but she will. It's a Glioblastoma. No one survives it. I think she's fooling herself, but I admire her spunk and we have a pact to help each other."

"Help each other with what?"

"Dying. We'll be there for each other." Indira wiped the corners of her eyes with the side of her hand. "Never mind. I don't think this is going to work."

The psychiatrist smiled for the first time. "The state requires a six-week evaluation process. Stop at the receptionist's desk and make another appointment for next week. We'll talk again. I've enjoyed meeting you."

"Really," Indira muttered as she walked out of the office, but she stopped at the desk and scheduled another appointment.

Chapter 31

Three hundred pounds of white-tailed deer cantered out of the woods, into the lane, and slammed into the truck Tom was driving at fifty miles an hour, too fast for country roads even on dry, sunny days. The impact knocked him back in his seat.

A full rack of antlers screeched across metal as the buck's body flipped onto the hood. Tom watched, helpless and stunned. His foot slammed on the brake. The rear of the truck sashayed across asphalt until it came to a shuddering stop. Airbags exploded, shielding him from glass flying off the fractured windshield as the buck's antlers crashed through it before the deer slid off the hood onto the asphalt.

He'd been thinking a million things, none of them about watching the road. He wanted to make Indira happy. If only they'd had a child who he could cherish after she was gone, someone who would remind him every day of her, although it was a good thing her death wouldn't devastate another human being. How would he keep his practice going when he was so tired he could barely drag himself out of bed? He would never be ready for her death.

It was too much. He couldn't cope. He would be an abysmal failure like his father. At the worst possible time, he would betray everyone, especially the people closest to him. Yesterday, when he tried to tell his mother what he was dealing with, she busied herself with the hem of her shirt.

"One day at a time, sweetheart," she'd said.

Insulted by the bromide, he said, "Mom you're not listening to me. My wife wants to kill herself."

She patted his hand and got up to pour him more coffee. "Things have a way of working out, sweetie."

"Oh, like Dad, right? That worked out okay, didn't it? Just turn a blind eye and Tinkerbell will sprinkle some fairy dust and we'll all fly away."

His mother put her face in her hands and cried and all he could do was sit there feeling like crap and wait until she calmed. He needed a solution, not dime-store philosophy. He had no one to turn to.

His uncle was no help. "Life can be shitty. Bury yourself in work, kid," his uncle said and slapped him on the back.

Tom wondered about his family. They were unable to relate to what he was going through. He had always thought of them as healthy, functional people. His impression was wrong. These days, he was wrong about everything.

He turned off the vehicle and walked around to the front of the truck. The animal lay on the road, wheezing. Its eyes rolled and fixed on him. Tom automatically estimated its injuries. Two legs were broken, probable internal injuries as well. Its belly heaved.

Tom shivered and closed his eyes. His grandfather's lever-action Winchester 88 rifle was in the locked chest in the back. He kept it in the truck more from nostalgia than for shooting, but it would do for this purpose even though it was more gun than he needed.

He couldn't save the deer. Unlocking the chest with shaking hands, Tom loaded two bullets into the magazine in case he missed the first time and walked back to the animal.

"Sorry, old man," he said to the deer. The animal eyed him as if it understood what he was about to do and forgave him. Tom took aim at the spot between the eyes where the bullet would enter the brain and kill the buck within seconds. He pulled the lever to load the cartridge and squeezed the trigger. The sound of the shot echoed through the woods. The deer's head sank to the ground. Tom crouched on the side of the truck and vomited.

Sometime later, he didn't know how long, he called for a tow and made another call to let animal control know they had a carcass to remove on Old Tree Road. It struck him as he was telling the dispatcher the street name and approximately where he was that if he felled an old tree there'd be much more paperwork and hassle.

By the time Tom opened the front door of his house, he was an hour later than usual. Delicious smells greeted him. He breathed in deeply and let go of his grief as his mind named the meal his wife was preparing— lamb, onions, thyme, carrots, garlic, red wine. Stew. He inhaled again. He could almost taste it. If Indira was cooking, that was a good sign that she was over her funk, wasn't it?

He walked through the hallway and into the kitchen. Indira stood at the stove with her back to him, stirring her stew in a large, turquoise Dutch oven. She had never been as precious to him as right now, her head bent, attentive to her cooking. Surely this was a good sign. Had she changed her mind about dying?

He walked up behind her and wrapped his arms around her, nuzzling her neck with his nose. "Rice or noodles?" he asked.

She laughed. The skin on his arms prickled. She leaned her head back against his shoulder and tilted her face up for a kiss. Instantly, he returned to the Cambridge bookstore, her face brimming with life, her radiance when she smiled. Could he have that all back again?

Indira reached up for his face and kissed him again. "Don't talk for a minute," she said and wrapped her arms around his waist.

If only we could go on like this forever. He buried his face in her hair, breathing in its sweet citrusy smell. He would never let go of her again.

"Rice," she said into his shoulder. He laughed. She sniffed his blue denim work shirt. "You need a shower."

He laughed again and kissed her. This was all he'd ever wanted. If they could stay in this feeling, he would never ask for more.

"I didn't hear your truck on the lane," she said.

He sighed, the spell broken. "I hit a deer, a big buck." He shuddered, reliving the impact. "The truck's in the shop. Max drove me home and dropped me by the mailbox." He couldn't tell her he shot the deer.

Indira put a hand on his cheek. "Oh. I'm sorry, honey. That must have been awful. Are you hurt?"

He rubbed his neck. "I'll be stiff for a while."

She went back to stirring the stew. "Want to make a green salad?"

Tom opened the refrigerator and pulled out salad ingredients. "How about I put artichokes in the salad?"

"Sure. There's a can of quarters in the pantry. Make the Dijon dressing you're so good at. I got one of those perfect crusty loaves of bread at the market. And there's another bottle of the Pinot to drink."

With his back to her, whisking together the mustard, salt, pepper, lemon juice, and oil, he asked, "What are we celebrating?" He hoped he hadn't forgotten an important date.

She pulled two white plates down from the cabinet, opened a drawer, and took out two forks and knives, and from another drawer removed two purple placemats. Gathering the place settings, she walked into the dining room and set the table so they could watch the sunset over the lake together.

Striding back into the kitchen as if she'd found the answer to his question, she said, "That I love you. Is that enough?"

"Yes. It's enough. It's always enough."

After dinner, both standing at the kitchen sink doing dishes, Indira said, "The psychiatrist is going to report I'm not in a fit state to receive the suicide meds."

Tom put down the dish he was holding and stopped moving. "You're sure of that?" He hoped he kept the swell of gratitude for that decision out of his voice.

"Yes. She said I needed more sessions to think this through, to understand ending my life is final. She reminded me there are no do-overs after I'm dead. Can you imagine a doctor saying a thing like that? As if it hadn't occurred to me."

He dried her soapy hands with the dishtowel. "That's the truth. After death, there's nothing, no chance at anything else. You can't take it back. We only have this one life." He couldn't keep the urgency out of his voice, his hope that she would finally hear him. "Or if we do, we might not find each other again."

She leaned into him and wrapped her arms around him, pulling him so close their hearts beat against each other.

"I want you to do it," she said into his shirt, her voice muffled.

Each word was an antler piercing his body.

Chapter 32

Indira pushed Anne's wheelchair out to the two chairs facing the lake. Now it was spring, this was their favorite spot. Whenever she sat here with Anne, she saw what her friend had seen all her life, smelled the layered aromas of the lake, and heard the birds and the wind in the trees.

The cool breeze buffed her cheeks. In this spot, Indira was all the people Anne had ever shared this view with as if their molecules had mixed together and settled in the grass beside her. She was instantly older, wiser, and a little melancholy.

"I used to play with my dolls on this spot," Anne said. "They were clever, my dolls. They knew things." She smiled at Indira. "It's nice, though, to have a real friend." She held out her hand and Indira took it.

Anne seemed physically smaller as if she no longer needed to project herself outside the earthly structure that housed her. Watching this transformation made Indira's heart ache, but she came every day and read her stories to Anne because she had promised. Today, a little stage fright gripped her.

"I started a new project."

Anne leaned forward to hear her better. "Do you know what it is yet?"

Indira laughed. "Good question. The answer is no. I have no idea. I'm taking what comes, finding the characters and place. It's only a first draft but I remember this feeling of magic, how a voice tells me the story like someone whispering in my ear and sending me messages in dreams. It's an intimate, exciting experience like the seduction at the beginning of a love affair. Want to hear a little about the main character?"

"Of course. I love being seduced." Anne leaned her head back against the wooden chair and gazed out at the lake. This was the way she listened as if her body whisked off to somewhere else and only her keen attention remained.

Indira straightened her back and began reading out loud. The pages rustled as she read. Birds called. The lake murmured. Her voice layered itself over the ambient noise.

Annabelle Lee lived in the house she inherited from her mother who inherited it from her mother and so on back to Sally Lee, the first of their line for whom they could find a record included in a census.

The house, which looked out over the river, was built by Annabelle's great, great, great grandmother and had been added onto by every generation until there were ten bedrooms, a guest house, greenhouse, living room, den, study, great room, a kitchen the size of a small town, and various other rooms she never went into.

Each woman who had ever lived in the house had added her own room, designed specifically to hold her, and built it by hand, board by board, nail by nail, filling it with her spirit.

At one point the family had a story for every room, passing them down with the deed to the house, generation after generation. Whoever lived in the house managed the job of keeping up the stories as well as the house.

It was a big responsibility and time eroded the edges of the stories the way it does monuments and mountains. Many of those stories were now forgotten, people being what they are. Some stories were abandoned because they were too sad. Some were too violent to be repeated. Some stories created such longing in the teller that she could only do it once and no one who heard them dared recite the words.

In addition to the stories, Annabelle thought, there was a ghost for every room in the house. She heard them walking around, whispering, knocking into things. Colluding with each other, making plans.

Certain mornings she'd find paintings on the floor, torn from the wall in the middle of the night as evidence of a ghostly quarrel, or discover a vase in a different spot as if some designer spirits were editing the room.

She played Billie Holiday records hoping the singer's haunting voice would beguile the ghosts into sitting and talking for a spell. She played Ella Fitzgerald to help them rejoice and Nina Simone to watch their forms sway in the smokey sound.

Annabelle lived with five cats and two dogs, but she was always on the lookout for a new stray. On story day at the library where she worked, she would tell the children that stray animals who, tossed out of their owner's cars onto the highway shoulder and wandering into town, consulted a central bulletin board that listed her address in large letters readable by any cat or dog.

The children laughed and said, "No! Animals can't read!" in one voice. But Annabelle would look at them over the top of her purple eyeglass frames and say, "How do you know? Have you ever asked them?"

The children looked at each other to see if anyone had been brave, or silly enough to ask. They shook their heads, eyes wide.

They would find the secret, Annabelle said, hidden in books.

Children who came to the library on story day always went away with a smile and an armful of books.

When she stopped reading, Anne said nothing for a while, as if waiting for more. Then she stared at Indira, her eyes wide. "This is completely different from what you did before."

"I know."

"Is there more coming?"

"I hope so. I think I'm supposed to find the story for every room in the house. It's like a treasure hunt. Then Annabelle gets herself in some serious trouble and the ghosts help her find her way out."

"You're inventing people." Anne closed her eyes. "What fun. I always wanted to do that. Real people can be so boring. Can't wait to hear more."

Tufts of white hair, grown back over her scar, lifted in the breeze off the lake. She seemed to be drifting off but instead leaned forward. "I've been thinking about memories, how people are always telling themselves stories about their lives. They think the stories are fact, but they're just as made up as fiction."

"That's an interesting idea," Indira said. "Tell me more about that."

"Well, it's like me. My whole life is a story I whisper to myself from another room."

"And you're the protagonist of your story?"

"Yes," Anne said. "Now I'm getting closer to the end, I can hear it better. I'm in a pickle, and it's my job to figure out what to do. I have to solve the problem. No ghosts are coming to save me. And I might get it wrong."

Indira was silent. They listened to the birds and the leaves swishing against each other in the breeze.

Anne leaned closer to Indira until their heads were nearly touching. "I'm going to die," she whispered as if she were revealing this fact for the first time.

"Yes." Indira's throat cramped and she couldn't say more than that.

"It's unbearable. I will miss everything, everyone. It's killing me that won't know what happens after I'm gone. I'm homesick already and I haven't left yet. I don't want to go."

Indira's eyes welled.

Anne gripped her hand. "And you. How can you tear yourself away from all this beauty?" She gestured to the lake, sky, trees, the world. "How can you abandon the work you're meant to do before you have to? Or leave your husband? I can hardly bear that you want to leave."

A moan rose in Indira's throat. "I'm so afraid of the pain."

"Ah. The pain. Well." Anne nodded and looked away. "Each leaf, the light, my children, they're all so precious to me. I can't let any of it go. What about your stories? If you're gone, who will tell them?"

Indira covered her face with her hands. "I don't know."

Anne pulled herself out of her chair, wrapped her arms around Indira, and smoothed her hair. "Oh, my sweet friend. You don't really want to leave."

Indira shook her head. "No," she mumbled. "No, I don't. But I'm terrified of the pain."

Anne kissed her cheek and murmured in her ear, "Me too, me too."

Chapter 33

Freddy watched Laura standing in his mother's kitchen, jiggling the way she always did when she wanted to say something cruel. He didn't know if his wife was imitating her five-year-old students or if she'd never outgrown this behavior. It didn't matter. Everything she did annoyed him.

He wanted to talk to her as well, but he could wait, and he wouldn't help her say whatever it was that she wanted to tell him. Their separation, which he pretended was a mutual and amicable decision given his mother's plight, had hardened his opinion about her. If she cared about him, she would have found a way to be useful. But Laura didn't care about anyone but herself and only found ways to drive him nuts.

Truthfully, he wanted her to go away and stay away, but the way he saw it, her willingness to stay away proved she didn't care about him. And if she didn't care, it was okay for him to dislike her. In his head, his dead father accused him of circular logic, but this was his opinion, and he was sticking to it. It didn't matter what anyone else thought about him. Even his father.

Freddy made them tea and sat down at the table. His mother was asleep, and Indira had gone to the market for him. The doctor turned out to be right. Having hospice nurses checking on his mother three days a week and helping with bathing her gave him some respite.

She was often awake in the middle of the night, babbling or crying. He gave her the anti-anxiety meds, but he worried that if he fell asleep, she'd wander out of the house, half blind in the dark and walk out in front of a car or fall in the lake. He wasn't sleeping much.

Outside, summer was in full bloom, and white sails dotted the lake as puffy cumulus clouds floated through the blue sky. They had a poster-worthy view. No wonder his mother loved sitting out here.

Laura broke the silence. "I have to tell you something . . ."

Freddy stared at her. She'd lost some weight, gotten a tan, and the top two buttons on her shirt were undone showing a little cleavage. This was a sexier look for her. He expected her to say she was divorcing him, she had a lover, he was a shithead. He was ready for any of that.

He'd be happy to have it over, to be able to forget he'd spent so many years trying to please her. She could have the cabin and everything in it. It was the only thing they owned together. He had never made her a principal in his business. He wanted to divorce her, but this wasn't the time. His mother was dying, and that came first. If Laura was going to save him the trouble of doing the legal stuff, though, he was good with that.

"Okay," he said. "What's up?"

Laura's face blushed to the roots of her hair. She closed her eyes, opened them, and glared at him. "I found some stuff in the shed."

"Yeah?"

"Letters. I found letters. From a guy named Colin McDowell to your mother."

He took a sip of tea. "Okay."

She sat down at the table opposite him and stared out of the window. "They're love letters. Your mother had a lover."

Freddy put his mug down on the table. "Good for her." What gave Laura the right to go digging around in his mother's past? "Why on earth would whatever old shit you found in the barn matter now? What is wrong with you?"

Laura leaned forward across the table, bringing her face as close to his as possible. "She had a lover when she was married to Howard and already had three kids."

Freddy pushed away from the table and walked across the kitchen to the door. "What are you saying?"

Anger glittered on her face. "You always were dense. I'm saying your sainted mother had an affair and you might not be Howard's son." She sat up straighter as if, delivered of her spite, she was now lighter.

He choked and coughed. His heart stopped for a beat. When it started again, it pounded so loudly his ears throbbed with its rhythm. He stood still in the room to get his bearings. Why should he believe her?

Laura was lying on purpose to hurt him. The lying bitch was making the whole thing up. His mother would have told him if this were true.

His hands closed into fists. "You unbelievable witch." He walked closer to her, fists at his sides. "You fucking bitch. My mother is dying, and this is what you have to tell me, what you're itching to tell me. What kind of person are you?"

His face was right next to hers. She didn't flinch. He couldn't imagine how he had ever kissed her. She smelled like alcohol. He backed away so he wouldn't hit her. "You're drunk. Get out of here. Don't come back. Ever. You're not welcome."

She stood. "Ha. That's what your mother said."

Freddy's eyes opened wide and his mouth gaped. "You talked to Mom about this? Jesus, Laura. Something is *wrong* with you. Don't you understand she's dying?"

"I'll prove it to you," she said. "You'll see. I talked to him to make sure. I know everything. And while you're waiting for a miracle to save your mother from dying, here's some reading material." She reached into her bag, tossed a stack of letters onto the table, and headed for the door.

"Wait," Freddy whispered. "You talked to who?"

"Colin McDowell, of course, her lover," Laura said with her back to him. "He's itching to see her again."

"Don't come to the funeral," he yelled, his heart banging in his chest. "We don't want you there." Freddy stared at the lake's black surface until he heard her car drive away. Then he read the letters.

When he finished them, he put them back in order and tied them with the ribbon. He didn't know what to think except he never needed to know this stuff. A stranger had loved his mother before he was born, loved her the way people yearned to be loved all their lives, the way he wanted to be loved. In a way, he was glad for his mother, that she knew what that was like. Why didn't she go with the guy? What was more important to her than love like that?

Freddy ran his hands through his hair. She should be awake by now. He pulled himself together and went to check on her. Anne smiled at him. "Luke," she said, and held out her arms to him. He hugged her anyway.

Freddy settled Anne in her chair and wheeled her into the kitchen. She could still eat solid food and feed herself. That was a blessing. He might lose his shit if he had to spoon-feed her. Mentally, he smacked his knuckles for being petty. She must have fed him when he was a child. All of them. Instantly he pictured a progression of small boys with their mouths open, the spoon sliding between their lips, his mother cooing, "Good boy." If she could do it for five, he could feed one.

"I made your vegetable soup, Mom. And Indira got some great bread at the market."

"You like Indira."

"Yeah, well, who wouldn't? Anyway, you don't see anyone from the family helping, do you?"

His mother's chin ticked up sharply. "Why don't you ask them for help? They think you don't want them here."

Her rebuke stung. Was he hoarding this time with his mother? Freddy busied himself filling their soup bowls and slicing bread and didn't answer her challenge. He brought the food over to the table and sat down opposite her. The issue of his siblings helping was a subject he didn't want to bother her with. One way or another, his brothers had shown they didn't have time to help right now. They didn't understand their mother was dying, and even when he told them about hospice, they thought they had all the time in the world to be with her and didn't listen when he tried to enlighten them.

"Not everybody does things the way you do," Arne whined when Freddy suggested he spend time with their mother.

He had refrained from telling his brother he'd be sorry later. Freddy silenced the argument with Arne going on in his head. "Mom, I have to talk to you."

"Not death stuff, I hope. Not while we're eating."

He laughed. Death was now an obscenity to his mother, all the words related to it, the idea of it. It was the one subject about which she wouldn't talk.

Anne sniffed the aroma of the soup and closed her eyes. "I can still smell! Wow, that's wonderful. The dill. Yummy. You made it perfectly."

Freddy took in the compliment and stored it away for when he would need it. They ate in silence for a while. When he glanced up from his bowl, he saw soup dripping from his mother's chin.

"You missed your mouth, Mom." He reached across the table with a napkin and blotted her chin.

"My mouth isn't where it's supposed to be."

He smiled at her, unable to think of anything funny to say in response. The sun dipped slowly behind the mountains on the other side of the lake, flinging vivid splashes of pink, orange, and red across the water and treetops.

"When I watch the sunset now, I see the earth turning instead of the sun going down," Anne said. "Makes me dizzy, like I should hold onto something, or I'll hurtle off the side of the planet into space. What month is it, anyway?"

"It's July."

His mother amazed him. Cancer was eating her brain like some out-of-control Pac Man and she was talking about the earth's rotation. Was that one of the delusions the doctor warned about? He hoped she was strong enough to deal with what he had to ask her. For a few seconds, he tried to convince himself it didn't matter enough to bother her with it. But Laura had put a worm in his ear, and it was slithering through his mind, making him unhinged. Lightning bolts were slashing through his brain. He needed to know the truth.

Freddy cleared his throat. "Mom?"

Anne covered his hand with hers. "Yeah, babe?"

Freddy's jaw hurt but he forced himself to speak. "Mom, did you have an affair with a guy named Colin McDowell?"

Anne sighed and moved her spoon in circles in the bowl. "I see what's-her-name has been up to her nasty tricks."

"Mom, you have to tell me the truth."

She stroked his cheek with her fingers. "Yes, I did. A long time ago and it's one of two things I shouldn't have done that I don't regret at all."

"But you were married to Dad."

"Yep. And I stayed married to him, regardless of what it cost me."

Freddy's face heated. "You cheated on him." He put their bowls in the sink. "That must have cost *him*. Don't you think? And Sam, Rob, and Arne. What about them? How could you do that to them?"

Anne's head shook. It was a symptom without meaning, but it seemed to him she was denying everything he said.

"I didn't do it *to* them. I did it *for* me. Anyway, they never knew so how could it hurt them?"

Exasperation made his bones weak. He rinsed the dishes and put them in the dishwasher. The silence lasted so long he worried she'd forgotten what he asked, and he didn't have the necessary ruthlessness to remind her. He glanced at her.

She was staring out of the window. "Colin was heavenly. I felt so alive with him, so fully myself. I could feel my body moving through space for the first time in my life like I had edges and wasn't invisible. My mind sizzled. I was graceful and pretty, and the whole world was different."

His stomach turned over. "Why didn't you go with him, then?"

She looked at Freddy with surprise, as if he should already know her answer. "He wasn't what my life was about."

"I don't get it, Mom. I don't understand any of it." He should never have started this miserable conversation. It would've been better not to know.

"I wish Laura hadn't told you about him. What's the point?"

Everything his mother said made him uncomfortable. This was the hardest thing he'd ever had to do, and now he wasn't sure he wanted to know anything more. She was suddenly a different woman and not who he always thought she was. She'd lied to them for all those years. He couldn't look at his childhood the same way without examining everything that happened. His breath was heavy in his throat, and his heart twisted in his chest.

"Laura is beside the point. I'm asking about you, about who you are, and about me—who I am." His throat closed as if he were allergic to what he was about to say. "Is Colin my father?" He waited with his eyes averted for her answer.

A mockingbird warbled from a nearby maple tree. The silence seemed to go on forever. When Anne finally spoke, she moved the words out into the space between them as if she had to find each one separately and figure out how to make her lips and tongue form it.

"Oh, sweetheart, you know who you are. It doesn't matter who your father is. You're you and you're wonderful."

Freddy threw himself back in the chair and flung his arms out. "Jesus, Mom, how can you say that?" he yelled. "Of course, it matters!" The top of his head was going to fly off. How could she not understand how important her answer was to him? He jumped up and paced in circles.

Anne scanned the kitchen, her eyes darting around as if she could find the words she needed tucked in the corners. She couldn't process it. The issue was too complicated. He ran his hand across his forehead. No matter how much he regretted starting this, he couldn't take it back now. "I'm sorry, Mom, I need to know. I'm trying not to judge you. This is about me, who I am."

"I don't think so, honey."

Freddy scowled, his red eyebrows ramming together over his nose. "What do you mean?"

"I mean you were born . . ." She stared at her hands. Her fingers jiggled as if she were using them to count. "Ten and a half months after Colin left. I'm fairly sure that makes you Howard's son."

"But all my brothers are dark-haired. Where did this red hair come from?"

She made a face at him. "My grandfather, I think. Recessive genes? I'm not a biology expert. Go look at his portrait in the office. You look exactly like him."

Freddy dropped his head and covered his face with his hands. He couldn't tell if he was relieved or disappointed. He felt empty. If he were someone else's son, that would explain why he'd never fit in with his brothers, and why his father never defended him against Luke. Now there was no explanation except that his father didn't love him as much as he did his brothers.

His mother calmly watched the lake turn purple and then indigo as if he'd never asked who his father was. Stars stippled the darkening sky.

"Mom, did Dad know you had an affair? Did *he* think I was someone else's son?"

156

Anne looked at him as if he had two heads. "Howard thought the sun rose and set with you, Freddy. He named you after his grandfather—Frederick Amos Morrow. When you were a baby, he carried you around and showed you off at the college like you were the trophy he won for being the best at everything. You were his Berggruen prize." She took his hand. "The way he looked at you like you were God's gift . . ."

Freddy took a deep breath and released it. Odd how a few words could make him feel better even when some part of his mind was still questioning everything. But he was angrier than ever at Laura for being a troublemaker, upset with his mother because she'd kept this secret all his life, and indignant at life in general because it had taken so long for him to recover from the feeling that he was less than everyone else.

Later, after Anne was asleep, Freddy called Laura and left her a message. "I'm Howard's son, you bitch. You made me drag my sick mother through shit to find out. We're done. Don't call me, don't come by, don't write. Sam will send you whatever the legal forms are."

Freddy was shaking when he clicked off the call. He wanted to get even, to crush Laura for forcing him to put his mother through the third degree, but he had no idea how to do that. Instead, he mopped the kitchen floor, scrubbing up all the grime that had accumulated over the last few months.

He was Howard Morrow's son. There was a logical solution to his Laura problem. First, though, he had to make sure she couldn't use the letters to hurt his mother again. He opened the woodstove grate, made a small fire, and fed them into the flames one at a time. No one else needed to know about his mother's brief indiscretion, and he certainly wasn't going to tell them.

Chapter 34

Indira sat in her favorite chair, one leg tucked under her, reading. Golden light from the lamp lit her skin. Her feet were bare, and the filmy edge of her long yellow skirt caressed one ankle as she swung her leg. Tom watched her for a while, imagining her foot in his hand, the feel of her skin under his fingers before she noticed him.

Although she looked fine, she was in agony. Not physical pain, not yet, but emotional anguish. She groaned in her sleep and sobbed in the shower where she thought he wouldn't notice her crying. When they had sex, she wept as if each time were the last and she was saying goodbye. This state of limbo between being alive and dead was killing her. To live, humans need to feel immortal, to have the sense that there was no end in sight, and anything could happen. Her diagnosis shattered that illusion and regardless of what he did, a little bit of her died every day.

She glanced up from her book. "What are you doing standing there?" She put out her hand for him.

He crossed the room, took her hand, and leaned over to kiss her. "How was your day?"

"Today Anne thought I was her sister, but Freddy said she didn't have a sister. Isn't that interesting? She invented a more intimate relationship than a friend to match her feeling." Indira stroked his face. "You look tired."

"I am. I brought you something. I'll be right back."

"What?" he heard her call as he ran down to the garage. She was standing when he returned with a dog in his arms.

"Oh, my God. What did you do?"

"This is Bo." The dog licked Tom's hand. "He's just like the president's dog." He put the furry bundle into Indira's arms. She buried her face in the dog's fur.

"Oh. He's so soft." Bo licked her hand. She smiled at him. "What am I going to do with him?"

"You're going to take care of him. He doesn't like being alone."

"But . . . I don't know anything about dogs."

"He'll teach you. He's very smart. You can go for walks together. He'll sit with you when you read or write. I'm gone so long every day—"

Indira put her fingers on his lips. "Thank you."

Tom sighed. It was okay. He'd done something right. "Something smells delicious. Is that cabbage?"

Indira laughed. "Yes! I'm trying Freddy's stuffed cabbage recipe. I thought you might like it."

"I might. I smell cinnamon and tomatoes. That's an interesting combination. You *were* Anne's sister in another life. You seem to have been absorbed by the Morrows."

"Do you mind? Anne's dying. She needs a companion, and Freddy needs support. I'm only there when you're at work. And now I can take Bo with me. Anne will love watching him run around."

He sighed. "I don't mind." He didn't. Taking care of Anne gave his wife purpose, let her inhabit her own life more fully, and he hoped that attending to something outside of herself would change her mind. He ducked his head so she couldn't read his thoughts. "I'll take a shower and we'll have dinner."

"Bo and I will get acquainted." She put the dog down on the floor. "Come on, Bo. Let's set the table." The dog scampered behind her as she walked into the kitchen.

After they put the dishes away, they took their wine glasses out onto the deck to watch the sun sink behind the mountains. Bo settled at Indira's feet. Nora Jones crooned in the background from an album Indira had selected from her playlist. He took her hand, pulled her into an embrace, and they danced.

He spoke softly into her ear. "Indira, I can't do it."

"Do what?"

He pulled back slightly to watch her face. "I can't be the one who kills you. It makes me frantic to think of it. I won't do it."

She leaned away from him and wrapped her arms around herself. "Why are you bringing this up now? I thought we agreed. I was feeling so calm. We already talked about this. You said you'd help me. It's only a matter of when."

Tom reached out for her. "No," he said, "we didn't agree. You said what you wanted. I never said anything."

She walked to the deck railing. "You can't do this to me! I need you. I trusted you. I can't do it myself. I don't have the courage to do it alone. How can you let me suffer? If you loved me, you'd do it."

"Oh, my God, do you hear yourself? How could you misunderstand?" He put his hands in his hair. "That's exactly it. I can't kill you *because* I love you. I won't do it." He held her shoulders and pulled her toward him. She jerked away.

Tom hung his head, trying to find a calm place to speak from when all he wanted to do was scream. "Everything in me says it's wrong. I'm going out of my mind thinking about it. You're all that's important to me. How can I end your life? Your life is worth fighting for, every minute of it. How can you ask this of me? If you loved me, you wouldn't ask me to do it."

Indira shook her head. Tears flew from her eyes. "So, basically you're too selfish to help me. You think this is all about you. This is so unfair. I counted on you. I'd finally found peace."

"Honey, you're confused. I can't do it because I want you to live, no matter what."

"You and my mother." She glared at him. "How do you not see? The two people who love me most in the world want me to go through hell so *you* can feel better." She raised her arms as if to implore the heavens to help her explain.

Tom took her in his arms and kissed her forehead.

Indira whispered against his cheek. "I don't want to have pain be the last experience I have. I'm afraid, but I also don't want to dope myself up with so much morphine that I'm a zombie. Because that's the only alternative, isn't it? For *your* peace of mind."

"Do you understand that even if I could bring myself to do it, I might bungle it? If I get the dose wrong, you're left paralyzed and unable to speak, or brain dead and still alive. It's worse than death. Doesn't that prospect terrify you?"

She pulled away from him. "I see what it's like for Anne. It's too much to bear. She's losing her mind, but she still knows she's dying. She's trying to be brave for her children, and it breaks my heart. You don't care what it will cost me to give you another six months or a year of my life."

"Of course, I care. Don't you care about being with me?" He knew it was a trick question and hated himself for asking it. Their whole argument was impossible. They were both right and wrong. Neither would win even if one of them succeeded in convincing the other.

"This isn't about you," she said finally and walked away from him into the house. The dog ran after her.

From the living room, she yelled, "I thought you were the only person who understood. If you can't help me, I don't want you here. I don't want to see you. I can't sleep in the same bed with you." She flipped off the music.

Breath caught in Tom's throat. "Indira, please, please understand. I don't want to leave you. I want to be here with you as long as we have. That could be a long time." He reached out for her, but she backed away and ran to the bedroom. The dog darted after her. The door closed and the lock clicked.

He knocked on the bedroom door. "Indira—"

"Go away!" she shouted. "Leave me alone."

Incensed, Tom grabbed his wallet and keys off the table in the hall, shoved his bare feet into his shoes, and left the house. He could hear his own breathing. His heart slammed against his chest. Everything about this was wrong but he was leaving anyway.

Tomorrow, I'll go back tomorrow, Tom promised himself as he drove down the lane away from the house. There had to be a way to straighten this out.

Chapter 35

The solution for saving the paper came to Anne in the middle of a restless night. She couldn't leave the job to others and, feeling herself failing more each day, it was now or never. The name of the person who could help her came to her mind as she sat up, as if those helpful remaining synapses had been working on the problem all on their own. She scribbled it on the pad next to her bed, left over from when she used to write to-do lists at 3 A.M.

The next morning, she called Molly. "Look for my stack, you know, the cardboard rectangles with people's names on them like small billboards with phone numbers. In my desk drawer."

She heard Molly walk through the office and open a drawer in a desk. The low buzz of people talking in the background made her homesick for the place where she'd spent most of her life. "It'll have a rubber band around it. It's thick."

"The middle drawer? Okay, got them," Molly said. "The business cards, right?"

Anne nodded although Molly couldn't see her. "Find the one for Maple. Lawrence. He owns a bunch of papers. Sorry, the cards aren't alphabetical. I saw him at the Suburban Newspapers conference last year. We were at the same table. He was tall."

She'd met Lawrence Maple at several conferences and shared a drink or two commiserating over the fate of newspapers. He was knowledgeable and calm. She hoped he was ready to buy another publication.

"I'll put you on speaker while I look," Molly said.

The slap of cards against a solid surface sounded deliberately loud as if Molly was slightly annoyed and wanted her to know it. Anne heard Sadie speak and Molly respond, "Not now." She should have remembered it was Wednesday and they were on deadline. Molly would be controlling her stress by intermittently taking deep breaths.

"I'm not paying you enough."

"Okay, found it," Molly said. "Have a pencil? I'll read it to you."

"Oh, wait. I'll get Freddy. I don't do numbers in the right order anymore. They get all mixed up."

Half an hour later, after taking deep breaths of her own, Anne sat in Howard's study and called Lawrence Maple. On the third try, she got the number right. His secretary informed her he had retired, and Keith Maple, his son, was managing the company. Anne squared her shoulders even though the woman couldn't see her and assumed her professional voice—the one that knew what it was doing.

"Please convey my best wishes to Lawrence and ask Keith to call me. I've got an opportunity for him he'll want to consider." She repeated her name, the name of her paper, and her phone number with all the authority she could muster, but she was shaking when she got off the call.

"I've still got it," she announced to Freddy when she shambled back into the kitchen.

Freddy grinned at her and pointed to a plate of Danish on the kitchen table. Her reward for saving the paper. She sat at the table and took a bite.

"I called them," she said around the sweet pastry in her mouth. Anne blotted her mouth with the napkin Freddy handed her.

"Who's them?"

"The Maples. Lawrence Maple. The guy whose telephone number you wrote down for me. He grew his company by buying up small weeklies all over the country as they went bankrupt."

Freddy looked confused.

"Of course, you haven't been following what's happening in the industry."

Freddy grinned. "Well, no."

"So, first the price of paper went through the roof, then the economy went soft, then computers and the internet changed everything, and finally the transition to digital news delivered twenty-four/seven and the social media revolution left many local newspapers in the dust. They couldn't compete with a zillion bytes of information on the worldwide web every second. The news cycle went from daily to hourly to now and now."

"Wow, Mom. I didn't realize it had been so tough. You made it look like anyone could do it."

Anne blushed at the rare compliment from one of her children. "We'll have to wait and see if I did or not. It's possible Maple has bought all the papers he has an appetite for."

Freddy stopped washing dishes and gaped at her. "You mean you're selling the paper?"

Anne nodded. "It's the smart thing to do."

Freddy put an arm around her and kissed the top of her head. The wet warmth from his fingers seeped through her shirt. "You're one tough old bird, Mom. I'm proud of you." For a few seconds, she basked in his admiration.

Two days later, Keith Maple called her back. "Dad says hello, he's glad you called. We *would* like to buy the *Queenscove Journal*."

Anne smiled at the phone. "I always thought your father was a smart guy. He had a good feel for the future of our business." She grimaced at the thought she had inadvertently given away her bargaining position, sucked in her words, and waited to see what happened next.

Keith laid out a process for how the acquisition might go without naming an offer. His voice on the other end of the phone crowded her. She was defenseless; they had the upper hand because they knew her situation. Everyone in the industry must know by now that she had terminal brain cancer. Reporters were notorious gossips. Somehow, she had to protect her legacy. She readied herself for a battle.

"No doubt you've checked my annual revenue, ratings, and online subscribers," Anne said. "We've been doing pretty well. What number did you have in mind?"

Maple's verbal offer astounded her—millions more than she ever expected. Her life's work, her family's life's work, now had a value beyond anything she had imagined. She hadn't done the job day after day for nothing. Instead, she'd built something worth taking into the future.

Struggling to hold in her glee, she told Keith Maple she'd call him back after she conferred with her legal team. She immediately called Sam.

"Could be a scam, Mom," her conservative lawyer son advised.

"I don't think so, honey. I initiated the call."

Sam cleared his throat, and in that sound, Anne heard his worry that she no longer knew what she was doing. Her oldest, smartest son thought she didn't understand what was happening because she had brain cancer, because she was dying. His doubt wiped away everything she'd built, every decision she'd ever made. For a few seconds, she shook with fury.

"I think it's real."

"Okay, Mom. I'll research their other purchases to get an idea if this offer's in the ballpark but let's wait and see what happens. Let them make the next move. See how interested they are."

Minutes later Anne thought she'd dreamed Maple's call. Dreams were now more vivid than her waking life. "Is this a dream or am I awake," she sometimes asked Freddy or Indira. They assured her if she was asking them, she was awake, but she wasn't sure they were right.

Another week passed as slowly as an eternity before she received the formal written proposal for the purchase of the *Queenscove Journal* from Maple Publishing Inc.

Freddy read the proposal to her and faxed the papers to Sam. Sam called twenty minutes later to congratulate her. "Looks like it's real, Mom. You were right. I'll get to work on the details."

"I've done it!" she exclaimed to her sons. "I've really done it."

She gripped Freddy's arm and grinned at him. In the next second, she was weeping inconsolably. He helped her walk out to her chair by the lake and sat with her. A hawk swooped over the lake and off into the trees. She pointed. "Was that a Caspian tern? Did you see that bright red beak?"

She flew aloft like the birds, soaring, and free. And then just as quickly her elation crumbled. She was a failure who had destroyed her family's legacy, giving away four generations of their work to strangers for a few measly dollars.

"I can't stay out here and gawp at the birds, Freddy. I have things to do."

He helped her back into the house and left her in the living room with Indira, who had just arrived. Anne called the paper's local attorney to double check the Maple Company's ability to make good on the offer. Selling the paper was like selling her soul. How could she do that?

"I'm worried I'm being snookered because a portion of my brain is gone and there's a loophole I don't see," she said to Indira.

She must have dreamed the whole thing. Sam's and the lawyer's confirmation aside, this was the worst time to have to understand complicated information. What if the Maples were deliberately taking advantage of her and there was no one to protect her?

"They seem to be good guys, Anne." Indira opened her laptop and pulled up one of the Maple-owned weeklies. "I did some research when you first told me about them. Take a look." She put the computer on Anne's lap and rotated the screen to face her.

Anne scanned the front page of a recent Maple acquisition, dipped into the inside pages, and flipped to the editorials. Their content strategy was as she'd recalled. She hadn't lost all her marbles. They were on the same wavelength as her Journal. They treated local news as important and not as sugar topping on the bad medicine of canned propaganda. Anne was impressed and reassured.

"Looks like they hire local people to run each of the papers," Indira said. "It's not prepackaged news. I googled the editors and staff. Some of them are holdovers from the original papers."

She tilted her head and checked Anne's face for her approval. "I made some calls to various papers to ask how the owners treat reporters and editors. I said I was calling on your behalf, so they'd talk to me. You have a good reputation, by the way. I hope that's okay."

Anne grinned. "Quite enterprising. You should have been a reporter."

"I think that's a compliment," Indira said. "Anyway, the editors say they like their jobs and the publisher doesn't meddle on the news side. I'm not sure what that means, but it sounded good." She opened her arms, palms up.

A goddess was sitting cross-legged on Anne's living room floor talking to her. "I must have already died and gone to heaven."

She hadn't done anything to deserve such a friend. Indira showed up one day for no reason she understood, and Anne now basked in her friendship. Later, or the next day—all days ran together—Anne asked Indira to call Sam and get him to explain how the purchase would work so she could explain it to her.

After their research, they all conferred using a phone conference as if she were back in the office—strong again, smart, and in charge. "Tell them we accept," she said to Sam. "Start the legal stuff going."

She had pulled it off, saved her paper and her employees. Her exhilaration carried her through days of feeling weaker minute by minute. She had the sensation that syllables weren't coming out of her mouth as words, that sentences were a puzzle where the edges of words didn't fit together the way they should.

Entire sections of the world her mind once mapped were missing. There were days she couldn't remember Howard's name and couldn't have said where the living room was. She took to referring to her dead husband as What's-His-Name and every place she wasn't in was now "over there."

With the contract finalized, she convinced Freddy to take her into the newspaper office. She wanted to see the staff's wonderful faces one more time and give them the good news, although she didn't know how they would take it. Change always made people anxious. They might be angry or sad. She shook her head, unable to solve the problem. *They'll have to deal with it.*

Everyone stood at the front of the office as Freddy wheeled Anne in the door. They applauded and greeted her as if she were the Queen of England. She smiled, bowed slightly, and hoped none of them would ask her a question she didn't know the answer to, which, now she thought of it, was how the Queen must feel at public events. Freddy positioned the wheelchair so they could gather around her in the reception area at the front of the office.

She inhaled the paper—old dust of her father's pride, rubber cement residue of midnight mockups, the sour sweat of fact-checking complicated stories at the last hour before the deadline. Like an archaeologist entering an ancient shrine, Anne recalled the office in her grandfather's day when she had imagined it as a dusky cavern with smoky torches fixed to the walls. She'd felt like an explorer among the desks, each lit by its own lamp, piles of newsprint everywhere, red pencils sprouting like bouquets from cups. She could smell her grandfather's pipe. Her throat swelled. *How could I have given this all away?*

The staff gazed at her expectantly. They were as dear to her as her family, and they were sad. Speculation must have run through the ranks with bets on what she was about to do.

Anne wanted to stroke their cheeks and tell them it was going to be all right. *They think I'm going to close the paper. It's worse than that. The paper will stay open and I'm going away.*

Overcome by her feelings, and unable to make the right sounds, she waved the papers from the Maple family. Molly put her hand on Anne's shoulder and took the document. Rolling her chair from behind her desk, she placed it next to Anne's wheelchair. The rest of them found somewhere to perch like birds sitting on different branches of the same tree. Anne smiled at them.

Molly studied the document. "It's good news," she said. She smiled broadly, but tears leaked from her eyes. "Anne's selling the paper to the Maple family. She's not closing us down."

She swallowed hard and flipped through the pages looking for the most important paragraphs. "It's quite generous. We stay in our current positions, at least until they evaluate us. They may appoint a new editor, but it looks like they're guaranteeing our jobs for at least two years. There's health insurance and a 401k with matching contributions for which we're eligible right away."

She focused on each staffer, amazement on her face. "If they're trying to buy our loyalty, they've got mine."

There was a murmur among the staff and Ozzie laughed even though tears streamed down his cheeks. Anne loved the way his face shone when he laughed. There was something in people they never saw themselves, a light that beamed out of them when they were happy or in love, or when they spotted someone they loved or arrived in a place they held dear. That light was pure energy, the constant that ran through everything and connected people to the universe and each other. She couldn't tell anyone this secret. No one would believe her anyway. If she were lucky, she would see that light a few more times.

Sadie leaned forward from her perch on Molly's desk. "Bottom line, the paper stays open and we keep our jobs?"

Molly read the letter again. "Yes. It will take a few months for the acquisition to be put in place. Looks like Anne put the paper in a trust a few years ago to protect it, so there's some legal stuff Sam Morrow, Anne's oldest son, will deal with. But after that, Maple Corp will put their handpicked publisher in here and we'll be their employees."

Sadie hopped off the desk and squatted next to Anne's chair. "I want you to know how much I value your mentorship." She waved her hand toward the other reporters. "We all do, all of us, going back to when you became editor all those eons ago."

Anne laughed. "Eons! Of course." She grinned at Sadie who kissed her cheek and, uncharacteristically red-faced, walked quickly to the kitchen at the back of the office.

Molly took Anne's hand and squeezed it. "Thank you. I knew you wouldn't abandon us." She rested her head against Anne's.

This was what it must be like to have a sister, Anne thought, this sense of complete understanding and solidarity, of sharing the same history. She gripped Molly's hand. "I always loved you."

Molly's astonishment showed on her face. "Me too," she said.

While the staff discussed all possible futures under the new owners of the paper, Anne drifted. The office phone rang. Molly spoke into the receiver, and watching her, Anne remembered another time five years before when Molly had called her on the office intercom.

"Anne, there's a woman here to see you. Do you want to talk to her?"

It had been almost a year since Luke died and Anne was still on automatic—get up, get dressed, go to work, put out the paper, go home, eat, go to bed—but she no longer had to remind herself to breathe. She sighed and looked toward the front of the office, dreading interaction with strangers. They never brought good news.

The tall young woman standing at Molly's desk had hair so dark it was almost purple. A little girl next to her had one arm looped around the woman's leg. The child stared at Anne with huge gray eyes. The woman turned. She was the spitting image of Luke.

A chill swooped through Anne. She swallowed, straightened her back, and strode up to the woman with her hand out. "Anne Morrow."

The woman shook her hand. "Margaret Morrow." Her tone was defiant.

Everyone watched them, some surreptitiously, others openly without embarrassment the way Anne would have done.

"Well, you'd better come back to my office." Anne led the way and closed the door behind them.

Margaret settled in a chair across from Anne and the child poked around the office. Anne opened a desk drawer and pulled out a deck of cards, a small metal car, a box of crayons, and a coloring book left over from when her sons used to visit her in the office. The girl plopped down on the floor and sang a little song as she colored.

Don't get attached to the child, Anne warned herself. "So. Why are you here?"

Margaret crossed her legs and leaned forward. "I'm Howard's daughter." She reached into her backpack, shuffled her hand around, and pulled out an official-looking birth record with a raised seal at the top. "Do you want to see my birth certificate?" Her voice was tense.

Anne ignored the paper Margaret shook in her face and stilled the quaking in her stomach. "There are lots of Morrows in the world. If you say that's your name, it's your name."

Margaret's face glowed red. Her green eyes blazed. "Don't you want proof? Look at the birth certificate."

Anne picked up the paper and handed it back to her. "When you tell me what you want, I'll know whether to believe you or not." She hoped her voice was calm, but the hammering of her heart muffled all sound.

"God, you're as much of a bitch as I was told you would be."

Anne smiled. Lots of people might think she was a bitch. It was a reputation she prized.

"Look, I'm only here because Howard stopped taking my calls," Margaret said. "I need the money he was giving me."

Anne leaned back in her chair and folded her hands. Margaret *was* running some kind of extortion scheme. "What money?"

"For rent, food, electricity, phone. You know. The basics." Margaret glared at Anne as if she should know this already.

"Why don't you go to his office instead of mine?"

"I tried. His admin wouldn't let me in. She threatened to call security." Margaret jumped up from the chair and paced around Anne's office.

Is she dangerous? "Look, Margaret, I can't decide what to do if I don't know what's going on. Sit down and tell me why he was giving you money."

Margaret shot Anne a sullen look that reminded her of Luke. "He gives me money because he's my Dad and he's supposed to support me." She seemed annoyed as if she'd had to explain it many times to many different people and was tired of hearing it herself. "He took care of me until last year, but he stopped all of a sudden. He never said why."

"Perhaps you hadn't heard. Our son Luke died."

"So? What's that got to do with me?"

Anne curled her fingers into her palms. *Stay calm.* "I suspect it has something to do with Howard's state of mind."

"Why should I care about that? I still have to feed my kid."

So, Howard's daughter turned out to be a total narcissist. That's interesting. "How old are you?"

"Thirty-one. What does that have to do with anything?"

Margaret was the same age Luke would have been if he'd lived. Anne rubbed her temples. Howard had had another family, for decades. The idea made her dizzy. *If I'd known about Margaret early on, would I have stayed with Howard? If I hadn't stayed, would Luke have run away?* It was impossible to guess. Her whole life could have been different if she'd known this one fact, if she'd been able to decide what to do about Howard's infidelity.

The child made large red and green circles on the paper.

"Why don't you ask the child's father for money?"

Margaret blushed. "That's none of your business."

A flicker of female solidarity passed through Anne. She ignored it. Margaret was the reason she had lost Luke. Her face turned cold. She wanted this woman to go away and never come back. "There's one way to find out the truth." Anne picked up her phone and called Howard. She put the call on speaker. *No point in having secrets now.*

171

Howard answered in the brusque voice he always used with her. "What is it, Anne?"

"Your daughter, Margaret, is here in my office asking for money. She says you owe it to her."

He coughed. "What? Uh . . . No . . . no." He coughed again and huffed as if he were annoyed at her.

"Dammit, Howard, be a man. Answer me."

"Uhm . . ."

"No, she's not your daughter, or no something else? Howard, are you talking to me or someone else?"

They heard a clatter as if Howard dropped the phone and it hit the floor hard, then a moan, and then nothing.

"Howard? Howard?" Anne raised her eyes to Margaret's face. "I think he hung up."

She disconnected from the call. Later she would wonder why she'd been so calm, why she hadn't screamed at Howard, or worried about his odd response to her question.

Margaret jumped up from the chair. "Well, what are you going to do about it?"

"About what?"

"About me. About how Howard has a daughter and a granddaughter and doesn't give a damn."

"I'm not going to do anything about it. You're *Howard's* problem, not mine. You're not related to me. I have no responsibility for you."

Margaret's eyes widened. Her mouth dropped open. "You bitch. I'll tell your sons. I'll tell everyone."

"Go ahead. Tell anyone you want. Take out an ad. It's twenty-five cents a word." Anne stood, indicating the meeting was over. "This is ridiculous. My seventy-year-old husband cheated on me thirty-plus years ago. How can it matter now?"

Margaret looked as if she intended to leap across the desk and strangle her. For a second Anne worried she'd have to call the troopers to escort the woman out of the office. She opened her office door. "I don't have time for any more of this extortion. You're thirty-one years old, for God's sake. Grow up and get a job."

Margaret took her child by the hand and strode to the front of the building. She opened the door and yelled over her shoulder, "You'll be sorry."

"I'm already sorry."

Anne was gathering up the crayons and coloring book from the floor when Howard's department chair called her cell phone. His voice was so strained, she could barely make out what he was saying.

"Anne, I'm sorry. Howard had a heart attack here in his office. A massive one. We found him on the floor and called emergency services, but . . . I'm so sorry . . ."

After a few seconds, his words broke through the buzzing in her head.

"Anne, can you hear me? Howard died, he's dead."

She couldn't think what she was supposed to do next. "Oh, thank you."

"Anne, who can I call for you?"

She had no answer. The person she would have called to find out what to do next was dead.

Chapter 36

The story Indira was reading to her was so complicated Anne couldn't follow it. She heard the sounds spiraling around her ear, going down, down inside it, but the meaning of each word evaporated to a hum before it reached her brain.

This was happening fairly often now, that she was in two places at once, her body in what everyone else called the real world and her mind adrift somewhere else.

Her tumor was a military outpost in a hot, dry desert. She imagined soldiers squatting atop crumbling mud walls, shooting at anything moving in the distant brush, obliterating everything sound by sound until the world was blank. Indira's words would have been rain on parched earth had they reached her. A small green oasis would have magically sprung from the ground. Anne saw herself lying flat on her stomach, thirsty and exhausted, her face in the water, drinking. She could almost feel the cool liquid on her skin.

Did Luke feel this way before he died—separate from everyone, parched and yearning? She should have gone to find him. That would have made a better story—the noble mother searching the earth for her sick child—instead of the one she'd really lived. There was nothing noble in giving up on him. She'd failed her son and had to live with the consequences for the rest of her life. Regret wound itself around her throat and squeezed.

"My own boy left home."

Indira stopped reading and raised her head. "Who?"

"Luke. He left. But really, we abandoned him first."

Indira put the pages down in her lap. "Tell me about him."

Anne adjusted the blanket over her legs and tried to get comfortable in the wheelchair. She was finally down to a size six and she couldn't even enjoy it. Her bones grated against everything. She leaned her head back and briefly closed her eyes against the glare off the lake. The sun was stronger than it should have been in autumn and at the wrong angle for this time of the afternoon. "This is fall, isn't it?" she asked.

"It's summer."

"*Hmph.* That explains why the sun's in the wrong place."

Indira laughed. "You were going to tell me about Luke."

"Oh, right." Anne decided it was safe to tell her best friend this story even if she'd never spoken about it to anyone else. She only needed to push it out into the world once, like a poisonous flower that blooms once in a lifetime and then dies. She could be brave enough, even if her throat was dry, even though telling it would reveal her worst regret, her selfishness.

"Luke was my fifth son, my baby boy." Her throat cramped.

Grief rampaged through her, but her lips drew themselves taut against her teeth as if she were smiling, and she was angry with herself. "Why do we smile when we want to cry? Who taught us these ridiculous . . . ?" Anne pointed to her face.

"Our mothers," Indira said. "I do it too. It's camouflage, meant to make our behavior acceptable to men, so we don't distress them with our emotions." She took Anne's hand. "So, Luke?"

Anne stared at her knees. "He died. Six years ago, suicide by overdose. Didn't I tell you this before? I thought you knew. I thought everyone knew."

Indira was so quiet Anne glanced up to see if she was there. It wouldn't have surprised her if she were sitting out here alone imagining that Indira was with her. That could happen now with her brain function disintegrating second by second. But no, her friend was here with her, as proved by the stunned look on her face. She squeezed Indira's hand.

Indira shook her head. "I . . . I don't know what to say. I'm so sorry."

"You don't have to say anything. He was troubled and I had no idea how to help him. I always thought he would come home. I imagined him dirty, half-starved, bedraggled, showing up at the door at Thanksgiving and pictured myself welcoming him home, taking care of him, and making him whole again, as if I had some kind of mother magic."

Her lips twisted and she was quiet for a while. "Obviously, that didn't happen. He was far away. Nebraska, of all places, in a town with a population of one-hundred-fourteen people, and even there he was invisible. The least I could have done was to be there with him when he died. But I wasn't. I didn't even know until after."

Indira sat silently, her hands in her lap.

Anne wiped her cheeks with the edge of her shirt. "Regret. That's all I have left."

The look of trust Luke used to give her when he was a four, his smile, that little spark in his eye when he tricked her, how his lips curled into a smile at her surprise.

"Tell me about him," Indira said. "Tell me about regret." She leaned forward to listen.

"He robbed us and took off in my car, and I watched him go, feeling completely helpless. It was a perfect June day, everything in bloom, the sun shining, the air still slightly cool. I called Howard to tell him what had happened, but he refused to do anything.

"The next day, I rented a car and drove through town, going up and down every street, every alley, parking lot, and town park and then all the rural routes thinking I'd spot him slumped against a wall or on a bench. At each turn, my heart twisted again until I was coiled so tightly I could barely speak. No one was camping on the mountain, the park police said. He hadn't been picked up for vagrancy or intoxication in any of the nearby towns. In Burlington, I searched unfamiliar streets, hoping to catch sight of him in an alley or crouched in a doorway. He wasn't anywhere. It felt like someone was scouring out my insides with steel wool."

After a minute of silence, Indira asked, "What happened next?"

"I hired a private detective using the paper's account. We sometimes hired one for background checks, so I knew a guy. I didn't tell Howard. He would've freaked out and told me I was overreacting. The PI found my car in a Detroit impound lot, completely bashed up as if Luke had gotten plastered, driven the car off a bridge, and flipped five times. The detective found no trace of Luke anywhere. No John Doe in the morgue matched his image. I lived with the idea that he had died for years before he did."

Anne opened her eyes and glanced at Indira. Her friend shook her head slowly. "Oh, God, Anne. What anguish to carry." She put both her hands against her chest.

They sat there at the edge of the lake for a while and watched light reflect off water.

"He was missing for thirteen years, and then he left a note," Anne said so quietly, Indira had to bend closer to hear her.

"It was written in pencil on the back of a restaurant receipt he left in his motel room. It said: *To Anne Morrow, Queenscove, Vermont. It's not you, Mom. You did everything you could. It's not your fault. I love you. Luke.*"

Anne held her face up for the sun to warm and let the memory envelop her. Captain Palmer, the state trooper assigned to Queenscove, had come to the house to inform her Luke was dead. He'd held out the note. His hand was so steady she could make out Luke's backward scrawl through the transparent plastic bag that encased it.

She clasped the baggy with the paper inside it between two fingers and turned it over four times. Dated March 11, 2011, the receipt showed that someone ordered fried chitlins and an iced tea for $6.95 plus tax.

At first, Anne pretended she didn't understand why Palmer handed her the restaurant receipt. "What is this? It doesn't make any sense. What does someone eating chitlins have to do with me?" But she knew as soon as she saw the officer at her door.

Palmer explained that the date stamp on the receipt gave the police a reference for when the death occurred, and the La Platte, Nebraska sheriff who found Luke's body had faxed a copy of both sides of the receipt to him at the Queenscove state police office.

He didn't tell her that Luke barricaded himself inside his motel room, that the local sheriff found her son in the bathtub, wrapped in the shower curtain, the needle still in his vein, and the mess of him neatly contained so it could be cleaned away with the least possible contamination. She learned all those details later from the police report she asked Molly to get, the report she wished she'd never seen, the images forever incised in her brain.

Anne put her hand on the trooper's chest and pushed him away. Palmer held out the faxed copy of Luke's long-expired Vermont driver's license and a photo of the body that the sheriff sent him. She jerked her face away so she wouldn't see it.

"You have the wrong kid," she told Palmer. That ruined face could not be her son's. "Someone stole his wallet. This is someone else's kid."

Looming up behind Anne, Howard interceded, holding out his hand for the morgue photo. He stared at Luke's gray face for a minute. Light blinked off the lake, and he put a shaking hand over his eyes. "What do you need us to do, officer?"

Anne stopped listening to them. She wandered outside, down to the lake to the view that always saved her. She wanted to crumple the note in her hand and throw it against the wall. She wanted to frame it and hang it over her bed. She wanted to light it on fire and run screaming in counterclockwise circles around the house to turn back time. She wished she were superwoman and that she had saved her son, but she was a failure and had let him go out into the world alone with no armor, no special powers, and no one to comfort him.

It's not you, Mom.

If it wasn't her, who was it who gave him permission to surrender? For a week after the notification, she walked through every room in her house yelling, "Why? Why? Why?" She sobbed in her sleep.

The day after his body came home—shipped in a plane like cargo and picked up by the funeral home—Anne stood by his coffin in the viewing room for four hours, numb and deaf to anything anyone said to her.

When she succumbed to wild weeping at two in the morning the day of the funeral, Howard tried to console her in his own way. He grabbed her by the shoulders and shook her until she stopped howling. "He had enough, Anne, he had enough."

"Enough what? Enough life? Can someone have enough life? You're his father. How can you say that?"

Howard closed his eyes and shook his head. "Do you think this is easy? Do you think I'm not suffering? That I haven't been suffering all this time? Life was torture for him. His way of living, his pain was killing me. Not the humiliation. I got over that a long time ago. The waste, that's what I couldn't stand. Didn't you see that? How could you not know?"

Shaking off her husband, Anne walked out of the house in her pajamas and wandered down to the edge of the lake. She checked to make sure the moon was in the right place as if everything in the universe would now be askew. Clutching a memory of her son's tiny hand in hers as they crossed the street, she remembered she once knew how to keep him safe. It used to be as automatic as breathing.

Howard followed her outside, wrapped her in a blanket, and secured her with his arms. "He was suffering, Anne," he said into her hair. "There were no veins left where he could insert a needle. He had daily hemorrhages from snorting anything he could crush into powder. God knows what hellish diseases infected him. Hep-C, TB, HIV, the whole fucking alphabet soup of killer illnesses. He had to steal, deal, or prostitute himself to pay for his habit. He had no friends left to borrow from. You know this. He was thirty years old, and he couldn't bear living like that anymore."

She struggled to free herself from Howard's arms. "How do *you* know this?"

"He told me."

"When?"

"On the phone two weeks ago."

Anne whipped around and faced her husband. "Luke called you and you didn't tell me? You didn't put me on the phone?" Rage blew through her. Her fists pummeled Howard's head and face. She howled. He grabbed her wrists and held her still.

"He called me at the office, collect. I let him talk. He needed to talk. I needed to hear what he had to say."

"Now you're paying attention. When it's too fucking late."

He whispered, "Thirteen years, Anne, he tried for thirteen years. He didn't want to inflict this nightmare on us, or on himself, anymore. Imagine the courage it took to end his life."

Anne flung herself away from him and yelled, "Are you mad? You call this courage? We gave up on him, so he gave up on himself."

She screamed until her voice was gone. Howard, astounded, let her be. She lay on the ground and pounded the earth with her fists. "Please God, please, don't let this be real," she prayed. "Let me wake up from this nightmare."

At the funeral, Anne was calm until the end. At the grave, as the casket was lowered into the ground she sank onto her knees and sobbed. For days all she could say was, "I'm sorry, I'm sorry, I'm sorry." And then for months, she couldn't speak at all.

Anne turned her face to Indira. "It wasn't my fault. He said so."

She put her hand on her chest where the pain of Luke's death had lodged all these years. Her palm rubbed against the smooth fabric of her shirt. The weight she'd become accustomed to carrying was gone, and in its place there was nothing.

For a minute she breathed deeply, as if her lungs needed to assess their new ability, then she squeezed Indira's hand. "Thank you for being here, for asking me to tell the story, for listening. It had to be you. I couldn't have told it to anyone else."

Indira rose from her seat and wrapped her arms around her friend.

Chapter 37

Freddy spotted Laura as she came in the door of the deli. He tried to conceal himself behind a stack of postcards in the cashier line hoping she wouldn't recognize her husband of twenty years if his back were to her. He held his breath and turned his face away. She spotted him anyway.

"Hey," Laura said, poking his arm with her finger. "I have something to tell you."

Freddy focused on the cashier. "I've got to get this."

He fumbled with the cash in his wallet, paid the tab, and picked up the bag. In it were all the weird things his mother and Marie wanted for lunch—avocado salad, Waldorf salad, tortellini salad, a spinach quiche—specialties the woman behind the counter hadn't even blinked about his ordering plus his normal roast beef sandwich on country white bread with coleslaw and chips. He walked out the door without saying anything to Laura.

Laura traipsed out of the store behind him and walked to his truck. The skin on the side of his body closest to her burned. He planned to ignore her for as long as possible. He planned to escape without exchanging a single word with her.

Laura put her hand on the door of his truck when he opened it. He wasn't going to get away from her without hearing whatever hateful thing was about to fly out of her mouth. He watched her lips. It astounded him now that he had once wanted to cover them with his own, to suck her bottom lip into his mouth, to lick her teeth. He gagged.

Sliding around her, Freddy put the deli bag on the passenger seat. "Didn't you have to get food?"

"No. I was looking for you."

She was standing so close he could smell her breath. "You're drunk." He climbed into the cab. "Don't you have better things to do than go looking for me, like make strings of paper cutouts for your class?"

Laura planted her hands on her hips, threw her head back, and laughed. "It's summer. No classes. I came to find you to tell you he's coming here." Her voice sounded like she was saying she was now president of the world.

"Who's coming here? A lawyer? Thank God."

"No, dummy. Your mother's lover, Colin McDowell."

He grabbed the armrest to pull the door shut. "What the fuck are you talking about?"

Laura did her little nasty jig. "He knows he's not your father."

"You're not telling me anything I don't know. Go away. Get a divorce." He could barely restrain his annoyance. He used to be wildly in love with this woman. Once upon a time, he couldn't stop touching her, thinking about her. *Mom knew she was wrong for me. Why didn't I listen to her?*

Laura glared at him and flipped her hair. "That's the thing. How does he know he's not your father unless he and your mother saw each other after the affair ended?"

Freddy started the engine. "So what? What difference does that make? Where the hell are you going with this? It has nothing to do with you."

Laura stepped back, away from the truck. "Oh, you'll care all right. I'll make sure of that."

He put the truck in gear. "There's no mystery here and you're no Nancy Drew. Leave it alone. We don't care what you find out."

Laura put her hands on her hips and raised her chin. "Anyway, I know about your girlfriend."

"What the hell? What girlfriend?"

"Keep up Freddy. You were always a little slow. I'm talking about that Indian woman, the professor. It's all over town about you and her."

Freddy shook his head. "You're out of your mind. They shouldn't let you near children."

Laura paled. "You'll be sorry."

Freddy jammed his foot on the gas and his tires skidded on the parking lot gravel. It took all his self-control not to run her over. He tuned Clutch Radio in on the truck's Bluetooth and punched up the volume. They were playing his song and the sound obliterated Laura.

Chapter 38

Laura drove up the lane slowly, trying to imagine the people who lived in this mid-century modern breadbox—long, low-slung, and opaque. Narrow casement windows marched across the front of the house. How did they get enough air inside to breathe? At least the skylights spaced at regular intervals along the roof gave them daylight.

Laura had bolstered herself for this encounter with a drink before she left home but took another sip from her flask to make sure she would remain calm for what she expected would be a heated encounter. She parked her ten-year-old gray Honda CRV in front of the two-car garage and walked up the slate steps to the front door. The woods surrounding the house were various shades of green. Birds chirped from every tree. The GPS map on her phone showed this property backed to the lake but it wasn't visible from where she stood.

She rang the bell and waited. When no one came to the door within the ten seconds she allotted for a polite response, Laura opened it. "Hello," she called out. "Anyone home?"

She listened. Silence. Outside a dog barked. Laura walked up five shining wood steps and found herself in a great room. Everything in the room surprised her beginning with the wall of windows facing the lake at the back of the house.

Light streamed in, making the space glow. The fireplace was set in a white stone hearth. Modern teal chairs and purple silk pillows popped against an oatmeal-colored L-shaped sofa. Large, brightly hued paintings occupied strategic walls. This home was as different from her own as caviar was from hotdogs. She had misunderstood who Indira was. Whatever did the woman see in Freddy?

A glass door on the back deck slid open and Laura heard a soft, low voice say, "Can I help you?" A dog bolted across the room and circled her, sniffing her feet.

Indira was wearing jeans and a white shirt with the sleeves rolled up. Even with her dark hair twisted up in a hasty bun on top of her head, she still managed to look magnificent. She squinted at Laura as if she were trying to place her and then smiled broadly. "Oh, I remember you. From the almost accident."

"Yes. I . . ." Laura swallowed. She understood now what had seduced Freddy. He loved this woman's beauty. Her sudden knowledge made her tongue-tied. "Yeah, well. That was before. I want to talk to you about Freddy, because . . ." She shrugged, giving up on anything she planned to say.

She could see now that Indira was her opposite. Where she had chosen homey, a place where a child would feel comfortable and a man could put his feet up, Indira preferred elegance. And yet here she was with no husband and no child, and this woman, not content with the life she had chosen, was stealing her husband, taking what she was meant to have. That was totally unfair.

Indira walked into the kitchen to the left of the dining area and pushed up the faucet handle with her wrist. She ran her hands under the water, squirted her palm with soap, and scrubbed her hands. "You're *Freddy's* Laura."

Laura nodded, watching her. Freddy was at the point in life when men decided they needed a younger model of the same woman they'd married years before or someone exotic who got their flagging blood pulsing. Laura had seen it happen: out of the blue, the husband would announce the marriage was over and abandon his wife who'd be left to carry on as if nothing had happened. Exactly that state of affairs left her principal flabbergasted for a year.

"I was putting in herbs in the garden." Indira dried her hands. "I hope I haven't done it too soon, or too late. This is my first garden ever."

"Oh, they'll survive. Almost anything grows in this season."

Indira held up a brightly colored mug. "Do you want some tea? I have some delicious walnut and cranberry bread from the bakery. I was going to have some."

Laura gaped at Indira in amazement. Freddy was obviously in love with this woman. He had discarded his wife of twenty years like she was yesterday's fast-food wrapper. She knew it even if he didn't. Indira must have knocked him out of his neutral emotional gear and made him remember how to be passionate. She was determined to rectify that situation. Even if she didn't want him anymore, Indira couldn't have him. He was still hers, and she still had a say in what happened.

"I came here to tell you to stay away from Freddy and you're offering me tea? I don't get you."

"There's nothing to get. Freddy and I are friends." Indira flipped the switch on the stainless-steel electric kettle and set a yellow ceramic teapot next to it. "We take care of Anne, each of us in our own way, and that's made us care about each other." She scrutinized Laura's face. "We're not romantic."

Exasperated, Laura threw her arms out. "But . . . but he's bananas about you. It's all over town. Everyone knows."

Indira pulled the bread out of a stainless-steel breadbox and sliced off four pieces. The sound of the knife crunching through the crust and the sweet smell of yeast and sugar would not placate Laura. She was determined to be angry, to demand capitulation from this interloper.

"Freddy's in pain because his mother is dying. He would be infatuated with anyone who was kind to him." Indira put the sliced bread on a hand-painted plate and brought it to the dining table. She glanced at Laura over her shoulder. "Sit," she said, and the dog sat.

Laura complied also, sitting in the chair Indira pointed to, and admired the view of the lake from the table. Indira brought over the yellow teapot and placed it on a tile trivet emblazoned with the image of a pink lily in full bloom. So many colors. Laura's head swam.

Indira handed her a purple mug and held up a yellow pot of honey with its own spoon. "Do you take milk?"

Laura nodded. No one besides her mother had been this kind to her in ages. This woman made no sense at all. Didn't she understand what was supposed to happen here? Her accusation should have humiliated or at least cowed her. Why hadn't she thrown her out? She must have brain cancer, like Anne. That must be why they were friends. Freddy said he didn't know how they became friends. Indira had simply shown up at the house one day.

"Where did you meet Anne?"

Indira spooned honey into her cup and stirred. "At the beach. She saved my life."

Laura choked on her tea. She had enough of this goody-two-shoes routine. Anne had never saved anyone's life. She couldn't imagine Anne putting herself out long enough to cross a playground to pick up a child who'd fallen off a swing. She closed her eyes and took another sip of her tea. The warm liquid eased down her throat, soothing her. "What kind of tea is this?"

"Peppermint. Good for indigestion."

"What do you mean she saved your life?"

"I thought I wanted to die." Indira spread cream cheese on a slice of bread. "I hesitated. She stopped me." She bit into the bread and chewed.

Laura shook her head. "That doesn't sound like the Anne I know."

"You don't know her."

Laura put her cup down and pushed away from the table. "I don't believe you. This is some kind of trick you and Freddy dreamed up." She stood, put her hands flat on the table, and leaned toward Indira. "Stay away from him. He's still my husband."

Indira put her hands on the table. "I will do whatever I need to do to help Anne, but you should be clear. I have no designs on your husband. He's a free man. He can do whatever works for him."

The nerve of this woman who barely knew Freddy telling her what to do. She wanted to slap Indira across her lovely face. Instead, she controlled herself, pivoted, and walked out of the house.

By the time she got to her car, her chest was heaving. Sobs started when she put the key in the ignition. She didn't even know why she was crying unless it was because she was so angry. After all, she had wasted twenty years and gotten nothing for it, because she had never been as close to her husband or Anne as this stranger managed to achieve in less than a year.

No revenge, no matter how big the blast, would change that. Laura drove home blinded by tears.

Chapter 39

Each day Indira brought Freddy his favorite bear claw pastry from the bakery. She walked outside the house and cut flowers from the many beds on the property, arranging them in colorful displays she put in every room. She sat with him for coffee and told him about the new novel she was conjuring. He imagined her as a magician chanting a spell to call a story out of thin air.

When he asked her about this, she smiled at him. "That's exactly how it feels, like magic. Very apt."

Despite everything happening with his mother, Indira's comment made Freddy's year. The person whose regard he most craved thought he was smart; his words were apt. Life couldn't get much better.

Then he recollected his mother was dying right in front of him and felt chagrined. Life, he thought, was too complicated for an average guy like him to understand. He couldn't keep his emotions straight: glad when he should be sad and proud when he should be humble.

As summer rounded the bend toward fall, Freddy decided he had to speak to Indira. If Laura was right and Indira wanted to be his girlfriend even though she never gave him any sign of that, he needed to say something. Her life was also upside down. His mother told him recently about Indira's cancer, how sneaky it was, how even though she appeared perfectly healthy, the cancer hid in her body and let her pretend she was fine.

He became convinced his love would save her, that being with him could heal her. He thought about it all the time. *If she loves me back . . .* He was like a teenager, one minute exhilarated, sure the best of life was ahead of him and he knew what he was doing, and the next minute scoured out by bitterness and confusion. He had to talk to Indira.

While his mother napped, they sat outside on the flagstone patio facing the lake, a view Anne and Indira never tired of, and sipped their tea. "I know it must feel a little crowded with Sam's wife, Marie, in the house," Freddy explained, "but you should keep visiting because Mom always feels better after your visits."

She nodded. "Of course, I will. I like Marie."

He put his hand on hers where it rested on the arm of the chair. "I like your visits too."

"Oh." Indira sighed and shifted in her seat. She squeezed his hand and withdrew hers. "You're a wonderful man, Freddy. I can see that in how you care for Anne, and in the way she looks at you." She smiled.

Freddy took both her hands. "You're so beautiful, inside and out. Everything you do is beautiful. Life is short. I just want to be with you. We shouldn't waste any time." He wanted to kiss her. He leaned closer. If she kissed him, he would have a future.

She leaned away. "Freddy. I don't feel . . . Not that way."

He paled, dropped her hands, and stared down at his knees, feeling like an idiot. His face flamed. He stumbled to the edge of the lake, his back to her. He was such a fool, thinking this amazing woman would reciprocate his feelings. If only he could turn instantly invisible. He couldn't look at her.

Indira walked up beside him. Light pinged off small waves. Multi-colored sails billowed over the water. "This thing we're going through, watching your mother die, all these emotions losing someone we love brings up, it upsets everything," she said.

Freddy nodded because there was nothing else to do and he couldn't speak yet.

"We're afraid we'll drown in our grief. We want to latch onto something solid we think will save us, to give our lives meaning. We know love will save us and so we look around for someone to love."

Freddy glanced down at her without saying anything.

Indira lifted her face to his. A breeze blew wisps of her shining hair around her head. If only he could take her face in his hands and kiss her.

"I have Tom," she said. "He's my life preserver, even if he doesn't know it. I would never betray him."

She was so clear Freddy had no choice but to accept what she said. He wasn't her life preserver. She wasn't rejecting him; she was clarifying her feelings. Bottom line, he'd lose his mother, and this woman would go out of his life. He felt caught in a landslide, suffocated by the mud.

He shook his head. "I thought you . . . You've been so kind to Mom, to both of us. I misunderstood. I'm sorry if I upset you."

"You didn't upset me. You've given me the most wonderful compliment. You think I'm worthy of your devotion. I'm honored." She put a hand on his arm and walked back to the house.

He wanted to grab her and embrace her, if only once, but her faithfulness was a wall he wouldn't breach. He watched her step across the lawn and open the door from the patio to the house. If she looked back, he thought, there was a chance for him. He held his breath, but she didn't look back.

* * *

Anne slipped past the patio doors, sneaking a peek outside at Freddy and Indira engrossed in a conversation, their backs to her. Her guardians were distracted. She was free! Glee raced through her body. She scooted through the house, grabbed her walking stick, and went out the kitchen door, bumping into the door frame on both sides as she struggled to figure out how to put her foot down on the step. She rubbed her arms.

"Cost of doing business," she muttered and stumbled forward across the grass to the shed.

Pushing the shed door open took all her ingenuity and strength but finally, it sprang apart. Inside it was as dark as a cave. She waited for her one eye to adjust. Dust motes danced in the shaft of light coming through the open door. Anne inhaled deeply and held the air in her lungs.

"That's our history, that smell." She grinned. Talking to herself was the best way to move her thoughts along. The sound of her voice kept her mind from scurrying off to some other topic.

"The riding mower." That's what she came for. The key was in the ignition. "Oh, Lord, how laziness does make theft easy."

What on earth are you doing?

"Shut up, What's-Your-Name. This is none of your business."

She scrambled up onto the seat and started the motor. Happy to find the mower had at least enough gas to start, Anne scooted up on the seat, jiggled the shift into reverse, and backed out of the shed. What a gift freedom was. Exhilaration was like champagne bubbling in her mouth. She needed to get away quickly before someone stopped her.

Anne gripped the steering wheel in both hands and putted down the driveway out to the street. The power of moving on her own, of seeing her neighborhood instead of the inside of her house, and the fresh air all enthralled her. She headed for the beach to take care of business.

The mower moved slowly, and Anne didn't feel disoriented the way she did in the car. She could keep track of things as she passed them. Nothing whizzed by her. She waved to Jim Stewart, who stood on his lawn with his mouth open and his hand half-raised as if he'd forgotten how to say hello. There was the Whitman farm, with all the sheep huddled together on the hillside munching the green grass. In the other direction, she saw Sally bundling her children into the car. Why hadn't she done this before? This was the way to get around.

She drove up onto the pedestrian path she always took to the beach and leaned her head back to watch the leaves above her. The sun planted patches of warmth on her face. She breathed in deeply. "Is this spring?" She searched the undergrowth along the path. Black-eyed Susan buds popped up everywhere and sunlight penetrated through the trees. "Huh. Must be summer. How'd that happen? I lost a season."

At the wooden bridge that led to the cove's beach, she stopped. The width was too narrow for the mower. Anne veered off to the left and back onto the road to get to the gravel parking lot above the lake. She pulled up to the gray, weathered log marking the lot boundary and pondered whether to leave the key in the ignition. Some teenager might take the mower for a ride and Freddy would never find it. She shrugged and laughed at herself. "Who cares?"

Anne stood at the top of the stairs and contemplated her descent. The drop seemed interminable. Her heart pounded. It was like stepping into a black hole. She drew back. Sticking her foot out into space terrified her.

"Where's your grit, girl?" she scolded herself.

Tucking her walking sticks under her arm, she gripped the railing, turned her body sideways so she could hold on with both hands and wouldn't see how steep the drop was, held her breath, and lowered her left foot. When it touched the next wood step below, relief flooded through her. She brought her other foot down to meet it.

"Good girl," she told herself, "you can do this."

By the time she reached the bottom step, Anne had sweated through her shirt. She sighed deeply. "At least I won't have to go back up." The water slurped gently against the shore, and she admired it for a while. "Blue all the way to the horizon."

Anne listened for whatever birds might be out this time of day. One was chirping but she couldn't remember the name of the bird. "That's okay," she consoled herself, "you don't have to know it." Forgiving herself, not having to be right, was such a luxury.

By the time she got to the water's edge, Anne was exhausted and weeping in frustration. Every stone on the beach meant to deliberately thwart her. She would never make it, but she had to keep going. This was the only way to lock up her deepest secret before she inadvertently mumbled it in her sleep. The lake beckoned, its blue deepening farther out, and she walked into the water. It slipped over her shins like silk socks. She was so tired, she wanted to lie down in it, to sink into the soft watery bed, and sleep forever. Holding her arms out away from her body, Anne inched deeper and deeper into the lake until her fingers trailed in the water.

A minute after going in the house, Indira came racing out, yelling. "Freddy, Freddy, she's not in the house. She's not in the house!"

Freddy ran to her and gripped her arms. "Slow down. Tell me."

"I went to say goodbye to her, but she wasn't in her room or the kitchen. I ran upstairs to see if she'd wandered up there, but she wasn't there either. Her walking sticks are gone from the corner near the kitchen door. Would she have gone out on her own?"

"Did she take the car?" he yelled as he ran into the house.

"I didn't look." Indira ran after him, through the house and out the kitchen door to the driveway.

Two cars and Freddy's truck were in the drive. "She's on foot," he said, his face grim, voice breathless. "You take Shore Road. I'll head into town. She thinks she's going to the paper. We'll find her."

191

Indira drove slowly along Shore Road, scanning both sides of the street, panic lodged in her throat. Sunlight shot between trees on the wooded lots, striping a white barcode onto the black asphalt in front of her. *We never should have left her alone. I should have known better.*

A kid passed her on his bicycle, standing on the pedals, light blinking off his red helmet. Random thoughts clicked together in Indira's brain. Anne wouldn't have come this way. *She went to the beach, the one where we first saw each other.* She would have taken her customary route.

Indira made a U-turn and sped past the stop sign, made a right, and headed for the beach parking lot. Anne would have avoided roads, using the pedestrian path to the cove. Indira pulled into the graveled parking lot, her tires spitting pea gravel as she skidded to a stop next to a riding mower parked nearby with the key in the ignition. Indira leaped out of the car, forgetting to turn it off, and flew down the steps to the beach.

Anne was already in the water, up to her waist. Small waves from the wake of a boat swooping through the cove jostled against her, and she swayed from side to side. She used her walking stick to steady herself. In a few steps, she would reach the point where the lake suddenly deepened. Indira pulled off her shoes and scarf and splashed into the lake.

"Anne, Anne, I'm here," she yelled. "Turn around. Walk to me."

The water dragged at her clothes, slowing her, pushing her back. Her heart was in her throat. She wouldn't make it in time. "Stop. Wait." Anne didn't seem to hear her. The water inched up her body.

What had Anne said to her that day on the beach? Those were the magic words. "It's a beautiful day out here, isn't it?" Indira called out.

Anne turned slowly and stared at her. Indira was within arm's reach. Another three feet and she grabbed Anne's hand and pulled her toward safety. "You know it's dangerous out here, don't you?"

"Do I know you?" Anne asked. "Are you my daughter?"

Indira slipped her arm around Anne's waist and half carried her toward the shore. "Yes, you know me. I'm your friend. I'm Indira, the one who reads to you."

When they reached the beach, Indira sighed with relief. Anne shivered and gazed around. "I remember now. Didn't I save you?"

Indira closed her eyes. "Yes. Yes, you did. You saved me." She wrapped her scarf around Anne's shoulders.

They picked their way across the stone-strewn beach to the steps and slowly climbed them. By the time they reached the car, Anne seemed to be herself again. She dropped onto the passenger seat. Indira tucked the blanket she always kept in the car around her friend and turned on the heat.

"Sorry to put you to all this trouble," Anne said, looking at Indira. She laughed ruefully. "I'm not sure what got into me."

Indira shook her head. "It's no trouble."

She picked up her phone and called Freddy. "I've got her. She's okay. She drove the mower. We're coming home right now." She heard Freddy sob before she clicked off. She imagined him covering his face with his large hands.

"Do you remember leaving the house?"

"Sure. I recall thinking this cancer was a fucked-up way to go. I was going to be a lot of trouble for the kids, and I shouldn't put them through all that shit. Everything was clear. I thought this would be easier, just leaving it all behind. But when I got out in the lake, I got confused. I couldn't figure out which way was the right way to go."

Indira kissed Anne's cheek and smiled. "Going home is the right way to go. We have a pact, remember? We're in this together. I'm supposed to go before you. Not the other way around. I'm not ready for you to leave."

She didn't add what she was thinking. *Not ever.* Her throat ached for days after with words she didn't say.

Chapter 40

Tom rolled over on the narrow cot in the bedroom they kept ready at the veterinary facility for nights when they needed to keep a close watch on a patient after surgery. He'd been living in this room for a week. *I might as well be in prison.*

Through the open window, he heard horses snorting and the low moan of a quarantined cow. In the moonlight, he made out his clothes on wall hooks by the door, his work boots placed below them, the hairbrush, and personal sundries he'd bought in a rush of irritation all laid out in a row on the table on the opposite wall.

My wife would rather die than be with me.

This version of what they'd said to each other made it possible for him to resist calling or texting her, kept him from driving by the house to see if she was okay. She had rejected him. She didn't want him to be around her. If anything happened to her, someone would call him. She had friends. Someone in the Morrow clan would check on her if she didn't show up for her daily devotions to their matriarch.

Bitterness will be all I have left if she dies without me beside her. Tom rotated to face the wall.

Everything about Indira's relationship with the Morrows puzzled him. He didn't even know those people. Their families had never been friends. How did his wife become so enmeshed in their lives? It was a symptom of her unwise decision making, of her panic over her diagnosis.

The Morrows were to blame for her certainty about taking her own life. No one in his family or hers, for that matter, would ever support such an idea. The answer to her question—the answer he couldn't say—was simple: no animal would wish for or plan its death. Death wasn't a choice.

He sat up in the bed and threw the blanket off his legs. It was clear he wasn't going to sleep anymore. He wasn't getting much sleep, anyway. The days were interminably long, and he dragged himself from farm to farm, not even noticing the road, the weather, and how nature conspired to mock his misery with day after perfect day. His actions were automatic, reading the animals' physical symptoms through his hands as if noting data on a screen.

He must look as wrecked as he felt. Staff asked every day if he was ill, and he was sure everyone talked about him behind his back. It made him angrier that the wake of his wife's wrong-headedness destroyed the calm equilibrium of his work.

"What the hell's going on?" Bruce asked him yesterday before he left the clinic for the day. "You're like a zombie and you never go home. This can't be about your Dad."

Tom waved his hand as if the gesture was an answer.

His uncle didn't give up easily. He put his huge paw on Tom's shoulder. "Look, kid, I know you've got some tough stuff going on, but staying here, moping, not talking to your wife—that's wrong. You're her husband. Toughen up. Take care of her."

"Jesus, Bruce, what the hell do you know about it?"

Bruce chuckled. "I know fuck all about your specific situation, my boy, but I do know life is a bitch and you can't hide from it. Being with someone you love, particularly someone who's going through hell, is better than not being with them. For both of you."

Tom had pressed his lips together, refrained from responding, and walked away. Bruce's wife was healthy. He had kids. He knew nothing.

Tom pulled on his jeans, a shirt, socks, and slid his feet into his boots. Walking through the darkened building to his office, it hit him. This was exactly what his life would be like after Indira died: empty, dark, quiet, and pointless.

He had to fix this. He couldn't mope around feeling sorry for himself, waiting for deliverance by some unknown divinity. He was the only one who could solve the problem, the one who could find his way back to his wife, to the feeling they lived in the same place and time, to being part of a partnership that mattered. But first, he had to take care of what had been in his way, all the indignation and angst about his father. He couldn't spend the rest of his life feeling humiliated. It was past time to confront him.

The entrance to the Northwest State Correctional Facility in Swanton appeared normal enough, complete with double rows of barbed wire topping a high fence. It took Tom an hour to drive there but when he arrived, the town made him feel like he'd never left Queenscove.

To undo the weird sense of being in a dream, he reminded himself that all the old towns situated near Lake Champlain had the same look—the brick buildings in the town center, the white steeple of a church, the village green, the smells of farms and open country around the town, a tractor on the side of the road with a "for sale" sign on it, and the deep smell of organic decay from a river emptying into the lake.

The prison itself, not pictured on the town website, could have been in any prison movie ever made. The tidy parking lot did not indicate that every kind of venal criminal was locked up behind those gates waiting for a more permanent cot elsewhere in the system. His father had been waiting for over a year. It appeared he might serve out his entire sentence in Northwest while he waited.

Does it matter where you are when you'd left everything behind in disgrace?

Tom took several deep breaths to calm down before he got out of his truck. He had called in advance to find out the rules, to make sure he could visit his father. Now he wished he'd never hatched this ludicrous idea, never driven out here. He vaguely hoped his father had transformed into a wise old man who could utter magic words that would unlock his misery and set him free. He laughed at the absurdity of his wish. *Only children think that way. Time to grow up.*

Tom slid out of the driver's seat and locked the truck in compliance with a posted sign saying the facility wasn't responsible for items left in cars. He hadn't told his mother or uncle he was coming here. He didn't want them to warn him off.

As far as he knew, no one in the family had seen his father since he'd entered prison. The words exile, outcast, and shunned rose in his mind like moths flitting around a light. Tom batted them away. His father had betrayed the family. The state said he was guilty, and a jury agreed. Who was Tom to question that decision?

In the visitor's lobby, Tom showed his ID, signed in, and put his jacket, wallet, phone, keys, pen, spare change, and any other flotsam from his pockets in a small locker. Waiting in line with the other visitors to go through the metal detector, he examined their faces. Mostly what he saw in them was despair, visible in the way they stood, the slouch of their shoulders, how their eyes were set in the middle distance, never meeting anyone else's. Everyone here had abandoned hope. Visitors, as much victims as anyone, were at the prison out of duty, or heartache, or a hidden desire for retribution, to say "I told you so."

Why am I here?

On the other side of a room fronted by a window on the visitor's side, long blonde wood tables divided the space. A wooden bumper in the middle of each table made it clear visitors could not touch the prisoners. Convicts sat on one side of the table, visitors on the other. This was the Tuesday, 9 A.M. visitation period.

His hand stamped, Tom waited for the guard to tell him he could enter. His face burned—an allergic reaction to following commands. Never mind the violations of basic privacy. To have someone tell you every day, every minute, what you could do and not do, to be under constant watch, was surely a punishment. Especially after you'd been king of the world, at least in their small county.

"Go ahead, Mr. Beale," the guard said tonelessly. He didn't get the honorific "doctor" here.

Tom sat where the guard said to sit and waited.

An elderly man came through the door opposite the one he'd entered. The man wore a white t-shirt outside his gray sweatpants and shuffled into the room in gray plastic slippers. Until the man sat down opposite him, Tom was unsure who he was. This couldn't be his father. There'd been a mix-up. They sent out the wrong inmate.

But the old man's eyes were his father's. He'd aged fifty years in two. Tom stared into his future.

"Hi, Tom. Good to see you, son. What are you doing out here?"

"I came to talk to you." He couldn't stop the testiness in his voice. Anger was his only defense against an onslaught of pity.

His father responded to what he didn't say. "I'm not guilty. I was framed. Friends are asking the governor to give me a pardon."

"Don't you all say that?"

His father groaned, leaned back in his chair, and folded his arms across his chest. He'd lost weight and his hair was white. Gone was the handsome, suave, confident prosecutor, the man who knew everything and strode across a courtroom sure of his win.

"I'm sorry I disappointed you, Tom," his father mumbled. "I never wanted to do that."

Tom recalled his parents waltzing at his wedding, their eyes alight, their delight in each other and their lives clear in every assured move. What a striking couple they'd been. Prison broke them both. Even if they paroled his father early, even if the governor pardoned him or commuted his sentence, he would never be the same. His life had already ended.

"Your mother came to see me."

"What? Mom did? She didn't tell me."

"She wants a divorce. I told her okay, go ahead. I don't blame her. She deserves better than this." He spread his hands out to include everything—himself, the prison, guards, the destruction of his reputation.

Tom put his face in his hands. "God, Dad." He breathed in the citrus smell of the soap he washed his hands with before he left the veterinary clinic. It reminded him of his wife and what he was here for. The guard watched him closely. He showed the guard his palms to prove he hadn't pulled a razor blade out of his mouth.

"I came here because I need the answer to something important. But maybe you're the wrong person to ask."

"Ask what?" his father said. "Ask me. Maybe I know. I used to know stuff." Charles pressed his lips together and smiled grimly.

"Indira has stage-three ovarian cancer. The bad kind that is almost always terminal." Tom watched his father's face go gray in an instant, surprised that he cared that much. "She had the surgery. She's refusing the chemo and radiation. Even with those treatments, she only has a forty-five percent chance of living another five years."

Charles' face softened. "I'm sorry, son. I didn't know. Indira's a lovely woman. So young, too young . . ." He wiped his mouth with his hand and didn't say the rest of his thought.

Tom brushed off the condolences. "I want to ask you about the law, about what happens if I help her."

"Help her? Do you mean under the Vermont death with dignity law? If she asks for it, her doctor can give her the prescription for the drugs six months before she's likely to die, usually around the time they recommend palliative care. It's a little complicated—second opinion, putting the request in writing, the timing. Stuff like that. She must self-administer the medication. To be safe legally, it's best if you, or someone, is there as a witness to record she did it herself."

"What if she wants to do it sooner, to avoid the pain? What if I do it, say, give her an IV of pentobarbital?"

"It's illegal. You could go to jail. They could charge you with an assortment of crimes, the least of which is assisting a suicide and at the worst, murder. You would lose your veterinary license. She must do it herself."

That was the father he knew, straight to the point and clear about what was legal and illegal. Tom folded his arms across his chest, imitating his father, breaking the rule about where visitors and inmates could put their hands in this glass cage. They were silent for a while. The guard scrutinized them as if they were plotting a jailbreak. Tom hoped the chatter around them covered his questions.

Opposite him was the man he'd always trusted to tell him the truth, to guide him. Now the person who had been his role model was a convict in prison, and his wife wanted him to kill her. Between the two of them, they had overturned every moral principle he'd ever learned. Could he trust what his father said or was he a liar? Tom suppressed a groan of frustration. He had to trust someone.

"Dad, what do I do? What do I tell her?"

Charles Beale put his hands flat on the table, as required by the prison visitation rules. Tom imitated him. They leaned forward, putting their heads as close together as they could without the guard forcibly separating them. For an instant, Tom remembered how his father would place his forehead against his and breathe with him when he was a kid. It had always calmed him and made him feel known all the way through.

"I'll tell you what you do," Charles Beale said. "You love her, son, you love her until there's not another breath left in her, until her last heartbeat. You love her even when she rails at you for not understanding. You love her and love her and love her until you're exhausted. And when you think you can't do it another minute, you love her more. Do you understand me?"

Tom put his face in his hands to hold down the sob in his throat. All his life he'd admired his father. This was the man he remembered. "I got it, Dad."

He pushed his chair back and signaled to the guard he wanted to leave. At the door, Tom glanced back at his father, who raised his hand in a goodbye salute before the guard grabbed his shoulders and pushed him out of the room.

Chapter 41

He was in the kitchen when Indira yelled from outside. "Freddy, come now, come right now!"

He dropped the knife on the cutting board and dashed out the back door toward them. Indira was leaning over, her hands under Anne's arms, straining to hold onto his mother's body.

"She's slipping," Indira called out to him as he raced across the lawn. "She can't sit anymore. She's falling out of the chair." Indira didn't scream or wail, but tears gleamed in her eyes, and he understood.

Anne's mouth and eyes were wide open in fear. She said nothing, no sound escaping her as if the skill of making words had disappeared. His mother's terror seeped under his skin.

He scooped Anne out of the chair and carried her into the house. Indira ran after him. "Her bed, I think that's best, put her in the bed." She sprinted through the first floor to the bedroom they had set up in Howard's old study, pulled back the covers, and propped up half a dozen pillows at the head of the bed. She grabbed a towel off the chair and spread it across the sheet. "Here, put her here."

"Wha?" Anne asked. "Wha?"

Freddy put her down gently. "It's okay, Mom, we've got you. Don't worry."

Indira removed Anne's shoes and adjusted the pillows under her back. Turning to Freddy, she said, "I think we need one of those beds where you can raise the head and foot with a button."

Freddy pulled his phone out of his back pocket. "Right." Hospice told him they could give Anne one of those beds, but he hadn't expected to need one for months. "I'll call them."

"She peed herself," Indira whispered. "I think she went unconscious for a bit. I'll change her while you're calling."

When he came back into the room, his mother was wearing dry clothes and was asleep, her face calm. Indira sat next to the bed in the wingback chair his father used to sit in when he read. She seemed so natural sitting there in his father's space, as if she'd always been with them, always been part of them.

"They'll bring the bed later today. And the hospice doctor will come to check on her." He sat on the edge of the bed and stroked his mother's hand. His throat ached. "Is this it? I didn't think it would come so soon. I thought I had more time."

Indira placed her palm on her chest. "I don't know. It seems abrupt. Maybe it's an episode of some kind and she'll recover. Ten minutes ago, she was carrying on a conversation."

Freddy hung his head. "I thought I had time to tell her how much she means to me when she could still understand." He put his hands in his hair and turned in a circle. With his eyes closed as if to dam up a flood of regret, he said, "I missed my chance."

Indira said, "You haven't missed your chance. You've been wonderful every day. She knows you adore her. Everything you do for her tells her that. She knows how you feel."

Freddy reached out his hand and she took it.

Indira drew in a ragged breath. "I don't want it to be now. I'm not ready. I'll miss her terribly. I want her to stay."

They sat hand in hand until Freddy wanted more than the touch of her fingers and let go.

Chapter 42

On a spectacular September afternoon with a sky clear blue all the way to the horizon, as his mother would say, Freddy opened the front door to a tall, slender man in his late sixties with white hair and beard, wearing jeans and a gray, quilted vest over a plaid shirt.

He stared at the stranger's face, inhaled fresh air wafting off the man like cologne, and tried to place him. He seemed so familiar, but Freddy was sure he'd never met him. Deciding the stranger wasn't a self-appointed missionary from the local church offering last-minute absolution for his errant mother, Freddy opened the door wider but didn't invite him in.

"Before you start your pitch, I can save you the trouble. If you're selling coffins, we're cremating."

The man stared at Freddy for a second and then broke into a laugh. "Colin McDowell." He put out his hand. "You remind me of your mother."

Freddy took a step back in surprise but grasped the man's hand. "Fred Morrow. Mom told me about you."

They shook hands and Colin pulled Freddy into an unexpected bear hug. "You know about me? I'm so glad." He pounded Freddy's back. "We don't need to be strangers anymore."

Freddy stiffened and pulled away. Had his mother lied to him, then? Was McDowell his father? "Frankly, I'm not sure what to think about you showing up here right now, Mr. McDowell."

"Call me Colin. Yes, you are definitely like your mother, forthright and plain speaking. It's a quality I always admired about her." He laughed again.

Freddy found himself admiring the effortless way Colin felt whatever he wanted to feel without embarrassment. He relaxed. *McDowell is right. It can't hurt to be friendly.* Despite the knot in his throat, and the sudden uneasiness that his mother might not have told him the truth about who his father was, neither of them had anything to lose by being courteous to each other.

"Come in. Mom's in her room. I warn you, she's not the way you remember her. Age and all. The tumor. She might not know you."

"Yes, I understand. It's okay," Colin said. "Think of me as an old friend of the family." He rotated in a half-circle in the hallway, waiting for Freddy to point him in the right direction. "Would you show me the way?"

Freddy led Colin through the living room to his father's old study, noticing how the man observed everything as if this were the first time he'd been in the house. The thought gave him comfort. His mother hadn't brought her lover here, into the heart of their family. She didn't sneak him into the house when her husband was at work and her boys were out playing. She protected her family, no matter how gonzo she'd been about him. Relief pulsed through him. Her family was more important to her than anything, even this man she'd kept secret from all of them for so long. He should believe what she'd told him.

As they walked through the house, Freddy mentally rehearsed how to introduce Colin to Marie, who was sitting with Anne. *This is Mom's old friend. No. This is the man who knew Mom. No. This is the guy Mom had an affair with.* He couldn't find the right words. By the time he reached the room, he felt tongue-tied. He shouldn't have worried. Marie stood up when she spotted them coming through the door and held out her hand.

Freddy waved his hand from Colin to Marie. "Colin McDowell, this is my sister-in-law, Marie, Sam's wife."

They shook hands, and Colin moved to the bed, his eyes fixed on Anne. He wasn't there for them. Anne was who he'd come to see, and she was hanging on for dear life, well past the three weeks from her fainting episode the doctor had given them for her death.

They'd been through three crises since then and each time they all thought that was the end. Each time, the entire family had gathered, sobs held in their throats. Anne hugged her grandchildren, kissed all her sons goodbye, and squeezed their wives' hands. But she came around, talking and laughing.

"Beat that sucker, didn't I," she said.

They had laughed, exchanged glances to say they knew that couldn't be true, and hugged themselves, torn between wanting to believe it was true and the grim certainty of another countdown.

The last time—the time they were sure had been the final goodbye—when they were all standing in the room around her bed, she contemplated each of them in turn. "You're my story," she said.

She smiled at the mystified look on their faces and tried to explain. "You are what matters, you are who I am, my legacy. I'm not making any sense, but you're the stories I won't write that exist anyway like ambulatory miracles. I wouldn't have missed a minute of you." Exhaustion hit and she slept.

Freddy had thought that was the end. She stayed alive long enough to bless them. He sat by his mother's bed holding her hand, letting go only when the hospice nurse insisted on taking her pulse.

"What's the point?" he asked, annoyed with the nurse's intrusion into his vigil.

"We have to chart her," the nurse said. "Hospice rules."

Freddy rolled his eyes and glanced at Indira, who smiled at him as if they were conspirators against some stupid bureaucracy. A few days later, Anne seemed to recover again, surprising them all, including the nurse.

"She's waiting for something," Indira had said, "one more thing she has to complete before she can let go. It could be she's waiting for you to forgive her."

"Forgive her for what?" Freddy had asked. "She was a great mother. I had a happy childhood. She was always on my side."

"What about Luke?" Indira asked. "She thinks she failed him."

Freddy hung his head. "We all failed him, and we don't deserve to get over it. Anyway, we can't forgive her for that." He glanced at Indira, temporarily transfixed, then blinked. "Only Luke can do that . . ."

Nevertheless, Freddy told his brothers Indira's idea about needing forgiveness for Luke, in case they knew what to say to comfort Anne. While he was at it, he told them about their mother's affair with Colin McDowell. No point in having secrets. His brothers had examined their shoes, raised their eyebrows, lifted their hands up as if to say, "Who cares?" and shook their heads.

"Good for her," Arne said, surprising everyone. "Pop could be a turd."

Only Sam was old enough to remember his mother being weird for a brief time one summer, but she had always been a little bit different from other moms, so what he recalled had nothing to do with her fling with Colin McDowell.

"She never forgot to pick me up from anything." Sam threw himself into a chair. "She was always there when I needed her, and she let me be as free as I wanted to be. She listened to me, paid attention to me, and encouraged me. As far as I'm concerned, she was a great mother." He glanced at Marie for confirmation and she nodded.

Now, Freddy watched Colin take in the frail creature lying on the bed with her eyes closed. Colin—that's what his mother had been waiting for.

In the last months, she'd eaten little and now she was tiny, barely a rumple in the blankets. Her nose, cheekbones, and chin jutted out away from her pale face, her white hair spread out on the pillow. Her breathing was shallow and sometimes faltered as if her brain intermittently forgot to send the right signals to her lungs.

Freddy pictured her young and strong, pulling him on a sled through knee-high snow, kneeling, and gathering him into her arms when he needed a hug. He saw himself spotting her across the schoolyard at the end of the day and running into her open arms. Now she was someone else, someone he didn't know. *What does Colin see?*

Colin spotted an extra chair and pulled it up to the bed. He took Anne's hand in his. "Anne, I'm here."

Anne opened her eyes. Her expression was blank, but she didn't pull her hand away. She licked her lips. Marie leaned across the bed to swab Anne's mouth with water.

Anne focused on Colin and her face lit as she found her memory. Her lips moved. She sighed. "Colin, oh, Colin. You're real. You're here. I'm not dreaming." She closed her eyes, smiled, and squeezed his hand. Colin leaned his forehead on the bed and sobbed. Anne combed his hair with her fingers.

Freddy pointed to the doorway and he and Marie left the room. "Whatever he needs to say to her, he can say it in private." Marie agreed.

Walking to the kitchen, they heard Colin talking to Anne, but they couldn't make out the words.

"Just as well we don't know what they're saying," Freddy said. "She should have a memory all her own to take with her. Don't you think?"

Marie shook her head. "You never stop astonishing me, Freddy." She stroked his shoulder. "I'll make some tea. Put out those cookies Indira bought. He'll need sweets to fortify him when he's done reminiscing."

Half an hour later, Colin walked into the kitchen and sat down at the table. His eyes were red, his face crumpled by grief. They understood. Marie handed him a cup of tea. He held the cup in his hands and took in Anne's favorite view of the lake.

"She's sleeping."

Freddy bent his head. "That's mostly what she does now."

"I should have come back sooner." Colin ran a hand over his face. "I should have come back after Luke died. I wanted to. She wouldn't let me."

Freddy sat in the chair opposite Colin. "You knew about Luke's suicide?"

"Yes, Anne told me. She was so distraught. She had to talk to someone."

Freddy's shoulders twitched as he blocked Laura's evil spell. "She knew where you were?"

"Yes. A few years after I left, she found me. I won a national book award, and she tracked me down." He smiled. "I always thought she was a good reporter."

"Did you meet up?" Freddy kept his gaze on the lake. He couldn't watch the man's face.

"We kept in touch intermittently. She would call me, but we never met again."

"So, after Luke died, why didn't you . . . ?"

"She said nothing could console her, not even me. I heard it as another rejection. Stupid, I know, self-absorbed. But that was the second time she'd told me to go away. I moved across the country to be where she could get to me quickly if she needed me, but she never asked, and I fought my impulse to go to her."

Freddy busied himself setting out ingredients for their dinner, his back to the man. Colin was so candid with them as if they were old friends. This guy talked like his mother had a right to do whatever she wanted, like she could have gotten up one day and left everything behind. Indignation burned in his chest like bile.

Colin seemed oblivious to the shock on Freddy's and Marie's faces. "When Howard died about a year later, I read his obituary in the paper. That's when I should have come, regardless of what she said. I'm so stupid. I let my pride get in the way instead of paying attention to what she was going through. I could've had five whole years with her."

Marie slid into the chair nearest the window. "Anne was seventy when Pop died." She took a sip of her tea. "What do you expect would have happened between you?"

Colin stared out of the window but whether he was seeing the lake, or a memory with Anne was unclear. "I expect I would have loved her with all my heart. I would have been with her every minute. I expect she would have loved me. We would have shared our lives. We would have talked, walked, traveled, read to each other, done everything together. That's all I ever wanted. To be with her. Love, the way she loved me, was the only piece missing in my life."

Freddy squirmed. Listening to Colin talk about love this way was like accidentally walking in on someone in the bathroom. "You don't think it would've been different from when you first met? You're both so old now it couldn't . . ."

He glanced around the kitchen imagining Colin in it with his mother. She would have been happy. He could see her singing and joking with the man. They would have shopped at the farmer's market, cooked together in the kitchen, read their favorite parts of books aloud to each other, and talked till all hours. They would have taken walks to watch the sunrise, held hands in public, and scandalized everyone in town. He imagined his mother's delight in the gossip and pictured her happy, a light in her eyes.

She knew what she'd given up. She used to stroke his face, brushing the hair off his sweaty forehead after a Little League game, and say, "You are worth everything, my sweet boy." Now he knew what everything was.

Freddy put a hand on Colin's arm. "Stay with her now. Be here with her for every minute she has left, for as long as there is." His eyes held Colin's. "If you want."

"Are you sure?"

Freddy silently checked with Marie. She nodded. "Yes," Freddy said, "I'm sure. Stay here with us. There's plenty of room."

Colin sighed deeply and closed his eyes. "She must be proud of you, of who you became." He stood. "If you don't mind, I'll go back and sit with her."

"I guess I should call Sam and tell him, so he's not surprised when he gets here," Marie said. "I'll make up Luke's room for you." She headed upstairs to Sam's bedroom to make the call.

Freddy sat for a while sipping his tea. This was the encounter he had worried about, the one Laura had threatened him with. She'd hoped meeting the man his mother loved would be horrible for him, demeaning and infuriating. Laura wanted it to wreck him, leave him broken, homeless, and orphaned. She had never been so wrong.

Colin was like a long-lost uncle, someone with whom Freddy was instantly in tune. While that didn't make any sense, it didn't matter. Not everything had to make sense. Colin worshipped his mother, and she was overjoyed to see him. That was what mattered.

Freddy sauntered out to the lake. Sunlight winked off the water. A few birds his mother would have known the names for flitted by. He pictured himself as part of this landscape, as if he could see himself from far away, and decided he was in the right place. Who he'd become, as Colin said, wasn't bad, even if he was confused.

Chapter 43

Indira heard Bo whining and the sound of his paws scampering across the floor before she saw Tom reflected in the dining area window wall, his face haloed by the sunset like a traveler in space, floating free of gravity, sighted from a distance.

She ran to him. He pulled her into his arms and kissed her. Indira clung to him, stunned by the electricity racing across her chest and stomach, the buzz in her head. What had she been thinking? Why would she ever let go of this?

He pressed his face against her hair. "I'm sorry. I'm such an idiot. I was so . . ." He held her face in his hands and put his forehead against hers. "I'm so sorry."

Indira breathed him in, the musky animal smell, cut hay, fresh air. "Me too."

She wrapped her arms around his neck and kissed his face over and over. She leaned her head against his shoulder. "Are you back to stay?"

Tom relaxed. "Yes. You're what's important to me. I want to be with you as long as you let me."

She held him tighter and spoke with her lips touching his neck. "I want that too."

He didn't ask what she meant.

They left words behind and relied only on touch and smell and taste and sound for the rest of the night and into the morning. When she woke at noon, Tom was still sleeping. She lay next to him and remembered how being with him was all she'd ever wanted. Words came to her. She rose from the bed, walked silently into her office, and began typing like her fingers were on fire.

Chapter 44

Laura walked through Anne's kitchen door expecting the room to be empty. There were a few cars parked in the driveway, but she'd thought everyone would be somewhere else at two in the afternoon.

The Morrows were always prompt about their weekend meals—seven in the morning for breakfast, noon for lunch, and six in the evening for dinner, including holidays, no exceptions. Laura didn't see any reason why that would have changed.

She planned to sneak into Anne's room and tell her all about talking to Colin and how she now knew he was Luke's real father. She'd changed her mind about whose father Colin was when she saw his photo on the backs of his books. The younger version of the man looked more like Luke—that hot body, the dangerous look in his eyes—except for the color of his hair.

Laura worked the dates out on paper. A year after Freddy was born, Anne and Colin must have gotten back together and conceived Luke. That had to be what happened, even if she were the only one who'd figured it out. Laura imagined their reunion—the heat, the gasps, and sighs—and resented them for it.

With two slugs of gin under her belt, she rehearsed her lines out loud as she drove to the house—"No wonder poor Luke killed himself. He knew he didn't belong in this family"—and imagined the stunned look on Anne's face, the halting rebuttals.

When she revealed Anne's secret, she would destroy all the Morrows at once. How she relished that idea. She imagined herself decked out in armor and carrying a lance, her sword strapped to her side. She only needed the right time. It didn't matter anymore what anyone thought of her, including her mother.

"Why are you so bent on torturing that poor woman and your husband?" her mother yelled at her over the phone this morning. "He's done everything for you. He built you a cozy house, gave you a comfortable life. What's your problem with him? As far as I'm concerned, he walks on water."

Pushed to the edge of her patience with her mother's infatuation with Freddy, Laura blurted, "He didn't give me a child. The one thing I wanted. My own child. And since the miscarriage, he hates me so much his sperm swims backward to get away from my uterus."

Laura heard her mother spit coffee all over her phone. "Jesus, Laura. You need a filter."

"What do you know about anything?" Laura had hung up the phone with that unsettled feeling in her stomach that meant she was about to do something she shouldn't.

Standing in Anne's house, Laura now realized that Colin McDowell, like the archenemy in a movie, stood at the stove cooking, completely at home as if this were his house. Laura stopped short. Her heart slammed against her ribs. She cleared her throat to announce herself.

Colin darted a look at her over his shoulder. His face registered shock. "I know you. We talked on FaceTime. I didn't ever expect to meet you."

She had surprised him, and he wasn't even bothering to be polite. "I . . ."

"I know about you now," Colin said. "Freddy filled me in."

Instantly infuriated, Laura tried to retort but no sound came out. She put her hand up to her head and decided to remain cordial. "Where is everyone?"

"They're out. I'm in charge. You're not welcome here."

That headmaster tone of his, so much for cordiality. The look on his face echoed his words. He wasn't joking. His superior attitude and his arrogance made her want to scream. Laura's face flushed. "I'm part of this family. I belong here. Unlike *you*."

Colin shook his head. "Legally you're on your last gasp as a Morrow. Sam has already filed divorce papers against you. I'm surprised you didn't get them in the mail by now. You only need to sign them, and all your pain is over."

He flipped over the cheese sandwich he was grilling. A tongue of sliced tomato stuck out at her. Laura stared at the sandwich.

This interloper, this adulterer who should have been ashamed to put his foot in the door, was telling her to get out of the house where she should, by right of marriage, automatically expect a welcome. "What, when, how . . ."

Laura pulled her phone out of the back pocket of her jeans and called Freddy. "Did you know Colin McDowell is in your kitchen making a grilled cheese sandwich like he belongs here?" she yelled into the phone.

Colin watched her, holding the spatula in the air.

Laura stamped on the floor, whirled around, and waved her arm as if she meant to propel herself off the ground. "What? You're what?" She checked her phone screen. "He hung up on me. He's going to get a restraining order against me if I don't leave now."

She glared at Colin. "How is this happening? You're the one who tried to steal Anne away from her family. How did I get to be the bad guy? You're the interloper."

The more words she said, the angrier she got. Umbrage made her lips stiff. "This is so unfair." Tears spurted from her eyes. She wiped her cheeks with the backs of her hands, her face frozen in a grimace.

Colin scooped the sandwich onto the spatula. "You know, I should thank you."

"Thank me?" Laura's voice squeaked. "For what?" She couldn't stand it if her clever plan for revenge had boomeranged and helped the Morrows or this guy. Imaginary ants crawled up her legs at the thought.

"Yes. If you hadn't called and told me, I wouldn't have known Anne was sick. I wouldn't have gotten here until I saw the obituary in the paper, and that would've been too late. I would have missed her."

Laura twitched as if a jolt of electricity shot through her body.

He put the sandwich on a plate. "You did us all a favor, Laura." He smiled. "You gave us an opportunity for closure."

The heat in Laura's face was unbearable. That condescending smile on his smug face. She wanted to smack him, hard. The nerve of him. She closed her eyes and screamed. "I did not help you!"

"Yes, you did. And we're all grateful."

She stamped both her feet. "You're supposed to be cowed. What the hell is wrong with you, with all of you? Don't you know what you did was immoral?"

"I think you need some quiet time." Colin's voice was calm as if she were a student in his school who needed a firm but courteous hand. "You should leave now before you embarrass yourself further."

Laura stood there with her mouth agape.

He turned off the stove. "That would be right now, this minute before the Morrows come back and find you here."

Pouring a glass of iced tea from the pitcher in the refrigerator, Colin took his plate and glass and walked out of the kitchen without looking back at her as if he fully expected her to obey his command.

Laura's chest heaved. *He's putting me in time-out. Like I'm some kid in his school.* She couldn't get enough air into her lungs. She whirled around and left the house, banging the door as hard as she could.

McDowell would tell everyone in the family about the encounter, how he sneered at her, her mortification, and they'd laugh at her, the way they always did. It was one of the things the Morrows had in common— they all laughed at her. She could see their faces, their mouths open in derision, their eyes closed to slits as they guffawed.

She held in the howling until she was home. In her own driveway, safe from prying eyes, she gripped the steering wheel, opened her mouth to scream at the windshield but no sound came. She was empty. No husband, no child, no future. They had taken everything, including her fury. Anne's death wouldn't make them even.

She dragged herself into the house, crashed onto the sofa, downed all the gin left in her flask, and fell asleep. She dreamed of a time at the beach when she was three, and she and her mother were flying a kite. Out of nowhere, a seagull flew at them, circling, screeching, swooping down toward their heads, over and over. Their day went from perfect to nightmare in a second. Her mother had grabbed her by the wrist and run away from the gull so fast Laura's feet left the sand. To her mortification, the people around them laughed as if her mother's fright were a spectacle in a TV sitcom meant for their amusement. She never forgave her mother for embarrassing her.

Chapter 45

For the last six weeks, Freddy thought he might as well be managing a bed and breakfast, but most of the time he was glad everyone was there. There was a vibe the family gave off when they were all together, a feeling that bent toward mirth and affection, and he sorely needed that.

The hospice booklet instructed them not to crowd Anne, so everyone took turns sitting with her, making sure that she was never alone. Even Arne, although terrified his mother would die on his watch and he wouldn't know what to do, sat with Anne when it was his turn.

"If it happens, just call out, man," Freddy advised.

Arne looked miserable. "I won't be able to speak. What if no one is home but me? How will I know what to do?"

Freddy hugged his brother's shoulders. "You get us. We'll know."

Arne smiled at Freddy and shook his head. "When did you learn how to say the right thing?"

They read to Anne, talked about their memories, rubbed her feet and hands with lotion, and swabbed her lips with water. Occasionally she opened her eyes and smiled. To avoid sadness they cleaned the house, attic, and shed, sorted old treasures, boxed them up, and weeded the flower beds. Keep busy, that's what she taught them about dealing with grief. And that's what they did.

One afternoon, Sam pulled Freddy outside and they walked to the lake's edge and sat in the chairs Freddy had made for his mother and Indira. When he sat in his mother's chair looking out over the water, it was as if he'd shifted into her body and could see the world the way she did. It looked different, more beautiful and mysterious.

"I've been going through all of Mom's bank accounts and the will." Sam shielded his eyes from the sunlight glinting off the lake. "She made changes to her will before . . . you know. Did she talk to you about those?"

"Nah. Mom never talked to me about legal stuff."

"Well, you know she sold the paper for fifteen million and we're all going to get a share of that."

Freddy nodded. "What's going to happen with the house?" The house was the only thing he cared about. His siblings could take all the furniture and stuff out of it, but this place was where he wanted to live, rooted in his family's history. He couldn't bear the idea that they would sell the place.

Sam raised his eyebrows. "You get it. The house, I mean. I wanted to make sure you understand the value of our share of the property gets subtracted from your share of the cash."

Freddy closed his eyes and sighed. His shoulders relaxed. He would still have his home. "Okay with me."

"But that's not the only thing I want to talk to you about."

Freddy laughed. "Okay."

"Do you know who Margaret Morrow is?"

Freddy shook his head. "Not a clue."

"Mom is leaving her a sizeable amount of cash."

"It's Mom's money. She can do what she wants with it." Freddy shrugged. "Morrow? Is this Margaret person related to us?"

"That's the thing. I went through all Mom's papers, even all the stuff from the newspaper that Molly sent over, and I didn't find anything. But when I cleared out Pop's desk, I found a folder with Margaret's name on it." Sam looked at Freddy in the strangest way. "There are documents. Like a birth certificate with Pop's name on it. She's his daughter."

"We have a sister?"

"Yeah, looks like it. By a different mother."

Freddy stared out at the lake. "Geez . . . Our parents . . ."

Sam threw his head back and laughed. "Freddy, you are the antidote to paranoid conspiracy theories." He slapped his brother on the back and went inside the house.

Late that afternoon, as they prepared dinner for fifteen, Marie abruptly stood stock-still in the middle of the kitchen, her face looking like she spotted a derailed train careening toward them and knew she was helpless to stop it or get out of the way. "I guess we're as ready as we're ever going to be," she said.

Indira put down the knife she'd been using to cut green peppers in half and hugged Marie. "I don't think you can practice for this."

Freddy washed his hands and dried them on a paper towel. "I'll never be ready."

He scooped cooked rice from the pot onto the chopped meat, broke four eggs into the bowl, and squished the mixture together with his fingers as if he were strangling someone. "There's no recipe for letting go of someone you love. We have to take it as it comes."

His brothers, sitting around the kitchen table, smiled into their beers. Arne mumbled, "At some point, Freddy, you became Yoda."

Marie blew him a kiss and began stuffing the meat mixture into green pepper halves.

This change in Freddy's reputation in the family from doofus to sage sat on his frame a little stiffly, like new clothes he was wearing for the first time. He was sure he would screw up at any minute and reinstate his nitwit status, but even that would be okay. He didn't mind anymore how they saw him. His mother said he was his father's Berggruen prize. That was all the reassurance he needed that he was okay.

Colin treated him as if he'd always been a smart guy even if his family were only now realizing it. Freddy felt like he'd known Colin forever. He didn't question their immediate alliance. They both loved Anne. That's all Freddy needed to know, it's what they had in common. Colin was someone he could count on and that was enough to make him part of the family.

Earlier that afternoon when Freddy checked on his mother, Colin was reading her favorite Emily Dickinson and Mary Oliver poems aloud. She was silent, eyes closed, and her breathing stuttered, but a smile lit her face. Occasionally, her eyelids fluttered open.

It was clear to him his mother was still waiting for something to happen and no one knew what. Whatever it was, that was fine with him. He didn't want her to die. He didn't want to think of what the future would look like when his mother was gone. It would be very quiet in the house without everyone around.

At dinner, they told stories about Anne. Arne's son told them his grandmother opened her eyes while he was sitting with her and said,

"Shit. I'm still here." They smiled at each other the way people who are grieving smile when a shared memory, destined to become part of the family's mythology and retold over and over, is born.

Midway through the meal, the screech of metal on metal coming from the driveway startled them. Freddy jumped up and looked out of the kitchen window. His unmanned truck inexplicably jerked across the grass. He opened the door and saw Laura's car smashed into his rear bumper, its wheels spinning on the driveway.

He ran outside, waving his arms. "Hey, stop! Stop."

The front tire on Laura's Honda exploded. The engine guttered out. Bumpers on the two vehicles tangled together. Coming up the driveway behind her was a stranger's car.

Freddy yanked open Laura's car door. "What the hell are you doing?"

Laura slid out of the car, breezed past Freddy, and hauled the woman who walked up behind her into the dining room.

"Hello everyone. I've been a busy bee. I found someone I thought you should meet." She swept her arm toward the woman entering the room with her. "Morrows, meet Howard's daughter, Margaret." Laura swayed a bit. The tall, dark-haired woman, the spitting image of Luke, looked stunned.

Freddy pushed Laura around to face him. "What are you doing? Why are you here?"

Laura jiggled her shoulders and hips and waved her arms. "Really. This is Margaret Morrow, Howard's daughter. She was born the same year as Luke. She looks like him, doesn't she? I found her in Burlington. Turns out she's a friend of George's, your college roommate, Freddy. In fact, she has a kid, your niece, with George that you never knew about."

Margaret's face grew bright red as she met the stares of every other shocked person at the table.

Laura put her hands on her hips. "She wants to talk to your mother."

"Laura, what the fuck?" Freddy tightened his grip on Laura's shoulders without any idea of what he could do to stop her from talking.

Arne grasped Freddy's arm to pull him away from Laura. "Come on, man. Let go of her."

"This is nuts. I don't need this." Margaret edged backward toward the door. "I didn't come here for this. I came to talk to Anne, to apologize for the last time."

"The last time?" Marie asked.

"I met her. A while ago, right before my dad died. I behaved badly. I wanted . . . Oh, never mind."

Laura yanked Margaret back into the dining room. "You stay right here," she said the way she would tell an unruly kindergartener what to do.

Laura faced Freddy. "I'm here to say goodbye to your mother."

"You're drunk." Freddy's anger made his ears burn. "You just crashed your car into my truck. You're not getting anywhere near my mother."

Sam sidelined Margaret and talked to her softly. Over the din in the room, Freddy overheard bits of that conversation. "Anne's will . . . death . . . your share." Margaret's shoulders twitched, and her blush deepened.

Freddy's head buzzed. More secrets. He didn't have the headspace to deal with all this.

Colin joined the circle around Laura. She flailed her arms and pushed them away. "You're all trying to intimidate me. You want to get rid of me, to pretend I never existed." She whipped around to gesture at Margaret. "Well, you can't get rid of her. Look at her face! She fits in here like a missing puzzle piece."

Margaret looked at her, her face expressing her fury, and ran out of the dining room. The kitchen door slammed.

"Laura, that's enough," Colin said in his sternest headmaster tone.

Laura stared at Colin and Freddy standing shoulder to shoulder. Her head tilted. "You guys could be father and son. I mean, really. Same height, same build, same eyes, chin." She smirked.

"Don't start that over again," Freddy muttered.

Recognition flickered across Colin's face. "Of course," he whispered and covered his mouth with his hand as if to keep the thought to himself.

Freddy looked away from him. He didn't want to know what Colin was thinking. He just wanted Laura to go away before he did something he'd regret.

A loud moan came from Anne's room. Colin dashed to her side. The soft tones of Colin's voice reassuring her filtered into the dining room.

Rob put his arm around Freddy's shoulders and pulled him toward the kitchen. "Don't do anything stupid, man."

Arne and Sam cornered Laura and talked to her in whispers. It didn't work. Rob joined them. "Don't touch her," Sam warned. "She's litigious."

"That woman stole my life." Laura pointed to Indira. "She's a slut, don't you get it. You worship a slut, an adulterer. She's the same as your mother."

Indira put her hands over her ears and stared at Laura.

Marie whispered, "Laura, you're not doing yourself any favors here."

Laura lunged at Marie, bringing them nose to nose. "Like you ever gave a damn about me."

"Of course, I care about you," Marie said. "We all—"

"Liar. You're all liars. You never knew her," Laura shouted. "Anne. The biggest liar of all. You have no idea who she is. All those secrets. You're a family of liars. Besides, she hates me so why should I care what happens to her?"

"Anne doesn't hate you," Marie said, guiding Laura out of the room. "She's a complicated person. Prickly sometimes."

Laura pulled away from Marie. "You don't know anything."

Sam, Arne, and Rob formed a cordon behind Laura and nudged her out of the house. Margaret, arms crossed over her stomach, stood next to her car with the front doors open.

"I don't know what I expected," Margaret said to Sam. "I'm sorry. I should have known this would be a mistake."

The brothers put Laura in Margaret's car and closed the door.

Margaret eased her car down the driveway as Laura bellowed out the window, "She stole my life! She took everything. That woman. That stranger stole my life!"

They watched the car drive away and then stood there in silence for a while, not looking at each other. Freddy broke away first. He couldn't talk and he didn't want to listen to their speculations about Laura.

Rob found him in the kitchen vigorously scrubbing pots. "What's Laura talking about?"

Freddy shrugged. "Who knows. She's drunk and confused."

His anger had dissipated. He bowed his head and concentrated on getting every square inch of the pot clean. His legs trembled. He didn't want Rob to see him in this state. Twenty years of effort had ended in farce. The humiliation was intense. He was embarrassed he'd married Laura in the first place.

"Do you believe that stuff about Margaret, that she's our sister?"

"Yeah. I might. I don't know what to believe except our parents weren't who we thought they were. But it doesn't matter now. We have our own lives, and we have to make them count." Freddy rinsed off the pot and handed it to Rob to dry.

"What are you going to do?" Rob asked.

"I'm going to call a garage to come out and get those vehicles untangled and hauled away to the body shop."

Rob considered his brother for a second and then concentrated on getting every drop of water off the aluminum pot.

Chapter 46

On the afternoon Indira finished her novel, she brought Tom to Anne's house for the first time. Freddy greeted them at the kitchen door with open arms. The men pounded each other on the back, grinning like old high school pals reunited as if they shared kinship without a word ever being exchanged.

Greetings completed, she took Tom's hand to lead him from the kitchen through the house to Anne's room in what had been Howard's study. Tom stopped short in the hall to admire the grandfather clock with its gleaming mahogany case inlaid with the scene of a pagoda and a man plying a river in a canoe.

"It's wonderful, isn't it?"

"It's a stunner," Tom said. "It must be worth a fortune."

Indira put her arm through his. "It's from a century when time was valuable, not just minutes to be tracked, used up, or monetized. There are many beautiful things here, but nobody boasts about them. They're just part of the environment."

Tom grinned. "Like you."

Indira tilted her head to acknowledge the compliment and led him into Anne's room. Marie put down her needlepoint when she spotted them in the doorway and welcomed Tom, kissing him on the cheek and clasping his hand as if she'd always known him.

Indira was sure he would understand now why she spent time with these people, how being part of their lives made her whole. They added to her life. Instead of taking her for granted, they took her as she was. She had come to them empty, without context or background, leaving everything else behind, and had been included as a part of their tribe. These were the people who saw her true self and reflected it back to her. She loved them for this.

A Turkish-blue handmade quilt hand-stitched with bouquets of pink silk roses and lavender sprigs covered Anne to her chin. The quilt smelled of fresh air and sun. Marie must have found it in a chest in the attic, washed it, and dried it on the line. *Another act of love.*

The hundreds of books Howard had collected over half a century lined the bookcases behind the bed. Sunlight streamed through the bay window and pinged off the lake. Flashes of light danced across the ceiling.

Anne's pale skin shone with a luster no one could explain. White light emanated from her and wrapped them in its aura when they leaned close to her. The grandchildren took photos of this phenomenon and posted them on social media. They whispered about it to each other.

Marie, her face drawn and eyes red-rimmed, whispered to Indira. "Her blood pressure is extremely low. We had a rough night. She woke up howling three times."

Indira wrapped her arm around Marie's shoulders to comfort her friend. The most helpful thing she could do was to share her sadness in silence.

Tom sat in the chair Marie vacated and cradled Anne's hand in his. "My wife has been telling me about you." He spoke in the same gentle voice he used to talk to sick animals. "She thinks the world of you."

Anne squeezed his hand.

"You saved her, you know," Tom said. "I'm so grateful. The writing and reading. Your friendship. You gave her time to find herself." He glanced at his wife. "I'll never be able to thank you enough."

Anne opened her eyes and stared at him. "Ah," she said and turned her face toward the sound of Indira's voice. Indira sank to her knees beside the bed and kissed Anne's cheek.

"How are you today?" Indira took Anne's hand in both of hers. "Are you up for hearing my new pages? This is the last scene. I finished the first draft!"

Anne seemed to nod. Marie and Freddy linked arms with Tom and took him to the kitchen. Indira settled herself in the chair next to Anne's bed and faced her.

"The pages are so new I haven't had time to edit them. I'll probably rewrite the end twenty times, but I wanted to read it to you while it's fresh."

Anne smiled and closed her eyes. Indira read out loud from her tablet.

Annabelle gave the cats a choice. They could stay in the house or go with her. When it was time to pack her little car, only two black and white cats remained to put in their carry crates. Figures, it's the females who are independent, Annabelle thought.

She loaded Harry and Will into the trunk of her orange hatchback along with her two suitcases and a box of books. For the dogs, there was never a debate. They were always going to go with her wherever she went. They were forever.

She opened the back door of the car and the German shepherd and the yellow Lab sprang onto the seat, sitting in their customary spots so each could see out of their own window. They looked at her eagerly. She started the car and drove slowly toward the street.

At the end of the driveway, Annabelle turned to look over her shoulder at the house. She had loved it there, the interior of every room, the view from every window. The house was everything she knew; it was how she knew herself. It had shaped her, reflected her, but it was time to go.

Homesickness instantly tugged on her heart, and a sudden emptiness formed in her belly. She needed to fill herself with something new.

"I'll miss you," she said to the house. "You've been a wonderful refuge. I'll be back when I have a story of my own to tell you."

She turned to the dogs. "Han, Leia, are you ready for our great adventure?" The dogs barked twice and settled down for the ride, noses stuck out above their open windows.

Annabelle pulled out onto the road, waved to the house in case any of the ghosts inside were watching, and drove away.

Indira put down the pages and took Anne's hand in hers. "What do you think? Is it the right ending? Does it work for you?"

She didn't expect an answer—Anne was well past speech—but Indira waited, because sometimes Anne would smile or squeeze her hand, or the ghost of an idea would flit across her face, and that was all the encouragement Indira needed to keep writing. Her friend's face was expectant, as if there was something more Indira was supposed to say.

Suddenly, Indira knew what Anne was waiting for. Laying her head on the pillow next to Anne's, she whispered through the tightness in her throat. "It's okay to go, Anne, it's okay. You kept your word. You did it. I release you. You can go before me. You can go first."

Five seconds passed as Indira held her hand, and then Anne took three deep, shuddering breaths, her chest rising high and collapsing, and on the last sigh, she lay completely still.

Indira waited in silence, not knowing what was happening. The grandfather clock in the hall ticked off the seconds. She placed her palm on Anne's chest. *No breath.*

"No breath." Indira gasped. No breath!"

Indira bolted upright. "No. I didn't mean it. No. Anne, come back, please . . ."

She stroked Anne's face. "I forgot to thank you. I should have thanked you. I never told you how much you mean to me, this friendship, the things you made me see. Oh, please be able to hear me. Please, please."

Before sobs overtook her, Indira whispered, "I'll miss you so much, how you listen, how you make me laugh. How you saw me." She gripped Anne's hand. "Remember everything. Next time I'll know you right away. I'll know it's you."

Indira gave herself a minute alone and then called out, "Freddy, Freddy come now!"

Feet slammed across the wood floor. Freddy burst into the room. "Mom?"

Indira raised her eyes to his and shook her head. Tears made her unable to speak.

Gasping, he sat on the bed, took his mother's hand, and pressed it to his face. "Mom!" He kissed her palm and closed his eyes. "Mom," he whispered. Tears spilled down his cheeks.

He looked at Indira, bewildered. "I never told her . . ."

"She knew. She loved you so much."

The rest of the family tumbled into the room. Tom appeared in the doorway, his arms open—her refuge. Indira took one last look at Anne and walked into the living room with Tom. This view of the lake and mountains always calmed her. She wiped her face with her hands and leaned against him. Tom rested his cheek against her hair. Light from the late afternoon sun flooded the room. On the other side of the lake, two loons took flight, their shadows rippling across the water as they called to each other.

Tom's arms tightened around her. She breathed him in and sighed.

"I'm staying," Indira said, her lips against his neck. "I'm staying with you for as long as I can." She raised her face to his.

Tom touched his forehead to hers and wrapped her hair in his hands.

Acknowledgments

Every word, phrase, sentence, and punctuation mark of this novel has been scrutinized by the wonderful writers in the Holey Roaders critique group—Frank Joseph, Solveig Eggerz, Katherine Lorr, Linda Morefield, Catherine Flanagan, Leslie Rollins, Bob Gibson, Stanley Whatley, and the late Phil Harvey—to whom I owe a debt of gratitude.

When I first joined the group a decade ago, I was uneasy about subjecting my novels to their thorough examination. Now, I would feel unprepared if I sent a book out into the world without their rigorous inspection. Fortunately, the gentler criticism of K.P. Robbins, Tara Bell, and Catherine Baldau buffered my tender feelings.

When I started this novel, I was thinking about stakes and desires. What could be higher stakes than life or death? What could be more important than love? What would happen if getting what one wants, or needs, destroys the people one loves most? What is the darkest secret someone can keep for a lifetime, and what happens when that secret is discovered by a child, or an enemy? (I'm still wondering about that.)

I want to thank Lawrence Knorr at Sunbury for taking on another of my novels and for assigning the thoughtful Gabrielle Kirk as my editor. So much depends on an editor's ear and heart and willingness to immerse herself in someone else's world.

Thank you to my extraordinary children who bring their own genius to bear on the many odd questions I ask as I'm writing. Always, they say exactly the thing that steers me in the right direction.

About the Author

Ginny Fite is an award-winning journalist and author of eight published novels, three collections of poetry, a collection of short stories, and a book of humorous essays on aging. A graduate of Rutgers University and Johns Hopkins University, her 40-year career in communications included posts in newspapers, government, higher education, and a robotics R&D company. Pushcart Prize nominated, shortlisted for the 2019 SFWP prize, a finalist for the 2020 Bakwin Prize, winner of the FAPA gold medal in fiction for *Thoughts & Prayers*, her stories have appeared in numerous journals such as *The Delmarva Review*, *Women Arts Quarterly Journal*, *Heartwood Literary Magazine*, and the *Anthology of Appalachian Writers*. Learn more at GinnyFite.com.

www.ingramcontent.com/pod-product-compliance
Lightning Source LLC
Chambersburg PA
CBHW011348010726
47493CB00011B/3001